THE
DOOMSDAY
DEPOSIT

THE DOOMSDAY DEPOSIT

STANLEY JOHNSON

Thomas Congdon Books
E.P. DUTTON · NEW YORK

For information contact:

E. P. Dutton, 2 Park Avenue, New York, N.Y. 10016

Library of Congress Cataloging in Publication Data

Johnson, Stanley, 1940–
    The doomsday deposit.

    "Thomas Congdon books."
    I. Title. PZ4.J716Do 1979 [PR6060.037] 823'.9'14 79-10509

ISBN: 0-525-09468-7

Published simultaneously in Canada by Clarke, Irwin &
Company Limited, Toronto and Vancouver

10 9 8 7 6 5 4 3 2 1

First Edition

THE
DOOMSDAY
DEPOSIT

1

It was her fortieth birthday. Aside from that minor cataclysm, the day had begun ordinarily enough. At eight-thirty that morning she had left her house in Bethesda to drive to work. She had turned east on the Capital Beltway, as she always did, then taken the Baltimore–Washington Parkway. A few miles on, she had passed an exit marked GODDARD SPACE FLIGHT CENTER— NATIONAL AERONAUTICS AND SPACE ADMINISTRATION (NASA) EMPLOYEES ONLY and slowed down at the checkpoint that guarded the center from unauthorized incursions. The sentry had recognized her and waved her through. All perfectly normal. Moments later she had been at her desk in the Data Interpretation Center, Building 6.

For the last six months Ella Richmond had been a program supervisor on the LANDSAT—Land Satellite—operation. Richmond had been made a supervisor because she was not only a gifted scientist but also an able administrator. She held a doctorate in physical chemistry from Berkeley and had numerous professional publications to her credit, but she was no ivory-tower academic. She had welded her subordinates into one of the most efficient operating units in the whole place.

She was a tall woman, strikingly handsome. She had thick and luxuriant black hair, a straight, proud nose, and the palest of skins. As she moved down the line of desks, where the various members of her team sat with electronic display screens in front of them, she was vaguely conscious of the current of interest she created. Heads turned as she passed, as they always did.

Just before eleven o'clock that morning, Shirley Lewis, a pretty brunette who was one of the latest recruits to Ella Richmond's team, punched the keyboard in front of her with a routine request and waited for the computer to search its memory. It was her thirteenth trace so far that day through the computer's storehouse of images picked up hours before by a NASA satellite as it circled the globe. She planned to go through another half dozen or so before lunch. She lit a cigarette and waited for the image to come up on the screen.

Finally it appeared, and Shirley Lewis gasped with surprise. In front of her, in the middle of the screen, was a glowing red blob, almost incandescent in its brightness.

She pressed the button of the supervisor's intercom on her desk. "Dr. Richmond? This is Shirley Lewis."

"What's up, Shirley?"

"I've come up with something I think you ought to take a look at. It could be important."

Richmond could see the young woman down at the far end of the room, on the right-hand side. She had just sat down herself after being called out on another query and she didn't want to move again if she could help it. There was a touch of impatience in her voice as, still speaking through the intercom, she asked: "What kind of thing?"

"Something like I've never seen before."

Richmond sighed. "Okay, I'll be right there."

She walked down the room and, pulling up a chair beside Shirley Lewis, leaned forward to look closely at the screen.

"Holy smoke!" Richmond exclaimed when she saw what was there. "What in God's name is that?"

Dr. Wilbur Silcott, a thickset man about forty-five years old with reddish hair and beard, was sitting at his desk in his office working on a paper he had been asked to present at the annual congress of the American Geophysical Institute. The Congress would not in fact take place for another eight months; there was still another five months to go before the deadline for the submission of papers. But Silcott was a punctual man (obsessively punctual, his wife would say). He liked to get things finished on time.

He shook his head, looked out the window, and turned back to his work. Thank God they gave him time for his own research! Otherwise he would never have stayed. He had told them, when they had offered him the job of head of the Geophysical Department of the U.S. Geological Survey, that he wouldn't take it unless they guaranteed him at least three working days a week for his own projects. He had driven a hard bargain but he had his formidable scientific reputation behind him. So far the bargain had stuck.

The only sound in the room was the scratching of Silcott's pen on the paper. He never used a typewriter. He liked to be able to see what he wrote as he wrote it, and to correct it as he went along. He used black ink and formed his letters with punctilious care. Nothing irritated him more than handwriting that was difficult to read. There was no excuse for it. It was just plain sloppiness.

At that moment, the telephone on his desk rang. Frowning, Silcott picked it up. It was his secretary. "There's a call for you."

"I'm not taking calls. I thought I told you that." He put the instrument down, with an impatient click of his tongue.

The telephone rang again. "I'm sorry," his secretary said. "It's Ed Mobley, at the Laboratory for Meteorology and Earth Sciences at Goddard, and he says it's urgent."

With a sigh, Silcott once more picked up the phone. One hand cradled the receiver, the other pulled rhythmically at his beard. He was relaxed now. Ed Mobley was a good friend. "Hello, Ed."

"Wilbur," said Mobley, "I know you hate to be interrupted but . . ."

"Forget it. I ask my girl to keep most of them out of my hair when I'm working, but that doesn't include you. You know that, Ed."

"Thanks." The other man came to the point. "Do you have a moment now?"

"Go ahead."

"You know we're involved in the LANDSAT program, among other things. We've come up with something this morning we think you should take a look at. It's urgent."

"Can you be more specific?"

"Not over the phone."

"You say it's urgent."

"Yes."

"I'll be over as soon as I can get there."

Half an hour later Silcott pulled up to the main gate at Goddard. The guard was evidently expecting him. "Dr. Silcott? Dr. Mobley is in Building 6."

A dark-haired, rather untidy man of medium height was waiting for him at the door. He held out his hand.

"Hi, Wilbur. Good of you to come. Of course we've got competent geologists on the staff here, but this looked like it could be something special. We'd rather have the Survey people in on it from the start."

"I'll be glad to be of any help I can, Ed. Tell me what's up."

Mobley paused before replying. "That's the problem. We can't really make it out. Come on, I'll show you what I mean."

They walked along the corridor to the Data Interpretation Center. Just before the main room, they turned off into another, smaller room. Like the main room, it was equipped with desks and display screens.

"This is where we view any sensitive material," Mobley explained. He flicked a switch. Outside in the corridor a red light and a sign that said NO ENTRY—VIEWING IN PROGRESS were illuminated.

Ella Richmond was already there, waiting for them. Mobley introduced her, and they joined her at the table. Mobley opened his remarks somewhat formally.

"Wilbur, we're very grateful to you for getting out here so quickly. I hope you'll agree, by the time we've finished today, that we were right to call."

• 4 •

Silcott smiled. "No problem. That's what I'm for."

For the next few minutes, Mobley described the LANDSAT system and in particular the spacecraft's remote sensing capability. "The sensors," he said, "observe approximately 6.5 million square kilometers of the earth's surface every day. These daily observations are converted into about 1,350 images at the Data Processing facility here at Goddard Space Flight Center. The satellite is in a near-polar orbit, and makes 14 daylight passes each day. Due to this orbit, LANDSAT overflies every point on the earth's surface at least once every 18 days. The fields of view of the 2 sensor systems are identical and cover a strip 185 kilometers—that's 100 nautical miles wide, directly underneath the spacecraft. Is that all clear?"

Silcott nodded. Mobley might look like a hippie, he thought, but there was obviously nothing wrong with his mind.

"Good." Mobley turned to the dark-haired woman beside him who had been waiting for him to finish. "Ella, would you care to take it from here?"

Richmond pushed her hair back from her forehead and looked at the two men. "Dr. Mobley has already mentioned," she began, "that the satellite sensors are working along orbital strips 100 nautical miles wide. My team began this morning by looking at some regional images from the 1057–16325 series. In other words, we were looking at an area that had been covered by 3 or more satellite passes, approximately 300 miles square. Perhaps you would care to see the composite image as we saw it today. I shall instruct the computer in exactly the same way as it was instructed this morning."

Richmond punched the keyboard at the end of the conference table and a few seconds later the image appeared on the display screen. She pointed to the incandescence in the center. It was small—this first composite image was, after all, covering a broad area—but even so it stood out clearly. Silcott's gaze fastened upon it.

"This blob, located more or less in the area of this river," she said, indicating a sinuous blue line, "was what attracted my programmer's attention in the first place. She called me in and I went to have a look. Frankly, I'd never seen anything like it. So I decided to examine it further. I took it next to a 100-by-100-mile basis."

Once more she worked the keyboard and new images appeared on the display screen.

"This time the incandescence of the infrared image in the middle is clearly marked, as is its position in relation to existing geological structures. We have here," she pointed to the screen, "a lineament of some sort, possibly a fold or a fracture, running through the incandescent area. There are also signs of a circular impact structure."

She allowed them time to contemplate the picture.

"Finally, I decided to look at the area on a 10-by-10-mile basis. I should warn you that the picture you will see is rather bright. There's perhaps some distortion in the reconstituted color. That's understandable—we don't usually deal with infrared images of such intensity."

Silcott stared at the picture in astonishment. He blinked as the bright red light filled the whole of the screen and burned into the room, then let out a long, low whistle.

"Man! Isn't that something! Where is it?"

"Northeast Asia. Manchuria. But the question is: *What* is it? What the hell is it?"

There was a long silence, broken only by the distant whirr of cars on the Balto–Wash Parkway. Ella Richmond switched off the screen; the image was too bright for them to keep looking at it steadily.

They turned to Silcott, as if waiting for him to reveal some magical formula. But the geophysicist was a cautious man. He never jumped to conclusions and he distrusted people who did. He was not interested in guesswork; he was interested in proper scientific assessment. And that meant not moving farther than the evidence itself permitted.

Their stares irritated him. "I'm not sure I know the answer," he snapped. "It's not really my field. I'm basically a seismologist now, you know."

Mobley pressed him. "You may be a seismologist, Wilbur, but

you also happen to know more about minerals and mineral formation than any other scientist in the United States."

Silcott accepted the compliment reluctantly. "Okay," he sighed. "Let's take the series again. Same order."

Once more they looked at the images. When he had seen enough, Silcott said, "Okay, that'll do. You can turn it off."

Richmond cleared the screen. The incandescent blob died away into a pinprick of light and then disappeared altogether.

They continued to look at Silcott expectantly. Instead of giving them an answer, he asked a question. "In your background presentation, Ed, you said the spacecraft carries sensors which, among other things, can measure sunlight in the infrared part of the spectrum, the part that's visible to the eye. You also said that the multispectral scanner is sensitive to a fourth band in the infrared, near 1-micrometer wavelength. But what about detection of *thermal* infrared? Does LANDSAT have a capability in that area?"

Silcott saw the glance that passed between Mobley and Richmond.

"Well?" He pressed the point. "Does it?"

Mobley spent some time examining his fingernails. Finally he looked up. "Wilbur, what I'm about to say shouldn't go beyond the four walls of this room. Is that clear?"

Silcott nodded. "Don't worry about me, Ed. I'm cleared for secret and top-secret material. You can check on that. I can give you a number to call now, if you like."

"I won't bother. I know you. I just wanted you to realize the area we were getting into."

After another pause, he continued: "You asked about LAND-SAT's capability to detect thermal infrared and, of course, you've hit the nail right on the head. LANDSAT 3 *does* have a thermal channel. This is a very new development indeed. To my knowledge LANDSAT 3 is the only resources satellite in the world with such a channel. The Soviets haven't got it. The Chinese haven't got it." He leaned forward. "You're a geologist, Wilbur. You can understand what this kind of breakthrough could mean. It's a quantum jump. If we can detect major mineral deposits by remote-sensing methods using thermal infra-red, we may have revolutionized the whole science of geological exploration. With LANDSAT 3 we're using orbital remote sens-ing to detect temperature anomalies due to geothermal heat. We are working on the theory that important concentrations of minerals in the earth's crust may either generate, or be as-sociated with, thermal anomalies of one kind or another." *

Silcott whistled. "Hell, I can understand why you give this program a top-security classification. If the theory is right, you could use LANDSAT to map the world's major mineral deposits in just a couple of weeks. How's it going so far?"

Mobley looked at Richmond. "Tell Dr. Silcott the snag we've run into, Ella."

Richmond took up the tale. "We believe the theory is correct," she said, "but the problem is that the very low heat flow in-volved in most mineral deposits means that temperature anoma-lies due to geothermal heat are almost invariably swamped by diurnal and seasonal effects.† Until today, we hadn't had a sin-gle reading that stood out clearly above background. *What* was so exciting about today—and this was the reason we called you in—is that the strength of the image we've just seen means that we are talking at least 3 or 4 degrees Centigrade above back-ground. Maybe more."

Silcott whistled again. "Hey, that's some anomaly! I can see why you all started jumping around. This could be the big payoff!" He turned to Mobley. "Okay, Ed. You've answered my question. LANDSAT 3 does have a capability in the thermal in-frared area." He picked up a pencil and, in his careful handwrit-ing, wrote down the various options. "Let's look at the possibil-ities. Before we start talking in terms of a mineral deposit, we've got to look at other possible explanations. What kind of event or situation could produce a thermal anomaly of 3 or 4 degrees

---

* Thermal anomalies, in this case, are temperature differences between one rock formation and neighboring formations; the formations are distinguishable because of differences in the amounts of heat each radiates.

† That is, the heat radiated by minerals, is usually so faint, in comparison to the temperature of the earth's atmosphere, that it is hard to detect.

above background? A forest fire?" IIe wrote "forest fire" on the pad and underlined it.

Mobley shook his head. "Those images were the result of several satellite passes over a period of months. The blob appears in all of them, in exactly the same place and to exactly the same scale."

"Okay, let's rule that out." Silcott put a line through "forest fire." "We can also rule out volcanoes." He wrote "volcanoes" on the pad and immediately crossed it out.

"Why?" asked Richmond.

"If it's a volcano in eruption, you'd be able to pick out the smoke in the visible spectrum. And on the images we've just seen there is no sign of smoke. All the volcanoes in the recent past have been detected by satellite."

"Right," Mobley said.

"I'd rule out hot springs too," Silcott continued. "Even in New Zealand at the Waimangu fields, where you've got some of the biggest geysers in the world, you've only got a degree or two above background. Plus, there would be other signs, such as steam clouds, which we don't find in the visual imagery."

"What about a magma* at depth trying to work its way to the surface?" asked Mobley.

Silcott thought about that one. "Unlikely on the evidence. If the magma is of sufficient intensity to produce a 3- or 4-degree temperature change at the surface, you'd expect to find also silica or carbonate deposits. Hot solutions, affected by pressures. And there's no sign of those."

No one spoke for a few minutes. Then Silcott said: "Very well. Let's suppose it *is* some mineral deposit. What kind of mineral deposit could it be? I'm familiar with the geothermal heat theory, of course, though I hadn't realized that you people at Goddard were testing it out operationally in connection with LANDSAT. The problem is that I can't at the moment think of any kind of deposit that could produce that kind of thermal anomaly at the surface."

As he spoke Silcott was aware that something was ticking

---

* Molten rock beneath the earth's crust.

away in his subconscious, some deep-buried magma was trying to thrust its way to the surface. He felt that the answer would come to him in the end, but he needed time.

"Let me sleep on it. We may be able to look at this from a different angle in the morning. In the meantime you should put a block on that series of images. Your security may be pretty tight. Even so, the fewer people who know about this, the better. I've got a feeling this is tremendously important."

"Can we do that, Ella?" Mobley asked. "Can we block it?"

"No problem," Richmond replied. "We'll just put a 'series unavailable' signal on the tape."

"Good." For the moment Silcott seemed satisfied. Preparing to leave, he shook hands all around.

"Nice to meet you, Dr. Richmond."

"Nice to meet you, Dr. Silcott."

"Call me Wilbur."

"Call me Ella."

They both laughed.

"You'll be hearing from me, Ed."

"Sooner rather than later?"

"You bet."

Silcott and his wife had to go out to dinner that evening, so it was not until he got to bed around midnight that he was able to continue his review of the possibilities. They had that afternoon ruled out man-made causes, as well as volcanoes, hot springs, and magmas, and he believed they were right. What was left?

His wife fell asleep beside him but he still tossed and turned, seeking enlightenment.

"What's the matter, Will?" His wife sounded irritated. "You're keeping me awake."

"I'm sorry. I can't sleep. I'm trying to work something out."

His wife sighed. She had had fifteen years to come to terms with Silcott's quirks.

"Do you . . .?" she began.

"No," he replied hurriedly. "Not now."

She turned away, pulled the sheets around her shoulders, and went back to sleep.

The moon rose and shone into the room. Silcott stared back at it and suddenly he thought he had the answer. The clue was to look not to the present but to the past, to the time when the earth and its satellite were being formed and history did not exist.

He leaped out of bed in his pajamas crying, "Oklo!"

His wife stirred. "What?" she mumbled.

Silcott, who had already found his dressing gown and slippers, repeated it. "Oklo!"

"Oh, I see."

"I bet you don't." With that he padded down to his study and to his library of books and scientific journals. His pulse racing with excitement, he went through the carefully arranged shelves until he found what he was looking for. It was a thick volume, about five hundred pages in length, which bore the title: *The Oklo Phenomenon (Proceedings of the Libreville Symposium, 1975), International Atomic Energy Agency, Vienna.* He took it down and slumped into an armchair. For an hour he read intently, jotting occasional notes. Once or twice he nodded as if satisfied that something he had suspected was confirmed by the evidence. Finally, he snapped the book shut and replaced it on the shelf. Though it was by now after 2 A.M., he went to the phone on his desk and punched out Ed Mobley's number. The phone rang five times and then a sleepy voice said: "Hello? Who is it?"

"Ed, this is Wilbur Silcott. . . ."

"Wilbur . . ."

"Ed, listen. I think I've got the answer on the thermal anomaly. I need to come on over and talk to you."

"You're coming now?"

"Ed, this could be big. It could be the biggest ever."

Mobley was by then wide awake. "Okay, Wilbur. You live in Chevy Chase, don't you? So take Wisconsin Avenue down into Georgetown and turn left on O Street. We're at the corner of O and Twenty-ninth."

"I know the way." Silcott put down the phone.

As he started the car, he was hardly aware of the fact that he was still in his pajamas and dressing gown. His mind, always active, was now keyed to a high pitch. He knew, as clearly as he knew anything, that he had just stumbled upon one of the greatest scientific discoveries of all time.

Twenty minutes later he parked by a hydrant, a thing he would normally never have done, and ran up the steps to the door of a pretty, shuttered house. Mobley had been watching for him and let him in before he had a chance to ring the bell. They sat in the sitting room while Silcott, hardly able to suppress the excitement in his voice, explained his theory. "My assessment of what we were looking at yesterday," he said, "is that the intense infrared images are an indication of a high degree of *radioactivity*."

Mobley was skeptical. "The satellite is not sensitive to radioactivity," he said.

The geophysicist was not put off his stride. "Agreed. The satellite won't measure radioactivity as such. But what it *will* measure under certain circumstances is the *heat* generated by radioactive ore bodies."

Mobley was still skeptical. "I don't know of any ore body that could produce that kind of thermal anomaly at the surface."

Silcott leaned back in his chair and lit a cigarette. "You've heard," he asked, almost smugly, "of the Oklo natural reactor in Gabon?"

"Vaguely. Tell me about it."

"The discovery of the Oklo natural reactor," he began, "for those who know about it, was one of the most exciting scientific events of this century. Back in the early 1970s, French scientists at Pierrelatte, France's main center for the development of atomic energy, noted they were getting uranium samples with a low U235 count. They were interested, because this was a completely unusual phenomenon. Normally, as you know, the distribution of the isotopes that make up uranium—U238, U235, and so on—never varies. So they did some pretty fancy detective work and tracked the source of the ore to a boat that had offloaded in Marseilles Harbor, and from there they traced the shipment back to Gabon in West Africa.

"After that," he continued, "the French scientists co-operating with the Gabonese authorities organized a field expedition to look at the uranium mines themselves in Gabon, and that was when they discovered the Oklo natural reactor. Basically Oklo was a huge uranium deposit that went critical* about seventeen hundred million years ago. The reactor shut off fairly soon, let's say after operating for a period somewhere between five million and one hundred million years. Do you follow me?"

"Perfectly."

"Now," Silcott continued, "what caused the deposit to go critical? The general feeling among the scientists involved was that there were two important factors. First, there was the composition of the uranium ore itself. As you know, normally U_3O_8, or uranium oxide, contains only 0.7 per cent of fissile U235 as against 99.3 per cent of nonfissile U238. But in Oklo scientists believed that they had a uranium body that contained a much higher percentage of U235 than we find today."

Mobley was riveted by the explanation.

"Go on."

"The second reason," said Silcott, "is that the deposit is free of the rare earth elements and this may have helped the reaction. The rare earths tend to act as a poison." †

"Why did the reactor shut off?"

"The best guess is that the U235 was depleted as a result of the reaction. If you examine the Oklo ore today—as the French scientists discovered when they first went to Gabon—it is almost entirely deficient in U235. The fissile element has, in other words, been thoroughly burned—which, of course, means that Oklo is of great scientific interest but not of much commercial or military interest."

"So you reckon that what we have here is an Oklo-type natural reactor?"

"I can't think of any other explanation."

For a few minutes both men were wrapped in thought. Then Mobley stood up. "I need a drink. Can I get you one?"

Silcott shook his head. "No, thanks." He had had quite enough stimulus for one evening.

---

* A radioactive mass is said to "go critical" when it starts a self-sustaining chain reaction—nuclear fission.

† A "poison" is a substance that retards nuclear fission.

Mobley came back to the sofa with a glass of brandy and sat down.

"You know," he said, sipping at his glass with a reflective look in his eyes, "I once heard Edward Teller give a lecture on his early experiences as a nuclear physicist. He was over seventy at the time but still a huge bear of a man. He had this ability to capture his audience completely. He never used notes, never hid behind a lectern. He just stood there center-stage and talked in his great roaring voice. In the middle of the lecture he told a story about how he had first heard of the possibility of nuclear fission. 'I was working in New York at the time,' Teller told us, 'since I had just fled from Nazi Germany. I was playing a Mozart concerto on the piano when the telephone rang. It was Leo Szilard, who was working up at Columbia University. Szilard said, 'I've found the neutron.' I remember the moment to this day.' "

Mobley paused. "I feel now like Teller must have felt then, as though somehow I've just witnessed history being born. I see why you said this might be big."

"I said biggest ever."

Mobley drained his glass and leaned forward to address his guest. "Is there a way of finding out for sure whether the deposit really is what you think it is?"

"Verify the hypothesis? Is that what you mean? Yes, of course we can do that. We can do what geologists have done ever since they invented the game. We can go out there and get our hands dirty and take a look. That's what they did with Oklo. They sent a team in. No reason why we shouldn't do the same."

"Jesus Christ, Wilbur!" Mobley exclaimed. "Don't you remember that when we were out there at Goddard we told you where this thing is? Those LANDSAT images were taken over the East Asian mainland. The area we've been looking at is in Manchuria, on the frontier between China and the Soviet Union—the one they're always fighting over. The river in the image is the Ussuri. That river is the Sino-Soviet international frontier. The thermal anomaly lies a few miles across the river on the Soviet side. How are we going to dig *there*?"

Silcott was silenced momentarily. Then he said, in a petulant voice, like a child deprived of a favorite toy, "I still think we ought to take a look. No scientific hypothesis is worth anything without verification. We need evidence, field data, and we can't get that while we're sitting on our backsides in Washington."

Mobley thought they had taken it about as far as they could for one night's session. "I don't disagree with you, Wilbur. It's a question of finding the right way." He held the door open for his visitor. "Good night."

"Good night, Ed."

"We'll talk tomorrow, okay?"

"You mean 'today'?"

"Yes, of course."

Silcott drove back home. His wife sat up in bed. "Where on earth have you been?" she asked.

"Uhuh," Silcott replied noncommittally.

There was a time to talk and a time to think. This was a time for thinking. He wanted to think first and then, if there was still an hour or two of the night left, he wanted to sleep.

2

Roberto Delgado slid into the driver's seat of his silver-gray Porsche and gunned the motor into life. He sat there for a second or two, revving the engine. Then, caring nothing for the peace of the night, he twisted and snarled through the back streets of Georgetown. When he hit Wisconsin Avenue, he headed north.

He was well satisfied with his evening. The girl—what was her name? Sheila? Shirley?—had been impressed by him, as he had known she would be. As a diplomat, he knew all the right moves. As the son of one of Brazil's richest industrialists, he had the money to go with it. When he had told the girl his name was Roberto Delgado, her eyes had lit up.

"Not *the* Delgados?" she had asked.

"Yes. *The* Delgados," he had replied. The effect was the same as one would have achieved, twenty years earlier, with the name Getty or Oppenheimer or Rockefeller. Nowadays even silly little girls knew the big money was south of the Rio Grande and above all in Brazil.

They had had dinner in town. He had told her about Rio and Copacabana, about his ranch in Matto Grosso and his private plane. She had asked him back to her apartment and they had gone to bed.

Easing the Porsche into the garage of his luxurious house near the cathedral, Delgado reflected that it had been a particularly pleasurable experience. In his life he had had more girls than he could count, and he hoped that would continue. But little Shirley—it *was* Shirley, he remembered now—was something special. He liked brunettes. And he had liked Shirley's hair particularly. It was soft to the touch, almost like velvet. When she had gone down on him, he had put both hands on her lovely velvety head while he writhed in ecstasy.

More surprising, Shirley had had something else to offer. During a lull, he had asked her what she did and where she worked. He hadn't expected to be interested—normally girls like Shirley seemed to lead working lives of the most ghastly monotony, which probably explained why they were so ready to go to bed. But in fact he had been quite engrossed by her description of her work out at the Goddard Space Flight Center.

"And you know," she told him, "there was some kind of crisis today. I saw the thing in the first place but then the supervisor came along and took a look and the next I knew I was being hauled off to the director's office and told I mustn't talk to anybody." She giggled and snuggled up to him in the bed, her hand moving to his groin. "Still, talking to Brazilian playboys doesn't count, does it?"

At first Delgado had pretended not to care. But later he had returned almost casually to the subject.

"That thing you spotted on the screen? What kind of thing was it?"

After a while, she told him what she knew. She couldn't see the harm. In any case, she liked Delgado, liked his Porsche, liked the idea of sunning herself on the Copacabana Beach. Perhaps she could keep him interested.

3

Ella Richmond, a mug of steaming coffee in her hand, came into the office of the chief of Goddard's Laboratory for Meteorology and Earth Sciences. "Here, take this, Ed," she said. "You look as if you could use it. What happened? More insomnia?"

Mobley received the coffee gratefully. "Silcott stopped by around two A.M. He had an idea about the image. Sit down. I'll tell you about it."

When he finished, Richmond was awestruck. "So," she said, releasing a breath, "where do we go from here?"

"I'm not sure. What do you think? Do we file a report in the normal way? Do we call a meeting? Do we go on up the line? I said I'd get back to Silcott this morning."

"Ed, I think I know what we can do. There are some personal factors involved here, though, and I'd like your judgment on those too."

"Go ahead, Ella." Mobley had known her long enough to know it was worth listening to whatever she had to say.

"Have you ever met Thaddeus Ricker?" Richmond began.

Mobley shook his head. "No. Why do you ask?"

"Because a couple of years back, before he came to Washington and became a bigshot, I ran into him at a conference on resources policy out in the Midwest. He was chairing one of the sessions and I was giving a paper. To tell you the truth"—she almost blushed—"he took me out to dinner once during the conference and I almost felt something would come of it. But I guess he was just bored and needed company, because when the conference ended, I never heard from him again." She shrugged. "I thought I might have."

"What are you suggesting?"

"I'm suggesting I might give Thaddeus K. Ricker a ring. Just for old times' sake. If we could get straight through to him, we could cut out the red tape and save ourselves a lot of trouble."

Mobley looked at her with frank appraisal. Of course he realized what Ricker must have seen in her. Ella Richmond was determined, self-confident, and successful in a field dominated by men. And somehow it all was reflected in her looks, in the way she held herself, in the way she spoke and thought. But Mobley had his doubts about whether she was on the right course.

"If you ask me, Ella," he said, "I think you're sticking your neck out. Why do you think he'll remember you?"

"Come off it, Ed. It's worth a try, isn't it? At the worst, I'll have some secretary hang up on me."

"And at best?"

"At best, we'll get some action on this thermal-image business a lot quicker than if we start writing memoranda to each other."

Mobley could guess why Richmond, who was usually so cool and collected, was sounding flustered. He teased her gently.

"And you may get to see Thaddeus Ricker? Isn't that right?"

"Damn you, Ed Mobley. If you hadn't drunk that coffee, I'd throw it all over you."

4

Thaddeus K. Ricker, United States Secretary for Energy, sat at his desk in his huge office on the seventeenth floor of the new Energy Department Building on Independence Avenue in Southwest Washington. He enjoyed being where he was. The flag mounted on the stand behind him, the framed and signed photograph of the President, the seal of his Department woven into the thick pile of the gold carpet that stretched from desk to door, the magnificient view over the Potomac, the private elevator, the layers of deputies and assistant deputies and deputy assistant deputies who existed, so it seemed, only to serve him— all these trappings of power and status he exploited to the full.

What was more, he enjoyed being *who* he was. He enjoyed his reputation as the toughest man in Washington; he enjoyed the respect in which he was held; the instant access to the President; the public recognition that he was doing a fine job handling the nation's crucial energy problems. The President had pulled him out of Milwaukee, where he had made a fortune as a businessman and financier, and had told him: "Get down there and shake 'em up. We have to turn this energy thing around and you're the man to do it."

Of course, he hadn't fully succeeded yet. The problem that

confronted him and the United States was too enormous, and he had been there too short a time to do more than a fraction of all that he hoped to do. But as he sat there, jaw jutting and thick mane of graying hair falling over his collar, he realized that he had made a good start. A damn good start. What he needed now was a bit of luck—a sudden fall in the price of oil, for example, or a breakthrough with fusion or solar energy. . . .

The buzzing of the telephone interrupted his daydream. His secretary, sounding faintly amused, said: "There's a woman on the line who wants to talk to you. She won't give her name. She says it's personal."

He spoke into the intercom. "Tell her I don't talk to people who don't give their names."

Seconds later, his secretary came back. This time the note of amusement was more pronounced. "She says her name is Ella Richmond. *Dr.* Ella Richmond. She says she met you a year or two ago in Dayton, Ohio, at a conference on resources. Do you want me to put her on to someone else or do you want to take the call? To tell you the truth, she sounds rather nice, Mr. Secretary."

An image was beginning to form in his mind, a pleasant image, featuring—among other things—a candlelit dinner and what for Dayton was passably good French food. Yes, he remembered the woman now. Tall, good-looking. More than competent. Gave one of the best papers of the session.

"Ask her if she works at the Goddard Space Flight Center?"

"She does. She already told me."

"Then put her through."

He picked up the ivory phone. "Hi, Ella," he said. "How are you? It's good to hear from you. How did you make out after that conference?"

At the other end of the line, Ella Richmond suddenly realized that she wasn't at all nervous. What difference did it make if Thaddeus Ricker was on first-name terms with the President? They had had dinner together—that was a bond, of sorts.

"Thaddeus," she said, risking familiarity, "I need to talk to you. Not over the phone. Do you have a minute in the next day or so?"

Ricker had a reputation for making decisions quickly. "How about lunch?"

"Today?"

"Well, they just canceled a Cabinet meeting so I've got a free spot. I remember you like French food. How about one o'clock at Jean-Paul?"

"Fine."

"I'll make a reservation. See you there."

He put down the phone and walked to the outer office. "Susanne, could you book a table for two at Jean-Paul for one o'clock today?" His secretary smiled.

He arrived at the restaurant ten minutes late. Jean-Paul himself came forward to greet the Energy Secretary. "Bonjour, Monsieur Ricker, 'ow are you today?" Jean-Paul's English was as good as Walter Cronkite's, but he laid on the French accent with a trowel.

"Fine, Jean-Paul. Absolutely fine. Has my guest arrived?"

"She is already 'ere, monsieur, waiting at your table." He permitted himself a slight wink. "A very good-looking lady, *n'est-ce pas?* I congratulate you on your good taste."

Ricker followed Jean-Paul to a quiet corner of the room. The other diners looked up as he went by. He waved at people he recognized and laid a hand here and there on a friendly shoulder. He was not a man who cared for anonymity.

Richmond stood up as he approached and held out her hand.

"Mr. Ricker. Thaddeus. This is a real pleasure. I can't tell you how grateful I am."

As Ricker sat down opposite her, he looked at her carefully and liked what he saw—the dark eyes, the fine nose, the firm chin. His glance strayed farther down and he liked that too.

"Don't be silly, Ella. The pleasure's mine. You saved me from sandwiches in the office."

She laughed and relaxed.

"Let's order first, shall we," said Thaddeus, "and get that out of the way?" They studied the menu and gave their orders to the waiter who hovered by the table. "I'm going to have a martini," Thaddeus told Ella. "What about you?"

"I'll stick to wine."

Thaddeus didn't waste time on small talk. If she didn't know what he had been doing since Dayton, Ohio, she hadn't been reading the newspapers. And if he wanted to know more about her, well, there would be time for that later.

"Shoot," he said.

Ella was about to plunge straight in when the waiter arrived with the drinks. She waited for him to finish serving before embarking on her story. Thaddeus took the point. As one of Washington's fashionable lunchtime restaurants, Jean-Paul had been witness to any number of indiscretions.

When the waiter had withdrawn, Ella said: "Ed Mobley knows I'm talking with you today. He knows we know each other. He thought it was probably the best step."

"Who's Ed Mobley?"

"He's chief of Goddard's Laboratory for Meteorology and Earth Sciences."

"Perhaps you had better start at the beginning."

So Ella told Thaddeus of the LANDSAT 3 program, of her discovery of the thermal anomaly, of the first evaluation of the satellite images, of Silcott's visit to the Goddard Space Flight Center, and of his preliminary assessment. She told him of the various hypotheses they had considered as they searched for an explanation of the anomaly. Finally, she told of the meeting that morning between Mobley and Silcott and of the startling suggestion Silcott had made.

Increasingly engaged by her story and anxious to persuade him of the urgency of the matter, she leaned toward him across the table. Though the background noise was at a high level as the lunchtime crowd finished its meal and relaxed over brandy and cigars, she lowered her voice. "You know," she said, "we might be dealing with the biggest deposit in history. I don't know, somehow it really frightens me. . . ."

"Frightens you?"

"To think of all that plutonium. Ever since Three Mile Island—we came so close to a real disaster. I mean, the *experts* were scared. The thought of hundreds of new reactors—it really unsettles me."

"But don't you see? Three Mile Island was the salvation of

nuclear power, not its downfall. It taught us the lesson we absolutely had to learn if nuclear power is to have a real future, that the safeguards must be far better than we'd let ourselves think. Believe me, I know the reaction in the scientific community—I talk to these guys all the time—and they've really got religion now. There was a lot of arrogance among the nuclear power people before Three Mile; they figured they were *it,* and they didn't have to explain or account to anybody. And so they got careless. Now they've banged their heads on the ceiling, and I can tell you, they're a hell of a lot humbler now than they used to be. There's been a tremendous tightening up of standards. The whole thrust is toward better safeguards, not more and more exotic equipment. I wouldn't worry about the use of the plutonium. The thing to worry about is who gets control of it."

Ella frowned.

"You don't look very convinced," Thaddeus said, smiling.

"I want to be, but what you're saying sounds like the kind of rationalization they always hand out after something like Three Mile. I find it hard to believe those people ever learn any lessons. Anyway, I just hope . . . well, at least for the time being we're the only ones who know about this deposit. The Russians don't, and the Chinese don't either."

Thaddeus came back sharply. "Are you sure of that? I thought some of that LANDSAT stuff was public domain! Don't you think someone else might have gotten wind of it?"

Ella shook her head. "I agree that it's U.S. policy that all LANDSAT images should be available on request to a bona-fide user. In practice what we do is this: We keep the master tapes in our central archives out at Goddard. The tape relating to the deposit area has, since yesterday, been taken from these central archives into a place of safekeeping. What is public domain are the photographs that have been based on the tapes, not the tapes themselves. In fact, photographs go out from Goddard to three Federal Data Centers."

"And those centers received copies of the photographs of the area you were looking at yesterday."

"Yes. Among thousands of others."

"I see what you mean."

For another twenty minutes Thaddcus questioned her closely. Then he looked at his watch and signaled to the waiter to pull out the table. In front of the restaurant his official car was waiting at the curb. "Can I give you a lift?" he asked Ella. "I'm afraid I've got to get right back to the office—I'm late for a meeting—but you could ride with me, and then Walter could drive you out to Goddard."

"Oh, thanks. I've got my own car. It's in the lot just around the corner."

"Well, maybe we could go limousine-riding some other time." He looked at her for a moment. "I'm glad you called me. And I'm glad you told me what you did. That was the right thing to do."

"Will Ed and I hear what happens next?"

"Yes, sure, I'll be in touch. It's an incredible situation. I'll call you."

"Good. I hope you will. Thank you so much for the lunch—it was lovely. Big change from the Goddard cafeteria, I can tell you."

"You're a big change from the types I usually have lunch with. I promise you that. A very welcome change."

"Good-bye, Thaddeus."

"Good-bye, Ella," he replied, wondering for an instant if it would be out of place to kiss her on the cheek and deciding it would. She turned and he watched her until she rounded the corner.

He realized his chauffeur was eyeing him. "Walter," he said gruffly, getting into the long, black automobile, "how can I get a nation to cut back on its energy consumption when I can't even get my own driver to switch his damned engine off while he waits?"

The chauffeur turned around and smiled broadly. "You're wasting your time, boss," he said. "Nobody's going to cut back on energy. You'd better get busy finding some more."

"You could be right, Walter." Thaddeus sank back into the seat. "You just could be right."

Back in his office, he made three phone calls on a secure line. The first was to Ed Mobley at Goddard. They talked for three minutes. At the end of it Mobley agreed to what Thaddeus asked.

"Okay," Mobley said. "I'll arrange for the master tape of that series to be lost. We'll take it out of the archives altogether. You realize I may be risking my neck."

"You'll get written authority in the morning."

The second call was to Lloyd Oakes, director of the Federal Bureau of Information. Without going into detail, saying only that the LANDSAT series was extremely important, Thaddeus came rapidly to the point. "In the event the photographs have been requested from one of the Federal Data Centers, we'll want all the particulars. Who requested them? And when? For what purpose? Surveillance if necessary. And I want all copies of the photographs still in the Federal Data Centers withdrawn. However unlikely it may seem, there may be some clue on the photos about the nature of the anomaly. That operation had better be clandestine. The less attention we draw to this series the better."

"Are you asking us to do a break-in job?"

"The Data Centers are Federal facilities. The Federal Government is responsible for them. We can't burgle ourselves."

Oakes sounded unconvinced. "Are you sure? We'll want something in writing."

"You'll get it."

The third call was to George Chisman, the director of the CIA. He dialed the "hot line" extension direct.

"George? I need to talk to you today. Can I drop by your office this afternoon?"

The voice on the other end of the line answered without any hesitation.

"Okay. How about four o'clock?"

At three-thirty he pressed the button on the private elevator that would take him direct to the garage. He was going to drive himself this time, in a smaller, less prepossessing government car. He took Memorial Bridge across the river, turning right on George Washington Drive. A few miles later he pulled into the Central Intelligence Agency parking lot. He parked but sat in the car for a time, looking out across the river, focusing his mind on the problem at hand. *Imagine,* he told himself, *that this is the Ussuri River, not the Potomac. Imagine that this is the Chinese side of the river and over there is the Russian side. Imagine that not far into the Russian side there may be a deposit of immensely valuable material but you're not really sure what it is. What the hell do you do? How do you verify the hypothesis? And, once you've verified the hypothesis, what do you do about it?*

After ten minutes, he looked at his watch, satisfied that it was time to go. George Chisman would be waiting for him.

The phone was ringing as Thaddeus opened his apartment door that evening. He ran to get it and immediately recognized the deep, booming voice of Lloyd Oakes, the FBI director

"You've got problems," Oakes said.

"What do you mean?"

"Someone requested and received those photos from the Federal Data Center in Suitland, Maryland, three days ago. A Brazilian outfit, based in São Paulo. Thought you'd like to know. The photos in the other centers are still intact. They've been 'lost' now. Like you asked."

"Thanks. Anything on the Brazilians? Are they bona fide?"

"They seem to be. It's a fairly large international consulting firm. Consultados Tecnicos do Brasil. They have a Washington office. New Hampshire and M Street. We're following up."

Replacing the receiver, Thaddeus kicked off his shoes and surveyed his luxurious bachelor apartment with some dissatisfaction. It was convenient—anyone who lived in the Watergate and worked in the White House could walk to work and even get back home for lunch if he had time. It was comfortable. He didn't have to cook if he didn't want to—the hotel would send up a meal. But he realized that, in spite of all the advantages, he was getting bored with living by himself.

He walked toward the refrigerator, hesitated, then turned back. He picked up the telephone and dialed a number.

"Ella, this is Thaddeus Ricker." He heard the little gasp of surprise. "I'm sorry I didn't get back to you before. I'm afraid I've been pretty tied up."

"It's nice to hear from you anyway."

"A new Chinese restaurant just opened on Connecticut Avenue, and I was thinking of going there to eat. Are you free by any chance?"

Just before nine, Thaddeus drove up Connecticut, past Dupont Circle, toward the Calvert Street Bridge. He glanced curiously at the blank façade of the Chinese embassy, which stood on the left just before the bridge. When he first came to Washington, the building was a hotel. What was its name? Royal Windsor? Windsor Park? Then the Chinese had bought it, and all the windows on the ground floor had been blocked in, and the compound at the back surrounded by a high wire fence. And then, after diplomatic relations with China had been restored during the Carter administration, the embassy had become one of the liveliest in Washington.

Ella was already in her coat when Thaddeus arrived to pick her up, and so it was not until they reached the restaurant that he saw what she was wearing. It was a dusty rose silk blouse, which seemed to cast a faint glow of the same hue upon her cheeks. He was stirred by the sight of her sitting across the little table from him, and he recalled how he had felt after their first meeting: the pleasure of having found someone to be more than expected, better than remembered, and the sense that agreeable revelations might be in store.

"You don't mind eating with me again so soon?" he asked, smiling.

"I assumed you had extremely important government business to discuss," she said playfully. "I'd be pretty upset to think you brought me to this lovely place for any other reason."

"I guess I could have handled the official business in a memorandum. You haven't lived until you've received one of my five-page memoranda."

"I'll take a five-page menu over a five-page memo any day."

"You know, I've almost called you half a dozen times today."

"Why didn't you?"

"Well, maybe I'm shy."

"That's not precisely my image of you."

"Oh, I'm very shy. I just cover it up with all this aggressive behavior."

"I'll have to take that under advisement. I'll let you know in a couple of months." They were both struck by that statement—by the overt suggestion that they might be seeing each other for months. He saw her expression change and knew she was wondering about him.

"I did, as a matter of fact, you'll be pleased to hear, have some business to discuss with you," he said. He told her about the checks they had run on the Federal Data Centers. "Why do you think a Brazilian firm requested that particular series?"

"Could be for lots of reasons. There are plenty of international consulting firms using LANDSAT photographs. Why shouldn't a Brazilian firm do the same? Brazil's a major economic power nowadays. How many other series did they request? Maybe they asked for several hundred photographs and they don't even know what they've got.

"And remember," she continued, "there's an important difference between the photographs and the tapes. Under the LANDSAT 3 program, we work with the tapes themselves, not the photographs. The tapes contain all the basic data. On the tapes there are sixty-four gradations in each intensity measurement. You can write a specific computer program to make what you want to see stand out clearly. It's really amazing. We call it image enhancement, using reconstituted color instead of real color. That way we can be much more subtle in our analysis of the data. If they don't have the tapes or interpretation capability we've developed out at Goddard, they won't get very far. You can't pick out a thermal anomaly from looking at photographs."

Thaddeus was reassured. "We'll keep a check on them anyway," he said, and then turned to the waiter to order drinks.

"By the way," Ella asked during dinner, "how did you get my number? I'm unlisted."

"I have my ways," he said, and then realized he had not said it as lightly as intended.

"Don't tell me," she replied, "that even the Department of Energy has its intelligence agents."

"Nothing as formal as that," he said, "but I can usually find out what I need to know."

"What else did you need to know about me?"

"Just the phone number, and . . ."

"And what?"

"Well, and whether you're married."

"And am I?"

Thaddeus thought he caught a note of irritation. "No," he said, trying to be jocular, "you're not. You were, but you're not. Isn't that right?"

She didn't reply, and she didn't raise her eyes.

"You don't mind my knowing that," he said, "do you?"

"I don't mind your knowing that," she said, "but I think I do mind just a little bit the way you went about finding it out. There's something so Washington about it—sending out spies to check up on people."

"I didn't send out spies. I just had someone make a phone call."

"Same thing."

"What if I'd just come right out and asked you?"

"I'd have told you."

He leaned across the table to her and looked at her steadily until she began to soften. "Ella," he said simply, "are you married?"

"I was, but I'm not."

"Me neither."

"I know."

"Aha! You sent out spies."

"No."

"You made a phone call."

"No," she said, laughing. "It was in the newspapers. Your divorce."

"You're telling me. Talk about things being 'so Washington.' Back home in Milwaukee, they don't put people's divorces in the paper."

"That would have been all I needed."

"Were you married long?"

"Twelve years, beginning the year we got out of grad school.

No children. Somehow I knew children would be wrong. We just didn't have a good enough thing going. One day I woke up and looked at my face in the mirror and said to myself: 'Ella, it's now or never. If you're going to make a break, this has to be the time.' So I just walked out while he was still asleep. He wasn't a bad guy. Just no imagination. All he really cared about was reverse osmosis."

Thaddeus was less specific about his own situation. He talked of "differences," and he hinted that his ex-wife had been a drinker. As he talked, Ella got the impression of an ambitious man so absorbed by his career that no wife could compete. But she also caught a hint of self-awareness, some signs that Thaddeus knew what his mistakes had been. He obviously enjoyed his rank and the perquisites of his job. When people at other tables looked over, recognizing him, she could see he was pleased. He was self-important, no question about that, but not really in the obnoxious sense. At least she hoped not. That night, after he had dropped her off, she sat in her kitchen for a while thinking about him.

5

When McNamara was running the Pentagon back in the sixties, the loudspeakers on the E Ring would announce that the Secretary would be on the squash court within ten minutes and expected a game. That was as good as an order. Twenty officers would leave their desks and sprint to the changing rooms. Clifford R. Bledsoe, the chairman of the Joint Chiefs of Staff, was less authoritarian. He preferred to play his Friday lunchtime game of squash with his normal partner, a military aide. The aide didn't go in for drop shots but played it long, which meant that Bledsoe could stay well back in the court—without running too much—and slash away with his powerful forehand.

This was more or less what he was doing when Otis Oman, the current Defense Secretary, summoned him to join a National Security Council meeting at the White House in thirty minutes.

He took a shower, ending as always with sixty seconds of ice-cold water. Then he dressed quickly. Twenty-five minutes later Bledsoe's car, flying the Joint Chiefs' pennant, was waved through by the guard at the White House gate.

By the time he arrived, still flushed from his game, the others were already there. The meeting was run by Gordon Kristof, the hard-nosed chairman of the National Security Council. He was a controlled, hatchet-faced man, intolerant of joking or frivolity. This afternoon he looked especially grim.

He gave them all a long, commanding stare. "Gentlemen, we're here to discuss a serious breach of SAG regulations. It appears that our Energy Secretary and our CIA director have taken it upon themselves to fly a remotely piloted drone over a sensitive area of the Sino-Soviet border. I am hoping they have an acceptable explanation!"

Thaddeus Ricker was not intimidated by Kristof's statement. Ricker knew the breach of rules would be overlooked when he told them what he'd found out with that drone. Still, he had to respond. "Gordon, if my head's on the line for this, okay, but the blame is mine, no one else's. I take full responsibility."

George Chisman smiled quickly at Thaddeus across the table. "Mr. Chairman, why don't we hear the facts before we start assigning blame? It might put all this procedural business into the proper perspective."

There was a murmur of agreement around the table. The other members of the National Security Council had no particular desire to see Ricker or Chisman browbeaten by Kristof. For all they knew, it might be their turn next week.

Oakes of the FBI also rallied to his colleagues' defense. He was a large, red-faced man whose stentorian tones and sometimes oafish behavior disguised a devastatingly sharp mind. "I agree, Gordon. Let's have the facts first. We can get the lash from the closet later if we need to."

Kristof shot him a sour look but conceded the point. "Okay, what *are* the facts? Let's begin at the beginning. Thaddeus?"

Thaddeus was brief and to the point. He sat up straight in his chair and told them the story in short, clear sentences. He included in his account a passing reference to the Oklo natural reactor in Gabon and ended with the recent attempts to verify the LANDSAT evidence at firsthand.

As he finished, expressions of amazement punctuated the stillness of the room.

"As for the drone," he continued, "we had a little help from our friends in the U.S. Navy. As a matter of fact, it turned out

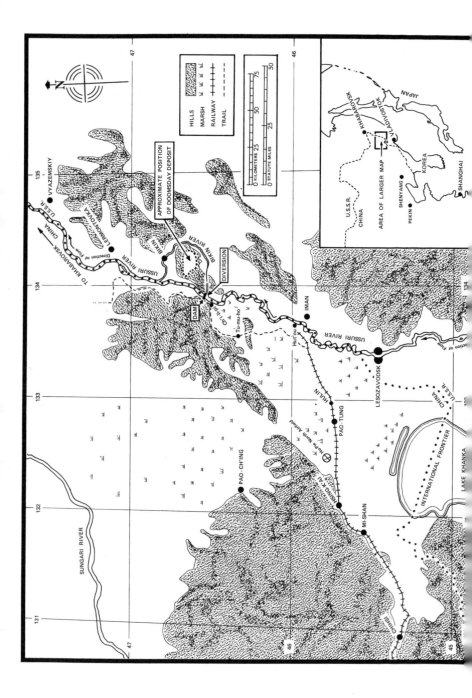

that the commander of the aircraft carrier we used as a launching base for the drone had been a classmate of mine in the distant past. Riverside High School, Milwaukee. Class of '48. You know how these things go."

There was a rustle of laughter in the room. Suddenly Kristof lost his temper. "Goddamn you!" he shouted. "This isn't funny. Why can't you people learn to play by the rules?" He banged on the table with his fist. "What if the drone had been spotted or shot down?"

George Chisman smiled benignly across the table. "This wasn't a big plane," he interrupted. "There was no pilot. We used a remote-control Paladyne machine with a unique delta configuration contributing to a very low radar cross section and low visual, acoustic, and infrared signatures. We're talking, by the way, about a drone with only an eight-foot wingspan, length about five feet, and average speed in flight around two hundred miles per hour. Frankly, it is highly improbable that the presence of our little drone in the border area was noticed at all and certainly not by anyone who matters."

As Kristof considered this information, Ricker took advantage of the silence to take control again. "With your permission, Mr. Chairman, I would like to ask Dr. Wilbur Silcott himself, who is attending today's meeting at my request, to present our findings. Dr. Silcott, as I already explained, has played a key role in the evaluation of the data."

Kristof, recognizing that the feeling in the room was running against him, gave in.

"Okay. Go ahead, Silcott," he said gruffly.

Although he gave classes twice a week at American University, Silcott had never lectured to a group like this. At bottom, he felt uneasy in the presence of so many politicians. He liked dealing with facts, not with the intangibles that went into political decisions.

He stood up and moved to a projector mounted at one end of the long rectangular table at which the men were sitting. He paused while they shifted their chairs to get a clear view, and he dimmed the lights.

"What I am projecting now is a USAF operational navigation

chart, scale 1 to 1,000,000—quite detailed enough for our purposes. It is fairly recent, mainly based on satellite reconnaissance supplemented by other sources." He paused and then added, "Satellites don't, of course, tell us international boundaries or the names of towns or rivers and so on."

He took a pencil flashlight from his pocket and directed the thin beam of light at the chart. "Let's start at the Ussuri at this point, about 40 miles north of the Forty-sixth Parallel, just above the village of Ch'i-li-pi. In this area, the river passes through a narrow defile. The 500-foot contour on both sides is right close to the river. About 10 miles farther on the defile opens up, the hills drop back on either side, and the river eventually flows out into the plain. On the Soviet side of the defile— as you know, of course, the Ussuri here forms the boundary between China and the Soviet Union—there is a piece of fairly mountainous territory. The map shows a high point of 3,586 feet. The area is bounded on the left, or west, by the Ussuri. For the rest it is more or less encircled by a smaller river, shown on the map as the Bikin."

Silcott turned back to his audience.

"What we were trying to do," he explained in case they had forgotten, "was to identify the source of the thermal anomaly. We were working under the hypothesis that, within the area I have just indicated, some substantial radioactive ore body was producing a temperature effect detectable in infrared by satellite. If this hypothesis was correct, then in our view there were certain effects that should be observable—and measurable—by a low-flying aircraft or drone. The most important of these, of course, is the natural radioactivity itself. In the past they used to sling Geiger counters beneath the wings and then try to count the clicks above the roar of the engine. Nowadays we have a more sophisticated device known as a scintillation detector, which was—in this case—built into the fuselage of the drone. Because of the efficiency of the scintillation detector in indicating the presence of gamma rays, it is possible to differentiate emanations from different kinds of mineral sources.

"On this particular mission, the drone flew about 100 feet above the ground. Because we needed to be able to correlate the readings we received, the drone made 6 passes over the area, on parallel tracks not more than half a mile apart and, of course, at a constant height in relation to the ground. I should add that all these passes were at the relatively slow speed of 100 knots."

Dr. Silcott paused in his presentation. "At this point I am going to run the film that the drone took with its miniaturized on-board cameras throughout this part of its mission. This visual information is important for geological purposes because it helps us correlate the instrument data with the observed geological configurations. It may also help you, gentlemen, to visualize the kind of terrain we are dealing with."

He switched on the machine, and the film began to run. "You will note that these are very high-quality images. The aerial cameras were specially mounted in the wings so as to minimize vibration. They were using high-speed film, with extra red sensitivity to permit high-speed exposures through filters. The cameras were directed so as to achieve a 60 per cent overlap, which means that we are able to view the results stereoscopically.

"What we are seeing now is the very first pass over the area. The drone is flying more or less due north, keeping the Ussuri on its starboard wingtip. Here we are over the Chinese village of Ch'i-li-pi. The plane is flying so low that we can see the dogs in the street and the first signs of movement as the village wakes up."

The only sound in the room, apart from Silcott's voice, was the faint whirr of the projector.

"Just past Ch'i-li-pi the drone was preprogrammed to turn east across the river. Here we are crossing the river now. You can see right away one of the reasons for the strength of the LANDSAT images. The ground below is virtually devoid of soil or vegetation, as though it has been cleared by a flash flood. So there would be no heat absorption."

They continued to watch in silence. The drone made its first traverse on a reading of 050 degrees. At the end of the run, it turned sharply to port and came back on the obverse heading of 230 degrees. After the fifth traverse, the drone banked to starboard.

"As we saw on the map," said Silcott, "that's the Bikin River coming in from the east to join the mainstream of the Ussuri. The drone is now going to circle to the east following the Bikin."

Through the eyes of the drone, they followed the Bikin upstream. The river curled around to the east of the deposit area, shrinking in size, until its headwaters were lost among the rocks. They could see how it had cut a channel back toward the main stem of the Ussuri. Barely more than a mile of rock separated the big river from its lesser tributary.

Finally, the drone flew one last pass, low and fast up the defile. By now the village of Ch'i-li-pi was well awake and they could see people moving in the streets and fishermen working the nets in the river.

Wilbur Silcott switched off the projector and resumed his seat at the table. "We had the tapes back in the USGS laboratory at Reston twenty-four hours after they left the aircraft carrier. The first analysis we made of the gamma-ray emissions recorded by the scintillation detector showed that we were indeed in the presence of a uranium deposit. We were picking up U_3O_8— that's normal uranium oxide—in very considerable quantities, particularly here in a location about three miles square more or less in the middle of the target area"—he pointed to the chart— "where the ground begins to rise to the peak. Now, this was interesting. Very interesting. Any substantial deposit of uranium oxide is worth looking at very closely indeed.

"What makes it even more interesting is that the signals we picked up show an abnormal distribution of the isotopes, with a high proportion of U235. We appear to have an Oklo-type deposit where the natural reaction—which in the Oklo case led to the eventual depletion of the U235 content—has not yet occurred. In other words, this is a deposit that contains thousands of tons of naturally enriched uranium."

There was a general gasp of astonishment, followed by silence.

"What could have caused that kind of deposit in the first place?" Kristof finally asked.

"That's a hard one to answer. One of the possibilities would be meteorite impact. We have evidence in the satellite photographs of a circular impact structure. It's possible that the effects of high-pressure shock waves, say in the 100- to 150-kilobar range, on normal pitchblende, might in fact produce new uranium-rich phases in which a reaction could occur. There was a time when meteorite-impact theories were put in the category of science fiction, like flying saucers. Not any longer."

There was a renewed buzz of comment and exclamation.

"Gentlemen," Silcott held up his hand, enjoying his moment, "that is not all. That is not nearly all. I must tell you about the results I got from another area lying just north of the peak, in fact, from this spur of land here"—he pointed it out on the map— "which runs back toward the river. These results were so remarkable that I almost didn't believe them myself. The gamma-ray emissions from plutonium are quite distinctive, and the indications are that the mineral composition on this spur of land has a very high *plutonium* content."

"Plutonium?" General Bledsoe couldn't suppress his astonishment. "Surely, plutonium is a synthetic element? Surely it doesn't exist in nature?"

Silcott looked at him, the academic stoutly confronting the military. "Right and wrong, sir. Right, it *is* a synthetic element. It was first produced artificially in 1942 at the University of Chicago. Wrong, because in fact plutonium does occur in nature, but in very, very small concentrations indeed. Glenn Seaborg discovered natural plutonium in concentrations of less than 9 parts per trillion. What happens in nature is exactly what happens in a nuclear reactor. Of course, in a nuclear reactor you have the neutron-slowing material such as heavy water, which acts as a moderator. A large proportion of the excess neutrons resulting from the fission of U235 is absorbed by the U239, which decays by two successive beta-particle emissions to Pu239. In nature, you don't normally have the moderator effect, with the result that the concentration of naturally occurring Pu239 is *normally* determined by the equilibrium balance between its rate of formation and its rate of radioactive decay."

"Why do you say 'normally' with such emphasis?" asked Kristof. "Are there abnormal situations?"

Silcott took his time before replying. "Let's look at the map again. This spur of land I was referring to juts out toward the river, doesn't it?"

They nodded.

"And the river floods regularly. In fact, the tip of the spur leads right down into the flood plain."

They nodded again. They could see what he meant.

"Now, ordinary water," continued Silcott, "also acts as a moderator in nuclear reactions. That's why we talk of 'light-water reactors.' Light water is ordinary water given a fancy name to distinguish it from heavy water. My theory is that in a situation where you already have a superrich deposit of uranium and a regular pattern of flooding, the natural formation of plutonium could be speeded up many thousands of times. In fact, you would have a natural reactor producing plutonium. The transformation could have taken place thousands of years ago or it could still be happening today. We could, in essence, have a natural plutonium factory here."

Silcott stopped. In his excitement he had slipped into the use of unscientific language. He stood up to write some figures on the blackboard, reverting, with an effort of will, to his more prosaic style of speech. "Say the ore in place has a specific gravity of 2 short tons per cubic meter, an ore body of 75 *million short tons*—I repeat, 75 million short tons—could fit into an area 1 kilometer square and 38 meters in depth. My own belief, based on the data we have examined, is that the deposit is a great deal larger than that. When you consider that a mere 20 kilograms of plutonium is enough to make a bomb of the size that destroyed Hiroshima, and that a few tons of plutonium or enriched uranium are enough to fuel a nuclear power station for a year, I think you will understand why I say that this deposit is so large it could change the world as we know it."

His voice died away to silence. No one knew what to say. They had been shown an incredible natural resource, which America and the world desperately needed. Only one catch: It was located in the worst possible spot. How could they get at it? And what were the risks? They had a lot to ponder, to analyze, and finally, to decide.

Gordon Kristof looked at his watch. "Gentlemen, it is five o'clock on a Friday afternoon. We have two choices. We can go on with our discussion now and if necessary run on into the weekend. If we do that, we risk giving the impression to the press and the public that we are in a crisis situation, and they'll start speculating as to just what the hell that crisis could be. The other choice is to reconvene on Monday in a normal continuation of today's session. Do you have any views?" He looked around the table. "My own feeling is that we should use the weekend to think about what we've just heard and come back to this on Monday. After all, the deposit isn't going to disappear between now and then."

No one spoke.

"Very well," said Kristof. "We'll all meet again on Monday."

As they left the room, General Bledsoe eased over toward Ricker. "Thank God for that adjournment. Listen, Thaddeus, I have an idea I think you can use. Can I get back to you this evening, after I've made a couple of calls?"

Ricker put his arm around the other man's shoulder as they walked to their cars. "Clifford, we're going to need all the help we can get on this one. If you've got an idea I'm ready to hear it. I'll be in the office until late tonight. By the way," he whispered, chuckling, "it looks like they've forgotten all about the illegal flight of the Paladyne drone."

6

Ricker opened the passenger door, greeted Bledsoe, and slid in. "Okay, Clifford. Enough mystery. Now tell me: Who is John McGrath?"

Bledsoe didn't take his eyes from the highway. As they drove west into the Virginia countryside, barns and white rail fences rolled past them. Horses and cows dappled by sunlight grazed in paddocks by the road.

"I first met McGrath," Bledsoe began, "during the Korean War. He was with the U.S. Army Corps of Engineers and I was with the infantry. We were both pretty young and green at the time, I guess, but somehow with McGrath, it didn't seem to show. He couldn't have been more than twenty-five but he had already acquired a wisdom and a compassion way beyond his years.

"One winter, when the Reds had us holed up north of Seoul, I came to know him well. He was at home in the East. That struck you immediately. He had this gift for languages. When I first knew him he could already speak Russian and Chinese fluently and he quickly added Korean to that. He also had an extraordinary ability to communicate with the villagers. Most of the military out there would roar in and out of the villages without any thought for the people and the kind of lives they led.

But not McGrath. You'd see him stop his jeep and get out and walk into the village square and really talk to those people. Even the village dogs seemed to love him."

Ricker watched the countryside go by and listened, beginning to understand why Bledsoe had suggested this Saturday visit to John McGrath's Virginia farm.

"During that winter in Korea, McGrath told me more about his background. His parents had been missionaries in China before the Second World War, and John was brought up there. He speaks the language like a native; in fact, he probably speaks two or three of the Chinese dialects, or used to. The elder McGraths moved around quite a bit, and young John moved with them. Edgar Snow claimed that there were no A-mericans on the Long March with Mao. But that's not true. The McGraths were there, and from what I can make out, young John McGrath—he must have been around twelve or thirteen years old at the time—played an active role. He won't tell you much himself because he's a modest fellow. But you learn how to read between the lines with him. Life must have been hard for all of them. He had to grow up fast."

"What happened to him after Korea?"

"After Korea, I sort of lost touch. I heard that he went back into China a couple of times at the invitation of the government. He was one of the very few Americans to do so back then, during the height of the Cold War and what with McCarthy and all. But by then McGrath had left the Army, after making colonel. He'd joined an international firm of civil engineers and was making his name as one of the world's greatest hydraulics experts. There's a streak of idealism in him, you know. Maybe he learned it from his missionary parents. He's the kind of man who likes to make two blades of grass grow where only one grew before."

"What's he doing now?"

"He retired a year or two ago, when his wife died. Then he came home to his farm in Virginia to raise horses and cattle."

"And we're going to try to persuade him that it's time to look the world in the face again."

"That's the idea," said Bledsoe. "John McGrath is too good a man to lose. Besides, I'm counting on him to come up with a solution to this uranium problem. If I know John, he won't be able to resist the challenge."

They drove into a private road that wound through hills until it opened onto the rambling, two-hundred-acre farm. The farmhouse was frame and brick, a lovely old Virginia building. A tall, sandy-haired man came out on to the porch to greet them, a pair of golden Labradors close on his heels. He greeted Bledsoe warmly. "Clifford, it's been too long."

Then he turned to Ricker. "Hello. I'm glad to meet you. I've heard so much about you." His handshake was warm and firm. "Come on in. We've got time for a drink before lunch."

McGrath's face was freckled and the lines around his eyes showed he had spent much of his life in the sun. He seemed peaceful and content, a man who was satisfied that he had done many of the things he wished to do with his life.

The sitting room gave out onto the mountains. Cattle moved into the meadow below the house, clustering around the pond.

"I dug that pond," McGrath said as they stood, drinks in hand, looking out at the rural scene. "When the children were small they used to swim in it. My wife loved it. Now it's mainly for the cows."

Thaddeus noticed a photograph on the table, a picture of the McGrath family some years earlier. A tall, handsome woman stood next to McGrath, behind a younger woman with two small children.

McGrath saw him looking at the photograph. "My grandchildren," he smiled. "I don't see enough of them. My daughter's living in Oregon and never wants to come East. They're always asking me to go out there, but now that I've retired I find I don't have the time. It's a full-time job being retired."

Ricker was still looking at the photograph. "And is that your wife?"

"Yes. She died three years ago. She was a wonderful woman. I miss her. We all miss her."

He stared out of the window at the cattle by the pond and then, deliberately changing the subject, he said: "Of course, building a pond is nothing. But I like to keep my hand in. I'll show you some little projects of mine after lunch."

They lingered over the meal. "All my life," McGrath told them, "I've been involved with dams and rivers and major engineering projects having to do with water. I was with the U.S. Army Corps of Engineers during Korea. Then after the war I spent fifteen years in various parts of Asia. I did a couple of jobs in China—on the Yellow River, and also on the Amur and Ussuri. We even blocked the Indus at Tarbela. Built the largest earthfill dam in the world. In the past, 80 per cent of the water of the Indus used to run waste to the sea. Now it's used to feed the hungry millions of Pakistan." McGrath smiled. "I still think about rivers. How to tame them, how to use them. Rivers are my lifeblood. To me the river itself is a kind of life force." Suddenly embarrassed by his enthusiasm, he rose abruptly from the table. "Let's go and see the place."

The dogs followed, barking happily, as they took off in McGrath's old jeep. He drove to a stream where they stopped and got out.

"Come and see my tank. I told you I liked to keep my hand in."

He showed them a flat earthbed about two hundred feet long and thirty feet wide, running parallel to the course of the stream. There was an inlet at one end of the bed and an outlet at the other. "This is only a model, of course, but you can scale it up as much as you like. You can create the Mississippi in here if you want to. Look."

He turned a stopcock and raised the gate on the inlet. Water coursed into the bed, finding its own channel through the dry earth.

"It's mostly mathematics. Other things being equal, the first bend a river makes in a flat plain will be perfectly reflected in subsequent bends downstream. This is classic meander theory. As long as you have the basic data, you can use models like these to predict the course of a river—any river—at any time in the future."

They watched the water run through the bed, cutting its own channel. After only five minutes, the first signs of erosion were appearing on the bank immediately opposite the inlet. A curve was beginning to form in the channel and, in response, an equal and opposite curve was being carved out immediately downstream.

"You mean rivers change course?" Ricker asked.

"Constantly. The meander is the most common phenomenon. But there are others. Take the case of what the hydrologists call 'stream capture.'" McGrath picked up a stick and drew in the sand. "You have a major river like this, draining—let's say—this side of a range of hills. The other side of the range you have another river, a smaller river. Over a period of time the channel of the smaller river cuts back into the main channel, and suddenly the whole lot is going down the channel of the minor river, and all you are left with where the main river used to flow is a dried-up streambed."

He turned off the stopcock. "Of course, this tank is just child's play. Nowadays, you run the big hydraulic models with a computer."

By the time they got back to the house, Bledsoe was ready to talk business. "John, I guess you've figured out that this isn't a social visit. Something's come up and the country needs your help. We're here to convince you to give it."

McGrath shook his head. "I'm an old war-horse, Clifford, and right now I'm out at pasture."

"You won't listen to us?"

"Aw, hell. Of course I'll listen. But I don't promise anything."

It took Ricker and Bledsoe two hours. They appealed to his patriotism, they got him intrigued by the project, and finally Bledsoe played his last card. "You know the country, John, you have experience, you know the people, you know the language. And what's more, you know Marshal Lu. He's an old man now. You may not have another chance to see him before he dies."

McGrath suddenly felt the pricking of moisture behind his eyelids. He hadn't thought of Lu for years.

"Oh God," he said, "that man was like a father to me once."

It was late afternoon when Bledsoe and Ricker returned to Washington.

"Could you drop me off at Bethesda?" Ricker asked.

"Sure."

Bledsoe dropped him on the Old Georgetown Road and drove on. Ricker walked a couple of blocks, then rang the doorbell of an old frame house. Ella Richmond answered it. "Hi, come on in. I'm glad you could make it." Thaddeus followed her. It was the first time he had visited Ella at home, and he liked what he saw. Rugs and cushions were scattered on the floor; there were plants and sculptures and books and records and a double bed in a room that opened off the living room.

"I wasn't sure you'd show up," she said, after putting him in a wing-back chair. "It sounded as if you might be too busy."

"How could I have sounded that way? I didn't even talk to you."

"That's my point—you had your secretary call. I don't think I've ever dated through a secretary before."

"Look," he said, "you've got to understand that I'm not some guy with an ordinary job."

"I know. You're one of the most powerful men in Washington. Tell me, Mr. Secretary, what does it feel like to be one of the most powerful men in Washington?"

"Powerful?" Ignoring the dig, Thaddeus turned and gazed out the window. "I say 'Come' and people come. 'Go' and people go. But I can be booted out of office from one day to the next, and what do I have to show for it? A signed photograph of the President and a couple of souvenir pens." He shook his head and then turned back to her. "No, I'd rather be McGrath. That man has real depth, real vision. I'm just a small-town hick who's gotten himself a nice office with a view—for a couple of months."

She waited a moment and then said gently, "I've met a lot of small-town hicks in my life, Thaddeus, and you're not one of them." She stood, her cashmere dress clinging handsomely to her body. "You make us some drinks, and I'll heat up the quiche, and then I want you to tell me all about McGrath."

He did, at some length, and his feelings about McGrath led to other, more personal topics, also discussed at length, and it wasn't until 11 P.M. that Thaddeus thought about the time.

"That's probably the longest I've gone in years without look-ing at my watch," he said.

"I'll phone *The Guinness Book of Records*," she said, patting his arm.

"And I'd better phone my service," he said. "There's so much going on, and as you know"—he smiled—"I'm one of the most powerful men in Washington." She kissed him on the cheek.

The answering service reported that Lloyd Oakes wanted him to call the special FBI tie line.

"Thaddeus? This is Lloyd Oakes. Where've you been all eve-ning?"

Ricker smiled into the phone. "Don't tell me you don't know, Lloyd. I thought you had tabs on everyone."

There was a snort at the other end of the line. "Do you think I can spare a tail for you? I've got other fish to fry!"

"Such as?"

"Such as your Brazilian friends."

"What do you mean?"

"You ought to know that a man named Antonio Galveas—he's a senior member of the consulting firm that put in the request for the LANDSAT data—left the country today on the one-o'clock plane for Rio. We got a look at his briefcase as he went through the security check at Dulles, and we think he's taken most of the photos with him. Of course, he's perfectly entitled to. After all, his firm paid for them, and they're the property of the firm. But I thought you'd like to know."

7

The men of the National Security Council filed into their meeting room on Monday morning. The somber, wood-paneled, green-carpeted room reflected their mood. They were up against a tough problem and they were ready to spend a long time finding a solution.

Gordon Kristof opened the meeting. Then he turned to Otis Oman, the Secretary of Defense. "Otis, perhaps you could lead this off. What about the military option? I assume we all agree we can't go in and grab that piece of land and hold it until we've mined all the minerals and shipped them safely back to the States."

Otis Oman, a small, dark-haired, rather wiry man, shook his head. "I'd have to ask General Bledsoe and his people for a full evaluation, but as a first reaction I'd say the military option is a nonstarter. Even if hostilities were limited to the immediate area, I frankly doubt whether the United States could hold the territory, assuming—and it's a fairly large assumption—we managed to take it in the first place. Remember, we'd be operating in a totally alien environment."

He leaned forward across the table and fixed Kristof with a hawklike stare. "Frankly, Gordon, I think we ought to take it out."

"Take it out?"

"Yeah. Blow the deposit up. Drop a bomb on it. That way even if we didn't get it, the Soviets wouldn't either."

"Destroy the deposit in order to save it, is that what you mean?" Kristof spoke quietly but there was a dangerous edge to his voice. He looked around the table. "Does anyone wish to comment on this suggestion?"

Wilbur Silcott, sitting back from the table in a second row of chairs, indicated that he wished to speak.

"Go ahead, Dr. Silcott."

"With respect, sir, the suggestion is absurd," he said, unable to keep the anger out of his voice. "We believe we are dealing with a deposit containing very large quantities of plutonium. Blow that up and you could create an explosion greater than anything the world has ever known. In a very literal sense this could be a doomsday deposit. The world could actually fall apart at the seams, or the whole globe could be poisoned irredeemably by the spread of plutonium, a powerful, toxic substance, throughout the atmosphere. I do not believe there is any merit in the suggestion. In fact, it reeks of irresponsibility."

Kristof looked thoughtfully at the geophysicist, sizing the man up. How frustrating it must be to be a scientist, a thinking man, and to have to witness constantly the inability of people to appreciate fully the intricacies of a problem.

"Sometimes," he said, hoping to soothe Oman's obviously ruffled feathers a bit, "I think you scientific gentlemen tend to be overcautious. However, in this case, I am inclined to agree with you." He turned back to the Secretary of Defense. "Otis, I don't think you're going to find any takers for that one." The nods around the table showed him that the meeting as a whole shared his opinion.

Kristof took them through other options. "We could, of course, do nothing. We could just leave the deposit where it is. Forget about it. Hope the Russians never find it. What do you think, George?"

"Negative," Chisman replied. "If the Russians haven't found out about the deposit so far, that doesn't mean they won't find out about it in the future. And, as you know, the KGB got hold of one of our satellite manuals not long ago. We know that they are in the process of developing a satellite that *does* have a thermal imaging capability. Or else they'll discover it with Geiger counters in the course of some routine geological traverse. And if they do discover it, the whole power balance will swing radically to the Soviets. They'll rule the world!"

"I agree with Mr. Chisman." Silcott, uninvited, spoke up from the second row. "This kind of anomaly cannot remain undetected forever. It's just a matter of time."

"Hell, gentlemen," Kristof snapped, the tension getting to him, "you're paid to be imaginative. Be imaginative. We haven't heard any viable ideas yet."

Ricker took that as his cue. He stood up. "Mr. Chairman," he said in a clear, strong voice, "you asked us to be imaginative. General Bledsoe and I believe we have been. I would like to outline to you all the elements of a scheme that I think may meet our essential objectives."

Kristof nodded. "Go ahead, Thaddeus. I'm glad somebody did some thinking over the weekend."

"As we all know," Ricker began, "the deposit is in Soviet territory, just across the border from China. My belief is that if the Chinese, as it were, owned this deposit and not the Soviets, the whole problem might be much simpler. Number one, the Chinese do not present the same kind of military and economic challenge to the United States that the Soviets do. Therefore the balance of power, or terror, if you like, is not affected to the same extent by their possession of the deposit. Number two, it's possible that the United States might be able to make a strictly commercial deal with China over the uranium or plutonium or whatever, the kind of deal that we could never make with the Soviets."

Gordon Kristof had listened to this with growing incredulity. "Thaddeus, you're out of your mind. You're suggesting the Chinese should cross a recognized international frontier and hold a piece of land on the other side so they can make a deal with the United States!"

Ricker looked at his colleague with unconcealed hostility. "Gordon, you ought to know better than to speak of the Ussuri as a recognized international frontier. Recognized by whom? Not by the Chinese, certainly."

He had their attention now. "Let's look at the facts. Why does China today speak about 'inequal' treaties? Why does China claim over a million square miles of Soviet Manchuria, *including* the area of the deposit? The answer is very simple: Over the last several centuries and particularly in the nineteenth century, the Chinese were forced under duress to sign border agreements, such as the Treaty of Aigun, that today they repudiate. In the sixteenth century, there were no clearly demarcated international frontiers. But by the end of the nineteenth century, Russia had encroached in Manchuria, coming right down to the Ussuri River. In fact, the Soviets rubbed it in when they built Vladivostok, which means 'Conquest of the East.'

"One of our most respected historians has written: 'It is still a principal aim of Chinese foreign policy to regain the full territory and standing of the Chinese Empire at its peak, and that includes the land across the Ussuri and Amur rivers.'"

Kristof looked skeptical. "Who the hell wrote that?"

"Well, Gordon, I hope you agree with it. You said it yourself. In fact, my entire historical presentation was really yours." He held up a dark blue volume and read the title: *"Historical Bases for the Foreign Policy of the Soviet Union,* by Gordon C. Kristof, Henry L. Moses Professor of International Relations at Columbia University!"

The laughter in the room was loud and prolonged. Kristof joined in the joke at his own expense.

"Okay, Thaddeus, I guess I can't quarrel with the historical analysis. Nevertheless, you must concede that at this moment the Ussuri is the de facto international frontier and the Soviets are hardly likely to shift from it. If the Chinese were to cross the river, the Soviets would treat it as a major territorial incursion and would certainly retaliate. We know that the Chinese don't want to risk a major war with the Soviet Union. They're simply not ready for it. But there's no way they could hold territory, even to a limited extent, on the wrong side of the Ussuri River, without such a substantial deployment of resources that they would effectively be in a war situation."

Ricker turned to wink at George Chisman.

"Gordon," he said patiently, "you're jumping to conclusions. I never said anything about the Chinese holding territory on the *wrong* side of the Ussuri River."

Kristof looked puzzled. "I don't understand."

The other members nodded. They were all bewildered.

General Bledsoe broke the lengthening silence. "Mr. Chairman, may I request that we bring in someone else not on the Council—Colonel John G. McGrath, a world-famous hydraulics expert, and incidentally an old friend of mine. I can vouch for him. I should add that Colonel McGrath is quite familiar with the deposit area and with the basic problems under consideration. He has certain ideas to advance at this time that I believe the Council will wish to hear."

Kristof looked around the room. They certainly needed help. "Okay, Clifford, bring him in."

McGrath followed Bledsoe to his seat. All eyes were on him, taking stock, noticing his graceful bearing and his quiet but forceful presence. McGrath set his pipe down carefully beside his papers as the introductions were made. Then he looked around to register where the main protagonists in the debate were sitting and turned to face the chairman.

"Go ahead, McGrath."

"Thank you. I gather you know the basic facts and have heard the historical analysis." Heads nodded. "Now, the Soviets have argued that the Ussuri is the de facto frontier. The precise boundary is, of course, the *thalweg*—the deep-water channel— in the river itself."

Kristof wondered what McGrath was driving at. As an historian, he was familiar with the old German concept of the *thalweg,* or downway, the track taken by boats in their course down the stream.

McGrath continued. "You would agree, wouldn't you, that if the river changes course, then in international law the frontier also changes, following the *thalweg* of the river? I could cite the case of Louisiana vs. Mississippi when the river suddenly shifted in 1912 and 1913, cutting off a large chunk of Louisiana, or, going farther back, to the Rio Grande affair in the last century where a change in the course of the river led to a change in the international frontier between Mexico and the United States."

They nodded their assent.

"Good," said McGrath. "Can we have the lights out, please? It will be easier to explain the idea I have in mind if we have the map in front of us."

The same map they had studied on Friday appeared on the screen.

"The area of the deposit, as we know, is bounded on the left, or west, by the Ussuri. We have also seen that a smaller river, the Bikin, comes off the Ussuri, drains the southern side of the high ground, then flows around to the east and north before joining up with the Ussuri again. It is my belief"—he paused to let his words sink in—"that it would be possible to engineer a diversion of the Ussuri River into the smaller stream running to the east. Thus there would be a new course for the river and a new international frontier that would effectively bring the deposit area within Chinese territory."

The Defense Secretary threw back his head and laughed out loud. "Tell me another."

McGrath drew himself up "Gentlemen, I hope you will hear me out."

The others looked at him with varying degrees of amazement. What was he saying? How could he be serious? Still, he was a respected engineer. . . .

Kristof rapped his gavel, bringing the meeting back to order. "We will hear Colonel McGrath. We owe him that courtesy."

"Thank you, Mr. Chairman," McGrath said formally. Once more he turned to the map. "I believe such a diversion could be achieved, gentlemen. And I shall tell you how."

8

Ella came by for Thaddeus at around eight in the morning. He had already breakfasted and was waiting for her. They took her car, since he didn't want to advertise his movements, and headed for Annapolis. "You look wonderful," he said simply.

She half turned her head and smiled without saying anything.

Soon after crossing the Bay Bridge they turned off U.S. 50, following a sign that said CHESAPEAKE BAY HYDRAULIC MODEL: U.S. Army Corps of Engineers.

Three miles down, a side road brought them to another, similar sign. On this sign, a notice had been superimposed: OWING TO MAINTENANCE PROBLEMS THE CHESAPEAKE BAY HYDRAULIC MODEL IS CLOSED TO THE PUBLIC. THE U.S. ARMY CORPS OF ENGINEERS, BALTIMORE DISTRICT, REGRETS ANY INCONVENIENCE THIS MAY CAUSE.

"They certainly do it big, don't they?" Thaddeus glanced at Ella as she drove. Her way of handling the car, calm and competent, was, he thought, a reflection of her personality. Why was it, he wondered, that some men were unwilling to let themselves be driven by a woman? He welcomed the fact that Ella had taken the wheel. It gave him a chance to concentrate on the project that was now underway, and on Ella herself.

They drove another mile, then parked in front of a huge building, like an enormous aircraft hangar, that sat beside the waterfront.

McGrath himself opened the door. Ella was immediately struck by the truth of something Thaddeus had told her—that McGrath had a strong resemblance to Gary Cooper. It was not so much a matter of features, though McGrath had the same kind of handsome, regular face that Cooper had caused to be associated forever with the American West and the same tall, lanky, rawboned frame. Rather, it was a sort of inborn modesty, a simplicity that was not in any sense simpleminded . . . something like a natural grace. "Come on in," he said, with a deep twang that only intensified the impression. "Welcome to the world's largest hydraulic model." He put his big hand out to Ella. "I'm glad to meet you, Dr. Richmond. I hear it was you who actually discovered the deposit in the first place."

Ella shrugged modestly. "I was just part of a team. Call me Ella, by the way."

They stepped inside and gasped at the sheer immensity of the cavern that confronted them.

"Yeah, it's big, isn't it?" McGrath was pleased at their astonishment. "It was one of the last jobs I was involved in before I retired. This shelter covers fourteen acres."

They stood together just inside the doorway, gazing into the inner depths of the enormous shed. Overhead lights illuminated the whole area. The whole place seemed to be deserted.

McGrath read their thoughts. "Don't be deceived. There are more people here than you think; you just don't see them. Let's see what it's all about. We're about to walk approximately seven thousand miles, the length of the tidal shoreline. Are you ready? We'll begin at Norfolk."

So they began at Norfolk, stepped across the Atlantic at the mouth of the Bay, and made the long trek up the eastern shoreline.

"I don't want to make any exaggerated claims," McGrath explained as they walked. "A hydraulic model is a precision device for the experimental investigation of hydromechanical phenomena. It can give reliable information only if its scales are determined according to certain definite rules—that is, if it is designed correctly. If the design is not correct, then the model is wrong. In that case, the employment of the most sophisticated instrumentation and measurement methods can only help to increase the accuracy of the *wrong* predictions."

"What scales are you using?" Thaddeus asked.

"On the vertical scale, 1 to 100. That means every foot on the model corresponds to a height differential of 100 feet on the ground. On the horizontal scale we are using 1 to 1,000. Time is a 1-to-100 relationship, which means that you cover 12.5 hours in approximately 7.5 minutes, or a year in 3.65 days. Stay here 3.65 days and you'll see the ebb and flow of the tides in Chesapeake Bay and the hydraulics of seasons of the year."

They walked up to Baltimore, then around the top of the Patuxent River and headed for the Potomac Basin. "Let's sit down for a moment," McGrath said. "I'm not as young as I used to be."

Thaddeus looked at him sharply, amazed that he would admit to being tired. The glint of amusement in McGrath's eyes told him that fatigue was not the only reason for the sudden halt in their progress around the Bay model.

McGrath walked down the river until he came to a spot where some chairs were conveniently placed. He lowered himself into one of them. Then he tore a piece of paper into pieces, like confetti, held out his fist above the water, and opened it. The bits of paper fluttered down and hit the surface of the water. They began to move with the current.

"What do you see?"

Ella studied the model, watching the direction in which the pieces of paper moved. "The river's flowing *upstream*!" she exclaimed.

McGrath was amused. "Ella, when you've been in the hydraulics business as long as I have, you'll realize that rivers never flow upstream. You think that river's flowing upstream because you think it's the Potomac and you know that the Potomac flows north to south. But that river is not the Potomac!"

"You mean it's . . ."

"Yes, it's the Ussuri! To my knowledge it's the first complete hydraulic model of the Ussuri that has ever been built!" He pointed into the depths of the shed, his finger indicating the line of the river as it ran north. "We've modeled it all the way up to the junction with the Amur at Khabarovsk."

"If this is the Ussuri, why are you showing a town here marked WASHINGTON, D.C.?"

"Just to confuse people. The staff here might get curious if they saw the word CHINA printed in large letters on the left bank and SOVIET UNION printed in large letters on the right.

"You may want to know how we set about constructing this hydraulic model. We were well supplied with topographic data. In addition to the satellite photography, we used the films taken by the drone. As far as hydrological data are concerned, we were able to get records of both annual and seasonal flows, as well as maximum floods. The Ussuri has been monitored, more or less thoroughly, over a long period, and the information was available in the literature. The Soviets produce scholarly papers in great quantities, which are published or presented to international conferences and seminars on hydrology. They were all in the Library of Congress files."

"You read Russian, don't you?" Thaddeus asked.

"In my field, you have to. It takes them so long to translate this stuff, that if you want to keep up to date, you've got to understand the language."

"Do you speak it too?"

McGrath shrugged modestly. "I get along."

He turned to Ella. "So you see, we have built this model of the Ussuri to enable us to make some of the most intricate calculations in the history of hydraulic engineering. Because, unfortunately, in this case, field experimentation is not possible.

"Let's look at the problem." He pointed to the river as it curled north through the defile. "Right now we're sitting on top of the deposit, at the high point, 3,586 feet up. We're looking due west across the river to the hills on the Chinese side. Over there in China, slightly north of west, is a peak of about 3,000 feet. In other words, this is a pretty substantial canyon. Now, what we have to do is block the river somewhere in the canyon so that, in effect, we shut off the channel, causing the water to back up and find a new channel off here to the right until it joins up with the Bikin River and curls back to the Ussuri north of the deposit area."

He turned to Thaddeus. "The other day when you were out at the farm we talked about a natural phenomenon known as 'stream capture.' Well, what we're trying to do here is give nature a helping hand—to speed up the process, if you like." He stood up from his chair and walked down to the riverbank. "The hydraulics of channel closure depend primarily on the way the material is deposited in the stream. Normally we can distinguish two methods. The first is the concentrated deposition of material by progressive lateral dumping from the banks of the river. The second is the transverse dumping of rock from a pontoon bridge, cableway, or conveyor."

He thrust his hand into a trouser pocket and came up with a bunch of pebbles. They watched intently as he dropped the pebbles into the middle of the stream. Some were immediately swept away by the current. Others stayed where they fell. McGrath pulled out a second handful of pebbles and dropped them in as well. Again, there was considerable loss, but this time the pile of remaining stones was appreciably larger—the beginning of a dam.

"Frankly," McGrath continued, "a lot of it nowadays is mathematics. You make an energy evaluation of the stream to be dammed; you look at the hydraulic-resistance criteria of the fill bodies; you work out the stability of rock in the fill and the characteristics of seepage flow through fill material; you look at the discharge capacity of potential diversion structures. And when you've done all that, you ask yourself: Given the operating conditions, can I dam this stream or not?"

"And can you?" Thaddeus asked.

McGrath took his time replying. "We haven't finished all the calculations yet but—yes, we think there's a way."

They could sense the excitement in his voice as he spoke, and they tried to get him to say more. But McGrath would not talk further.

On the way back to Washington, Thaddeus took Ella to lunch at a ramshackle old inn on Chesapeake Bay. Their table overlooked the water, the sun shone, and the soft-shelled crabs and chilled white wine seemed extraordinarily good. Thaddeus reached across the table and enclosed Ella's hand. "You started all this, you know," he said. "McGrath was right."

"Sometimes it frightens me."

"It doesn't frighten me. When I think of those millions of tons of uranium and plutonium out there, I think of what it can mean to humanity if we put it to proper use."

"That's exactly it: *If* we put it to proper use. Just the fact of its being there changes everything—the whole of human history, probably. One way or the other—and I hope it's not the other."

"We can't let it be the other. That's why we've got to get to it first."

"I just keep thinking of that glowing spot on the videoscope. I see it when I shut my eyes at night."

"Don't let it get to you. It's going to be okay."

"Yes."

"Come on. Let's go. We ought to be getting back."

"I know. Do you want to go to your office? I'll take you."

"No. I've got a meeting at five, and I can't go in these clothes. Not dignified. Could you drop me off at my place?"

But she didn't drop him off. When they arrived, without either of them suggesting it but both of them implicitly wanting it, she parked the car and came up with him. In the elevator they stood very close.

"Hey," she said, when he showed her the living room, "for a bureaucrat you've got an awful lot of books." She looked at the shelves. "Poetry?"

He was faintly embarrassed. "Yeah, I've been getting into poetry a little bit lately. I find I can manage a few lines before I go to sleep at night."

"Who's your favorite?"

"I range pretty widely. I've been going through Matthew Arnold. He's nineteenth-century English."

"I know. I went to school too."

He laughed. "Right. Do you know his 'Dover Beach'?"

"I haven't read it in years. I can barely remember it."

"It's really some poem," he said. "Someday I'll recite it for you."

"Why not now?"

"No," he said softly, "not now." He put his hands on her shoulders and, looking into her eyes, drew her slowly to him. He kissed her hair and then her cheek, and when she raised her head he met her lips with his. Then there was a rush of eager, mutual kisses.

She pressed her head against his shoulder and held him tightly. "You know where this is going to lead, don't you?"

"Do you mind?"

"Mind?" she whispered. "I've been thinking about it for hours."

Gazing at him, she pulled his shirt from his trousers and brought her hands up under it, feeling his chest. He removed her blouse and undid the catch of her bra and lifted the bra until her breasts were suddenly free of it and hot against him. And then there was too much urgency for slow undressing. They stood apart and rapidly disrobed, letting the clothes fall on the floor. And then they hurried into each other's arms, hands and mouths moving everywhere, desperate for everything at once.

Deep in a sensuous languor, she barely felt him inching his arm from beneath her. She opened her eyes. He was looking at his watch.

"I've got that meeting," he said.

"Oh, no."

"I'm the chairman. I've got to be there. It's the regular weekly meeting of my Department heads. It's reorganization time. You know, I was just lying here thinking about it, and all of a sudden I figured it all out—how to switch my two deputies without losing either one of them or even making them particularly unhappy."

She came wide awake. "Well, you're making me particularly unhappy, I can tell you that. You mean to say you've been lying there thinking about your job?"

"Well, I wasn't really thinking about my job, I was . . ."

"You've just finished making love to me, and you're back to thinking about your goddamn job?"

"I was thinking about you . . . about us . . . about how wonderful it was. But then I had this random thought. It always happens to me. Right after I finish making love, suddenly I'm thinking about twice as clearly as I did before. I've had some of my best ideas like that."

"You can't imagine how that makes me feel."

He raised himself to one elbow and looked down at her. Her expression made him instantly contrite. "Ella. I'm sorry. I'm terribly sorry. It's just something that happens to men. I read about it—it's called postcoital acuity."

"Postcoital acuity!"

"That's what they call it. PCA, for short. Suddenly you're tremendously sharp. But it goes away pretty soon, and then you're your old stupid self again."

She looked at him sternly and then shook her head, and finally she gave in to a wry smile. "That's really something. *You're* really something, do you know that? PCA—is your PCA over yet?"

"Nope, not yet. I still feel brilliant, and my brilliant insight of the moment is that you are the loveliest, sexiest woman in the world with the world's most beautiful tits. . . ."

"Ah, that's better. In fact, that's wonderful." She brought his hand up over her breast. "But maybe that's *pre*coital acuity. Could that be possible?"

"I think it's possible," he said, pulling off his wristwatch and letting it drop to the carpet.

9

The boyish excitement Ricker felt when he boarded the Presidential plane for the trip to China was a marked contrast to McGrath's reflective, nostalgic mood. The two of them were comfortable together, though, eating, sleeping, talking, and watching the clouds float by beneath them. McGrath enjoyed Ricker, amused and impressed by his enthusiastic, unbounded energy. For his part, Ricker was calmed by McGrath, beginning to learn the importance of letting some things follow a natural course.

They caught their first glimpse of China as the plane began its descent to the Peking airport. The country looked vast and unpopulated. Ricker turned to McGrath. "Well, how does it feel to be seeing all this again after so many years?"

"It feels like coming home," he replied.

They landed in Peking in a fanfare of publicity. It had been a long time since a ranking member of the U.S. administration had paid an official visit to China. Crowds had gathered on an airport balcony to watch the arrival of the American plane. The Boeing was strangely small but its gleaming elegance gave it a certain aura of power, and it was the latest thing off the production line, with a number of impressive technical improvements. The long, sleek craft, nosing its way to a halt with its cargo of high-level officials, was the visible symbol of the might and the wealth of the United States of America.

The red carpet was unrolled while a band of honor played. Ricker appeared at the top of the steps, blinking a little in the bright sunlight, and squared his shoulders to the view. As though on a signal, the crowd burst into applause and a posse of balloons was released skyward. Ricker grinned, waving at the crowd, and started down the stairs. Followed by McGrath, Wilbur Silcott, and the eighteen other members of his party, he stepped for the first time onto Chinese soil.

After the official welcoming ceremonies at the airport, the U.S. Ambassador to China, W. Smith Mason, drove Ricker's party into the city. The Cadillac, flying the Energy Secretary's personal pennant alongside the U.S. flag, looked out of place on the crowded streets. The driver kept one hand on the horn, weaving in and out of the throngs who walked or bicycled along the narrow, tree-lined roadway. Peasants pushed handcarts laden with agricultural produce; others threshed piles of grain on the shoulder of the road. The wheels of the car scrunched through the remnants of the harvest, and oxcarts loaded high with bundles veered out of the way as they approached.

Ambassador Mason was a career diplomat with an encyclopedic knowledge of China and her people. He was somber-suited and gray-faced, sitting in the back of the car commenting on the various sights. He was having some trouble keeping to himself his doubts about Thaddeus Ricker's mission. It just seemed to him too unorthodox, too farfetched.

As the road widened and the density of building increased, he told them: "This is the beginning of the Boulevard of Lasting Peace."

"And what's that?" Ricker asked as they passed signs of excavation by the roadside.

"That's the Peking subway system. They've built fourteen stations already. The stations and the tunnels will be used as air-raid shelters in the event of war."

"War with the Soviet Union?"

"They don't say. They speak of the 'hegemonistic superpowers.' But the Soviet Union is what they mean."

Suddenly Ricker saw his visit in a new light. Sino-Soviet confrontation was not just a theoretic possibility to be ventilated by academics like Kristof during classes on political theory. To judge by the evidence of his eyes, it was a fact of everyday life. The operation that had brought him here might affect the balance of power between the Soviet Union and China in a very real way.

The official banquet that night was held in the Great Hall of the People in the Central Square of Tien An Men. This was the place where the body of Chairman Mao had lain in state for eight days in September of 1976. For those eight days all Chinese flags flew at half mast. On the final day of mourning, a solemn memorial rally had been held, and at 3 P.M. precisely the whole country had come to a halt. Instructed by official decree, people in all organizations, Army units, factories, mines, enterprises, shops, people's communes, schools and neighborhood communities, wherever they were, stood at attention in silent tribute for the space of three minutes. During that period, ships, trains, and factories throughout China blew their whistles and sounded their sirens.

As he walked up the marble staircase to the marble-floored and many-columned foyer of the Great Hall of the People, Ricker wondered what the new leadership under Chairman Yang was like. Ricker had had access to the best possible briefing material before he left, and probably knew as much about Yang and the other members of the Politburo as they knew about him. Possibly more. But nothing could substitute for personal contact, the face-to-face meeting, the man-to-man discussion. He looked forward to the chance to form his own firsthand opinions.

From the foyer, he went up a second red-carpeted staircase to the main floor. Halfway up he paused before an enormous painting of sunrise over the mountains, dated 1959. It carried a line of text.

"What does that say?" Thaddeus Ricker asked the interpreter who walked beside him.

"It is a line from one of Chairman Mao's poems. It says 'How beautiful is the landscape of our homeland.' "

Ricker walked on, entering the banquet hall. He saw that the dais on the south side was already festooned with microphones. On the dais, a long table had been set with twenty-two places. All of them faced into the room, so that the dinner guests could see the honored celebrities. On the other side of the table were a number of upholstered stools for interpreters.

In all there were thirty tables seating more than four hundred people. Ricker was placed on the dais. As he took his seat, he noticed that other members of his team, both those with bona-fide business in China as well as those who were involved in the operation, were spread about the room at various tables, well interspersed with their Chinese hosts and other guests.

The place cards showed that on his right would be seated the enigmatic Chung Feng. Ricker's briefing had given him some information about Chung. He was by far the youngest member of the Politburo—he was still in his forties, something of a miracle in this land where gerontocracy was the norm. The briefing had also pointed out that Chung had risen in the Party hierarchy faster and farther than anyone except Mao himself. Once a lowly Party secretary in Shanghai's No. 17 Cotton Mill, he had made his name in Tibet as a tough political operator soon after the Chinese takeover, and then, at the Tenth Communist Party Congress in 1973, he had been made both a member of the Politburo and one of its five vice chairmen. Intelligent, personable, and ambitious, Chung had been an organizer of the radical Red Guard during the Cultural Revolution. Apparently he came from a peasant background and lacked a college education. This gave him appealing credentials as an authentic proletarian. Ricker's sources in Washington, though, had warned him about Chung. They thought Chung might give him trouble.

Ricker had just taken his seat when Chung himself appeared. He was youthful but poised and held himself with what Ricker concluded was an air of self-importance. Chung's star might not yet be the brightest in the firmament—he was a radical at a time when the moderates held the center of the stage—but he was clearly looking to his own future. Ricker stood up and shook hands.

Everyone was seated when a hush fell on the room. The silence extended first to one minute, then to two.

"Why are we waiting?" Ricker asked.

The interpreter placed a finger on his lips as though warning the American not to talk too loud. "We are waiting for Chairman Yang," he whispered. "He is about to arrive."

Suddenly there was a sound of several hundred chairs being pushed backward at the same time. The guests rose to their feet applauding as Chairman Yang, the leader of one quarter of mankind, entered and took his place at the top of the table.

Ricker observed him carefully, noting every detail of his face and dress. Who was this man? Was he only a symbol or a figurehead? Or did he have real power in the land? When they had analyzed it back in Washington, they realized they knew very little about Yang. The CIA, and other professional China watchers, had admitted that they didn't even know how old he was. As the stout, dumpy figure made his way across the room, acknowledging the applause with a slight wave of the hand, Ricker tried to estimate Yang's age; he was in his early sixties, Ricker decided. He could have been a good deal older, though— it was hard for a Westerner to judge the age of an Oriental.

Yang came up to Ricker, to welcome him and shake hands. The guests stood while a military band, on the north side of the room, played "The Star-spangled Banner" and the Chinese national anthem. Then they sat down again and the banquet began. Several cold hors d'oeuvres were served, some readily identifiable, others less so, but all delicious.

As protocol demanded, Ricker, speaking through the interpreter who sat opposite them, addressed himself first to Chairman Yang. "This is my first visit to China," he began.

"We will try to make sure you enjoy it." Yang was in a very good mood. The general thrust of the complex U.S.–China trade agreement, which Ricker had come to negotiate, was clearly— in Yang's eyes—favorable to China. The Americans seemed ready to be exceptionally generous, offering low prices on food commodities, grains, and advanced technology, and fixing high foreign-exchange prices for goods the Chinese might offer in return. Uncle Sam, in Yang's experience, was usually a tough customer to deal with, although lately, with the softening relations between the countries, it was easier. When the Politburo was discussing Ricker's forthcoming visit, some members had expressed surprise and a certain cynicism. There was perhaps more to this visit than met the eye. Chung Feng in particular had warned them against falling into a trap. His quotation from Mao—"A revolution is not a dinner party"—had chastened them, but they had gone ahead with preparations for the visit.

"I am sure we will have useful talks over these next days," said Yang.

"I certainly hope so," Ricker had replied, wondering how it would go when he finally broached the real reason for this visit to China. It had been agreed, before he left Washington, that this was something they would have to play by ear. They would, after all, be treading on extremely delicate and tricky ground. The Chinese were a proud, sensitive people who might not like being told that the United States had a better view of their mineral resources, or potential mineral resources, than they did themselves. If he raised the subject at the wrong time or in the wrong way, Ricker might be sent packing.

Hors d'oeuvres were followed by the hot main dishes, each one more delicate and exquisite than the last. The food was perfect, Ricker thought, but there was a certain lack of alcohol. He found himself knocking back glass after tiny glass of sweet red wine without assuaging his considerable thirst.

Yang, himself a teetotaler, observed his American guest with mild amusement. "Try some of this," he said, pushing over a bottle of the more potent mao-tai.

Ricker filled his glass and drained it and, Chinese-style, held it upside down to prove it was really empty.

Yang applauded.

"Kanpei! Kanpei!"

"What does that mean?"

"Bottoms up!" the interpreter replied, laughing with them.

When the time came to turn to his neighbor on the other side, Ricker found the going considerably more difficult. Chung was stiff almost to the point of being uncommunicative. Yes, he might create difficulties for them.

"This mao-tai is a pleasant surprise," Ricker said finally, trying one last time. "I half expected to see Coca-Cola everywhere, the way it is back home."

Barely moving his lips and staring straight ahead, Chung appeared to be speaking to the interpreter and no one else. "It is a tragedy," he said, "that Coca-Cola has been allowed into this country, to poison the Chinese people just as it has poisoned the American people. It is very poor nourishment, the least healthful form of sugar, and it will cause massive problems of dental hygiene. It is typical of your society that it permits some people to make money by injuring the health of others."

Ricker was stunned at first. "Well, as a matter of fact," he stammered, "I more or less agree about the food value of Coke. Most intelligent Americans are coming to see that sugar is pretty bad stuff and are discouraging their kids from using it."

"But it is all right for 'intelligent Americans' to sell this poison to China?"

"Why is China buying it, if you feel that way?" Ricker retorted.

"I am not the one who made that decision. Or the other decisions of 1978. We shall see how they work out."

"Other decisions?"

"Western technology at any price—even the price of the purity of the Revolution itself, the price of the integrity of Chinese revolutionary culture. It is a question of values."

Ricker was amazed by Chung's candor. "It strikes me," Ricker said, "that you could not be speaking this way about the present regime had not a new atmosphere been created in 1978 and 1979, more freedom of speech?"

Chung, who had been fingering his chopsticks, stopped all movement, and his mouth drew tight. The interpreter seemed embarrassed as he looked to see if Chung would reply. Grimly Chung said: "There are so-called friends, self-styled friends of the Chinese people, with honey on their lips and murder in their hearts."

"Let's see how the cookie crumbles," Ricker said. "We may all end up friends after all."

The interpreter quizzed him: "Cookie?"

"Yeah, as in fortune cookie. Chinese fortune cookie."

"Ha!" The man nodded vigorously several times and bounced the comment back across the table.

Chung suddenly stood up and left the banquet. Ricker shrugged, assuming that his neighbor was trying to make some political point, since his departure would not go unnoticed. He looked down the table and saw that Yang had studiously ignored Chung's calculated rudeness.

Halfway through dinner, there was another stir in the hall. Once more the guests rose to their feet as an old man in a crumpled blue suit, a scarf tied scruffily around his neck, limped into the room with the aid of a stick. He came up on the dais and shook hands with Chairman Yang, who introduced him to Ricker. So this was the legendary Marshal Lu, in his seventies now—according to Ricker's sources—but still a power in the land. He was a vice chairman of the Party, had a seat on the Politburo, and was both Minister of Defense and vice chairman of the Party's Military Committee. His credentials as a loyal cadre member were flawless: He had joined the Party in 1927, accompanied Mao on the Long March, and was a top military commander in the resistance against the Japanese occupation. He was recruited into the Party's highest echelons in 1971 when Chou En-lai asked him to purge the Army of followers of Marshal Lin Piao. Lu had been a persistent advocate of U.S.–Chinese rapprochement and was one of Peking's representatives at talks with Kissinger in the early 1970s. He was also supposed to have a spectacularly beautiful daughter who at the moment was one of China's top interpreters. Ricker looked around trying to spot her. Surely she would be at such an important event. And sure enough, across the table from Marshal Lu, perched on one of the interpreter's stools, was a strikingly attractive woman, with thick, dark hair and the palest of skins. Ricker noted the smile that flashed between them.

Just then, Lu pushed away the plate that had been set before him. He gazed out into the body of the hall. Ricker, intrigued, followed his eyes and caught the old man's sudden start of pleasure. He watched with amazement as Marshal Lu hobbled off the dais, down the steps, and over to the table where John McGrath was sitting. McGrath saw him coming and rose to greet him. The two men clasped each other in a warm embrace and exchanged a few words. Then Lu slowly turned and returned to the dais.

This little cameo did not attract much attention. The banquet was far advanced and had already reached that relaxed stage at which incidents of considerable significance can pass unnoticed. It had occurred to Ricker, however, that perhaps this was the channel they were looking for. The personal link between Lu and McGrath might be used to lay the groundwork for the project they had in mind. In the end, all diplomacy was a matter of trust. And it was clear, from the scene he had witnessed, that trust existed in full measure between Marshal Lu and John McGrath.

As these thoughts crossed his mind, Ricker's eye once more fell on the woman who sat opposite Lu. Yes, surely it was the old man's daughter. There was a family resemblance that even the difference in their ages could not obscure. Once or twice, as he watched her, she half turned in her seat to glance toward the table where John McGrath sat.

There were speeches from both sides. Chairman Yang spoke for ten minutes; Ricker for five. There were toasts. There was applause. At 10:15 P.M. precisely, it was all over. Big cars carried passengers away from the Great Hall of the People.

The American delegation was staying at the Peking Hotel, which was central and convenient. "Let's walk," McGrath said. "It's only across the square." So they sent the official transport away and instead walked across the square, skirting the Monument to the Heroes of the Chinese People, then cutting diagonally across to the Boulevard of Lasting Peace, the great street that swept through the heart of the city and on which their hotel was situated. Although the night was balmy, there were very few people in the streets. It was a late hour for the hardworking Chinese.

McGrath suddenly broke into Chinese, reciting in a soft, lilting voice.

"That's lovely—what is it?" asked Ricker.

"A poem."

"Can you translate it?" Ricker asked, thinking suddenly of Ella and their last hours before the trip.

McGrath's sentimental mood had returned. He said:

> Our mission, unfinished,
> May take a thousand years.
> The struggle tires us, and our hair is gray.
> You and I, old friends, can we just watch
> Our efforts be washed away?

"Who wrote that?"

"Mao did. In 1975. It was his last poem."

They walked on in silence.

"It must have been quite a time here, when you were with Mao and Marshal Lu. I thought I saw Lu's daughter at the banquet. She must have been a little girl when you saw her last," Ricker said after a time.

"Yes," McGrath answered. "She was a pretty little schoolgirl, in a neat blue uniform with her hair in braids."

McGrath remembered how pleased she had been when he spoke to her in Chinese. "Why do you speak Chinese if you are an American?" she had asked him. "Why do you not speak American?"

"Americans don't speak American," he had corrected her gently, "they speak English."

This was hard to understand, so he had explained that once upon a time, long ago, King George of England had thirteen colonies in what was now America, but now nothing was left of the English in America except the language itself.

"So was England a hegemonistic superpower?" she had asked.

"Oh, little Li," he had replied, "I wouldn't bother about all that if I were you."

She had run off, calling after her, "One day, Ma Ga't"—it was difficult to pronounce the name McGrath—"I shall speak English as well as you speak Chinese."

McGrath shook his head and focused again on Ricker. "I could hardly believe that the young woman at the banquet was little Li. But she has certainly learned to speak English."

"I saw you talking to Lu," Ricker said. "You know, that may be the way in."

McGrath nodded.

They went through the hotel lobby and to the desk to pick up their keys. A short, rather swarthy man was ahead of them. The desk clerk was having trouble with the man's name.

"Galveas," the man said impatiently. "Antonio Galveas. Room 229."

"Ah yes, Room 229. Of course."

Ricker, listening to the dialogue with half an ear while his mind was on other things, wondered vaguely where he had heard the name Galveas before.

As a member of the Politburo, Chung Feng was allowed to rent a private house in Paichekiao Street, a once-fashionable avenue, not far from the Zoological Gardens. The location pleased him. One of his rare diversions was to stroll along to the zoo in the late evening, when the usual crowds had dispersed for the day, and watch the pandas waking up. He found himself in some sympathy with the panda's manner of life: sleeping by day and going out at night. More and more, he found himself working straight through until dawn, reading, writing, and, more recently, plotting. The little house on Paichekiao Street had become the nerve center of the radical faction, with Chung the acknowledged leader. At all hours of the day and night came a succession of visitors and messages. Slowly but surely Chung was preparing to take over from China's moderate leaders. He had an instinctive feeling that the visit of these Americans might give him the springboard to power he was looking for. First he had to discover the real motivation behind the American overtures.

On a purely personal basis, the American presence was a vexatious business. Li Lu-yan had told him that, while the Americans were in China, she would not be able to come to him.

"My father needs me. Ma Ga't is an old friend. When I am not working, I shall have to stay at home, to be the hostess."

Chung was annoyed. He had come to depend on those visits by Li Lu-yan. Until he met the young interpreter, he had not thought much about sex. Love and lust had been subordinated to politics. His first meeting with Li convinced him that it was perfectly possible to combine both work and pleasure.

He frowned as he sat on the veranda waiting for his breakfast. Did she really have to run home to her father just because this McGrath fellow was in town? What was so special about McGrath? Li must have been a child the last time McGrath was in Peking. Did she once have a girlish crush on the American or something like that?

The frown on Chung's face deepened but was soon replaced by the beginnings of a smile. An idea had occurred to him. If Li had decided to stay at home; if, for whatever reason, she was interested by McGrath, then perhaps he could find some way to turn this to good account.

A woman with heavy black spectacles and hair tied straight back came out onto the veranda. A servant, now called a member of the Revolutionary Household and Kitchen Committee, she had been with Chung for ten years.

"Your visitors are here."

Two men, both of dark complexion, were getting out of a taxi.

"Perhaps you had better tell the taxi to wait," Chung said to them, speaking faultless English. "In this city they're hard to find."

The first Brazilian came up the stairs and shook Chung's hand. "My name's Delgado, Roberto Delgado."

Chung noted the vital complexion, the dazzling teeth, the dark hair that was beginning to grizzle slightly around the temples. "How do you do, Mr. Delgado?"

"And this is my colleague, Antonio Galveas." The second man was shorter, somewhat corpulent, and flushed from breathlessness.

"Come in, gentlemen, please. Won't you join me for breakfast?" He gave instructions to the woman. "Now," he said, when they were seated on the porch, "what can I do for you?"

Delgado spoke first. He told Chung that he had learned of the existence of some sort of geological anomaly in the Sino-Soviet border area. He explained how his colleague, Antonio Galveas, who worked for a Brazilian consulting firm in Washington, had through perfectly orthodox channels been able to acquire a set of the relevant LANDSAT photographs. He went on to say that they had taken the material to Brazil in an attempt to assess its importance.

"With what result? Where exactly is the geological anomaly? What is the explanation for it?" Chung was patently anxious to know more.

The two Brazilians exchanged glances. They were now in a negotiating situation and did not wish to give away too much of their hand before knowing what they could get in return.

"Our problem," Galveas explained, "was technical. We had access to the photographs, which are in the public domain, and we knew what series to request. Of course, we requested several other series at the same time, not wanting to excite suspicion. The difficulty is that the LANDSAT photographs themselves do not necessarily contain all the data. The photographs are based on information that is tape-recorded by sensors on board a roving satellite. The tapes themselves contain the complete information, which doesn't show up on the photographs."

"What kind of information?" Chung asked sharply.

"Well, we don't know enough yet about all the new American techniques," Galveas replied, "but we know from an informed source that the Americans themselves consider this discovery to be very, very important."

"How much *can* you learn from the photographs?"

Delgado opened his briefcase and took out a set of large glossy prints. He spread them on the table. "As you can see," he explained, "these photographs show a hilly area crossed by a river of substantial size. The geological anomaly is located somewhere in this area. As you see, these photographs bear no indication of the geographical co-ordinates. We will tell you that they were taken somewhere along the four-thousand-mile Sino-

Soviet border. We might be persuaded, however, under certain circumstances, to reveal the precise location of the area that these photographs depict. This information alone will be of great interest to China. You will at least know where to start looking."

"Is it possible for you to acquire a copy of the tape as well?" Chung asked.

Delgado seemed doubtful. "We could try. I am not sure if we shall succeed."

Chung took a sip of tea. "You want to make a deal, is that right? You want me to pay for the material?"

Delgado leaned forward and said in tones of the greatest sincerity, "Sir, the world has been told that China and the United States are in the process of negotiating a treaty of economic and cultural co-operation. We feel there is more to their visit than meets the eye. One of the things they have come here to talk about is this geological anomaly and what it might mean."

Chung nodded. It made sense. Maybe it would even explain the suspiciously favorable treaty agreement. "Go ahead," he said.

"After all," Delgado continued, "we know that the Americans are aware of this anomaly. They must have some plan. But, sir, I must tell you our true identities and the real reason for our coming to you. We represent a strong and well-organized but little-known revolutionary force in Brazil. We have been watching and waiting for the right time to move against the military dictatorship of our country. In the meantime, many of us have taken jobs in government and business in order to infiltrate the power centers. This has finally paid off, and we think we are ready, with your help, to launch the revolution in Brazil. This valuable information we can give you would be small payment for the liberation of the Brazilian people. And, of course, you would have good friends in power in the largest South American country." Delgado leaned forward, hoping for a positive response.

"Why did you come to me?"

"We thought that you would best understand our point of view. Today China is led by revisionists, friends of the West, men without revolutionary principles. But this will not always be the case."

Chung smiled, accepting their flattery and working out in his mind the possibilities of co-operation. They talked for another twenty minutes. When the Brazilians said good-bye they left the photographs with Chung. Reflexively, Chung wondered if other members of this Brazilian organization were in Moscow giving a duplicate set of photographs to the Soviets and, if so, what the next step would be.

10

Old Marshal Lu cast a last contented look around his sitting room. Everything was ready. The little porcelain cups were set out on the low lacquer tables; the Ming vases were filled with flowers; the cigarettes—Chinese, Turkish, even English—nestled in boxes inlaid with rare woods and precious stones. Two priceless screens were set at either end of the room. On the walls hung silk tapestries from the middle Ching period, together with three exquisite fans hand-painted in the classic style. There were, Lu thought, some advantages in being old and venerable. Few people dared, or were in a position, to dispute his right to surround himself with beautiful things. He had earned these small pleasures. He decided, since this was a very special occasion, that he would produce a box of his best cigars to set alongside the cigarettes.

He limped out onto the balcony and stood, hands on the rail, looking out over the city. How much the view had changed over the years! When he had built the house on this little hill, it looked out over true countryside. On the way to his office in the city, he used to pass through fields where livestock grazed and peasant families worked out their livelihood. Many of these families he had known well. His own garden had backed onto the fields, and his livestock—pigs and poultry, mainly—had mingled with theirs. Since then the town had swelled outward as the population grew, and suddenly the little hill where he had settled so many years before was a desirable suburb, much sought after by upper-echelon bureaucrats. Of course, the rampagings of the Red Guard during the Cultural Revolution had had a certain effect, and the more extravagant lifestyles had been toned down. Even so, "The Village of the Summer Palace," as the area was known, still displayed a touch of class in this otherwise classless society.

Lu listened to the darkening city, a multitude of sounds fusing to become one long distant hum, like the sound of waves breaking on a far-off coast, broken from time to time by the clatter of an oxcart or the yell of a child. He turned as his daughter came to stand beside him. "He's coming tonight," he said simply. "After all these years, he's coming tonight."

"I'm glad. May I stay with you?"

"Of course. Perhaps he will remember you."

She laughed. "I was only a child the last time he was here."

He placed a hand on her shoulder. "My dear, to me you will always be a child."

As the dusk gathered, the old man yielded to the memories that forced their way into his mind, seeing events of forty and more years ago. When was it, he wondered, that he had first met the elder McGraths? He was sure it was after Mao and his people had crossed the Tatu on their Long March west. They had fought their way over the Snowy Mountains into the Great Grasslands. What an epic struggle that had been! Over five thousand miles of hazardous terrain covered at nearly twenty-four miles a day! Fifteen whole days devoted to pitched battles; every day, somewhere along the line, a skirmish or two. And always the relentless pressure to press onward, ever onward.

They had spent the winter of '36–'37 in the hills of Shensi. It was not until the New Year—it came back to him now—that he had first met the three Americans. Precisely what their status was had not been clear to him at the time. The couple had apparently, with a bravery that bordered on foolhardiness, made their way through the Nationalist line to present their credentials as "medical missionaries." It had fallen to Lu, then commanding the XV Red Army Corps, to receive them and their son, young John McGrath, who was living and traveling with his parents.

During that long winter, huddling in caves on the hillside to escape from the bitter cold, barely scraping together enough food to keep alive, he and the McGraths had come to know each other well. McGrath, Sr., had taught Lu some English, and he in turn had taught young John McGrath Chinese. Partly because Lu had no son of his own, he and young John became very close. When Lu rode through the lines on his pony, the boy would come with him. Young McGrath was quick and brave. By the time he was fifteen, he could fire a gun and skin a sheep. He carried messages to the front and joined whatever scouting parties offered the most promise of action. The boy became virtually one of the family, almost an adopted son of Lu and his wife, Wen Shu-chen. Wen Shu-chen was a beautiful young girl, scarcely twenty years old, full of warmth and a vigor and vitality that enlivened every occasion. Young McGrath grew very close to Wen Shu-chen. On his own initiative he tried to teach her English. Lu remembered how Wen Shu-chen's face would screw itself up into strange shapes as she tried to pronounce the unfamiliar sounds. Then, invariably failing, she would burst into fits of uncontrollable girlish giggles. Yet Wen Shu-chen could handle a machine gun with the best of them; she was often seen, at the height of some battle, exhorting her people that all sacrifices, however great, were to be suffered for the cause.

When she fell ill, in the spring of '37, Lu took her to McGrath, Sr., who had gained considerable respect for his work as camp doctor. None of his remedies, however, could cure Wen Shu-chen. Her mysterious disease was never diagnosed. Lu remembered how he and McGrath, Sr., had sat on either side of her as she lay on the floor of the cave, each of them holding a tiny white hand as her life ebbed away. The boy, burying his face in his hands and sobbing, had watched them.

The events of those years had created a strong bond between McGrath and Lu. When McGrath came back to China in the early fifties, Lu felt as though a long-lost son had come home.

McGrath had visited his house in Peking and had met his second wife and little Li Lu-yan, the child of this marriage. After McGrath left, there were many changes in China. The chaos of the Cultural Revolution had convinced Lu that he would never see this young man, almost a son, again. He felt absolute joy, therefore, at seeing McGrath at the banquet. His delight had infected his daughter as well. She would act as hostess for her father. He did not entertain much; since his second wife's death, of cancer, he had led a rather quiet life, saving his energies for work. When guests did come, he liked things to be done well, in the old style. Li knew his tastes, she could prepare the dishes he liked best—peach-blossom rice, crisp and soused with a sizzling ragout, and *guo giao mia,* sliced prawns and meat cooked in scalding chicken broth. He was proud of her and glad that she shared his pleasure in McGrath's visit.

As soon as he saw the car, Lu walked down the steps to greet him. Li watched from the balcony as the tall American got out of the car and embraced her father. He must be very special to Lu, she thought, if her father would kiss him.

"It was very good to see you at the banquet," McGrath said in Chinese. "You've become a great man."

Lu laughed. "There are no great men. There are men who survive and others who do not survive."

They walked to the house.

"It's the same as I remember it." McGrath looked around. "Just the same."

"And my daughter, is she the same?" Lu smiled proudly.

McGrath started. "I thought I recognized her at the banquet. Little Li Lu-yan. I remember when you were knee-high to a grasshopper, and now look!"

Li Lu-yan blushed deeply, gave a little bow, and smiled a warm, radiant smile. "Welcome to our house. My father has often spoken about you. I feel I know you already."

"You do. You were eight or nine years old the last time I was here. I remember you doing your lessons on the balcony. You were so earnest, so determined."

Lu interrupted with paternal pride. "She has done well. Today she is one of the top interpreters for the Politburo. She is much more important than I am!" Once more he laughed and they went inside.

They ate the splendid meal Li had prepared, and talked about the old times, people they had known, places they had seen, things they had done.

"Do you remember," said Marshal Lu, "when we had to capture the Luting Bridge? If we had failed, it would have been the end of the Long March. We received the order from Marshal Lin Piao. 'Our Left Route Army has been given until the twenty-fifth to take the Luting Bridge. You must march at the utmost speed and act in the shortest possible time to accomplish this glorious mission!' The twenty-fifth! The twenty-fifth was the following day, and we were still eighty miles from the bridge. A tremendous march. And we had to fight our way through strong enemy resistance."

"Yes, I remember. That was some battle!"

"Sometimes," Lu reflected, "things go better when you are really under the pressure of time."

After dinner they sat side by side in the deep armchairs in the sitting room. On a lacquer table between them were the cigars, cigarettes, and glasses of Chinese brandy.

"I shall bring tea," Li Lu-yan called out. No occasion was complete without tea.

She brought a thermos flask—McGrath noted its charming panda design. The leaves were already in the cups, and she poured hot water from the thermos on top of them. The green and black particles swirled and turned in the water and then settled back to the bottom. The girl passed McGrath a box of cigarettes, and McGrath felt the faintest flutter of her fingers on his hand.

He smiled at her and said in Chinese, "Thank you."

She nodded and smiled back, then got up to leave the two men to talk together, setting the flask between them so they could help themselves when they needed replenishment.

"Are you going now?" McGrath was sorry; he would have liked the chance to get to know her better. But he also had to talk privately to Marshal Lu.

"Yes. I still have work to do in town. I am learning to fly and tonight there is a theoretical class in navigation procedures. All that trigonometry is quite difficult."

"I'll have the car take you, if you like."

"Thank you. There's no need. I have my bicycle."

She left them and a few minutes later they heard the tinkle of her bicycle bell as she set off down the hill.

Lu poured out more tea, carefully recorking the flask.

"We're getting on in years, now," he said, looking affectionately at the younger man. "Even you. You are not a boy any longer. I remember when you could run after a rabbit and catch it. And we needed those rabbits too! There wasn't much else to eat in the caves."

McGrath answered, " 'The struggle tires us, and our hair is gray.' "

Lu, moved, completed the quotation. " 'You and I, old friends, can we just watch our efforts be washed away?' "

They sat in silence for a while, enjoying each other's company. It was like old times.

"Now, my son," Lu said at last, puffing on his long cigar, "tell me why you and the Americans are really here."

So McGrath outlined the story up to this point. It took a long time, since Lu asked many questions and sought exact answers. When McGrath finished, Lu sat puffing on the stub of his once impressive Havana and contemplated the possibilities. When he spoke, his voice indicated that he had already made up his mind. "We need to be sure. I cannot take the responsibility unless we are sure. Completely sure."

"But we have the results of the scintillation analysis."

Lu shook his head scornfully. "You cannot ask me to take such risks on the basis of American evidence and American analysis. How do I know your people may not have made a mistake? How do I know your drone was correctly programmed? How do I know your scintillation detector, or whatever you call it, was working correctly?"

"You can see the films. We can show you the films."

But Lu was adamant. "It's my country. My Army. It would be my war."

"There will be no war."

"Are you quite sure?"

McGrath nodded. "If we do it right, there will be no war."

Lu came halfway to meet him. "I like your plan. I like this scheme to divert the Ussuri. It is the kind of stratagem that appeals to me. But I want to be sure, absolutely sure, that the deposit is where you say it is and that it is what you say it is. Otherwise our efforts will be in vain."

McGrath knew what the old marshal had in mind. "You want a proper survey. You want us to take samples. It would be risky."

Lu stood up, speaking firmly. "I am Minister of Defense and I am a marshal of the Chinese Army. I know what risks are to be run and what risks are not to be run." His voice softened. "Remember Kansu, old friend, when Chiang's airplanes bombed us all day? Remember this?" He pointed to the wound on his thigh, which was the reason he still limped.

McGrath remembered. His own parents had been killed in that same raid.

"My people wanted us to move out, didn't they?" Lu continued. "Even Lin Piao wanted to move out, back to the caves. But I told them that if we moved back now we would lose a year and that Chiang's planes would soon run out of fuel. And was I right?"

McGrath had to agree. "You were right." As he spoke, he could see his parents lying together on the cold hillside, their eyes closed and an expression of joy on their faces. Those who had fought the good fight had no fear of death.

"And I shall be right again," Lu insisted.

With that McGrath had to be content.

"You know," Lu said, "I can authorize the reconnaissance across the Ussuri River, and I will do so. But even if the results of the reconnaissance are positive, I cannot authorize the operation itself. That decision must be taken collectively, by the Politburo as a whole. And we will have to watch out for Chung. Chung Feng can block your scheme."

"Can't we do something about Chung?"

A glint of amusement appeared in old Marshal Lu's eyes.

"Why, perhaps we can," he said. "After all, *les absents ont toujours tort, n'est-ce pas?*"

"Hey," McGrath exclaimed, "I didn't know you spoke French!"

Marshal Lu feigned surprise. "You didn't know I was with Chou En-lai in Paris, over half a century ago? Your big black briefing books didn't tell you that, eh?" Lu leaned back, prepared to tell McGrath yet another story of the Revolution.

The U.S.–China Trade Conference began the next day. The two delegations faced each other from opposite sides of a long table covered in green baize. Photographers and reporters lurked in hallways and antechambers trying to get pictures and comments from anyone who left the meeting room.

The UPI correspondent in Peking, an earnest young man starting his career with an assignment in the Far East, managed to grab Thaddeus Ricker as he went into the meeting. "Mr. Secretary, do you think the United States is ready to sign a treaty with China?"

"The United States signed a treaty with China after the Boxer Rebellion," Ricker replied. "No reason why we shouldn't update it now."

The negotiators talked all day the first day, all day the next. Plenary sessions were followed by working groups, which in turn set up drafting groups, which reported back to the working groups, which reported back to the plenary. Translations of texts were made and revised. The search went on for the correct concordance of terms; a word that meant something in one language did not necessarily mean the same thing in the other. They covered energy, agriculture, commodities, cultural and sporting ties, even human rights. In almost all fields the Americans were unexpectedly open and forthcoming.

During one of the breaks, the UPI correspondent was again able to buttonhole Ricker. "The way it's coming out, Mr. Secretary, do you think Congress will ratify? The Chinese seem to have all the advantages. What's in it for us?"

"I can't speak for Congress," Ricker said, "but frankly, when they're fully informed I don't anticipate any problems on the Hill."

At the end of the third day, the Americans asked for an adjournment. They said they had traveled halfway around the world and they needed a break. Besides, the conference's technical services needed time to get documents ready for final approval. They wound up the afternoon session on Thursday and agreed to meet again the following Tuesday.

Before they adjourned, Ricker asked for the floor. "Mr. Chairman," he said, addressing Chairman Yang, who had himself presided over many of the negotiating sessions, "you have very kindly invited some of us down to Tibet for the long weekend while the people here get the papers ready. I must tell you how happy we are to accept this invitation. Speaking for myself, I've always wanted to try my hand at giving a prayer wheel a whirl."

Ricker took advantage of the little gust of laughter that greeted this joke to spring the trap he had laid. "I understand," he said, "that the runways in Tibet are quite long enough to take our new Boeing. I would therefore like to invite those of our Chinese hosts who will be accompanying us to Tibet to ride with us aboard our plane and to sample at firsthand some of the aspects of advanced American technology that we have spent so much time talking about in this conference. If I may be so bold, Mr. Chairman, I would like especially to invite Mr. Chung Feng to come along. We understand that Mr. Chung's immense knowledge and practical experience of Tibet would make him an invaluable guide."

Ricker saw Marshal Lu lean across to have a few words with Chairman Yang. At the conclusion of the exchange, Yang nodded. "Mr. Ricker, I think your suggestion is an excellent one and we shall be happy to agree to it." He looked pointedly in the direction of Chung Feng, who was seated amid the Chinese negotiating team. "Comrade Chung Feng will take charge of all necessary preparations and will himself accompany you on your first visit to Tibet."

Chung Feng felt himself scowling and quickly produced an insincere smile. He scented that he was being set up, but he wasn't quite sure how. All he knew was that there was something forced in Ricker's enthusiasm for his company. After all, he had given Ricker no reason to like him. He had to go, however. He decided that he would take all possible steps to secure his interests in Peking during the time he was away.

Ricker and McGrath walked together to the car at the end of the day.

"Congratulations on the way you handled that—getting rid of Chung," McGrath said.

"Thanks, but it was your idea and Marshal Lu's. I just hope that with Chung out of the way, and assuming everything goes well on the survey, we can get a favorable decision out of the Politburo."

"Lu thinks there's a very good chance," McGrath said. "But a man like Chung isn't easy to fool. His views run against those of the current leadership, yet he maintains his power and position. That takes some doing. I have the sense that he's biding his time."

11

Huddled inside the troop compartment of the strange vehicle, sweating in his airtight clothing, Wilbur Silcott was not only uncomfortable but also frightened.

Saturday morning he had been called into a secret meeting with Marshal Lu, John McGrath, and a young Chinese geophysicist, Fu Pu-po, who was director of the Geophysical Institute at Peking. Marshal Lu wanted hard evidence of the deposit, and he wanted that evidence verified by competent people on his own side.

As a scientist, Silcott saw merit in Lu's proposal. He recognized that the Chinese were perfectly justified in asking for on-the-ground verification. There had never been a mineral discovery that did not have to be confirmed by digging boreholes and taking samples. No matter how sophisticated the initial methods of detection, in the end you had to go out into the field, and that was all there was to it. He was certain the deposit was there, and that it was a lode of substantial magnitude. But, although he had examined the LANDSAT images with the utmost care and had attempted to correlate his readings with the data produced by the drone, without a ground traverse there was no way of establishing the precise dimensions of the deposit, or of assessing its contours and configuration. How far south, for example, did it extend? How deep did it go? They had some superficial information, but if they were to conduct these investigations in a proper manner, they ought to have a great deal more.

Professional considerations, however, could not suppress his fear. "Do you really think it's necessary," he said, "for me to go along? Imagine the political consequences if I'm captured by the Soviets."

McGrath answered him. "We're going to have to take some risks. I, for one, have to go in there. We still need to confirm some of the hydraulic information—flow data, for example, and the scouring characteristics of the riverbed. We made some calculations based on the literature but we need solid up to date information. Even a 10 per cent difference in the rate of flow can throw the sums off. As far as I'm concerned, crossing the river is an ideal opportunity to firm some of these things up."

Once McGrath had thrown his weight behind the expedition, Silcott was reluctantly forced to agree. It was true that they needed his expertise and familiarity with the available data.

And so just past midnight Silcott found himself inside a Chinese amphibious vehicle, about to cross the Ussuri River into the Soviet Union. Thanks to a periscope with night vision he was able to follow their route. He had studied the maps and could relate the observed topography to what he already knew of the area. They were traveling about due east. Their speed, as he estimated it, was well over twenty miles an hour. They were following the line of the little one-track railroad, skirting Pao-Tung and Hulin to avoid notice.

Two or three miles from the river, they turned due north. Past Hut'ou the ground began to rise and they had to cross a saddle before dipping once again to the plain. After Tu-mu-ho, where a dog barked at their passage but no one else appeared to take any notice, the track cut in between two hills and then curled right to run through the village that was situated virtually on the riverbank, Ch'i-li-pi.

Silcott moved away from the periscope and turned to McGrath and Fu Pu-po, who were with him inside the troop compartment: "This is a pretty nice little vehicle, isn't it? What do they call it?"

"They call it the Panda. It's based on a Soviet weapon, the Soviet Army's BMP or Bocevaia Machina Piekhoty, which the Chinese captured in a border skirmish. It's a pretty faithful copy of the Soviet BMP, light-armored, combining the features of a light tank, antitank guided-missile carrier, and amphibious personnel carrier. It's smaller, lighter, and, I believe, cheaper than either the German Marder or our own MICV—mechanized infantry combat vehicle—even though its antitank firepower is considerably greater."

"How does it compare with the Soviet vehicle it's based on?" Silcott asked anxiously.

"It's better. We may not run into Soviets tonight, but if we do, at least we're prepared."

Silcott was a little relieved.

McGrath and then Silcott looked through the periscope at the village of Ch'i-li-pi. They remembered the films that had been taken by the drone, showing people in the square and the nets of fishermen. McGrath knew that, if all went according to plan, he would become quite familiar with Ch'i-li-pi over the coming weeks.

"I like the look of that place," he said, turning away from the periscope. "It's a long time since I've lived in a Chinese village. It will do me a lot of good. Being retired has made me too soft."

Beyond the village a narrow path ran on through the river canyon, but it was impassable even for a vehicle as versatile as the Panda. It clung precariously to the cliff face, sometimes rising steeply, at other times falling away, almost disappearing toward the river. It was no place for mechanized transport.

The four Pandas lined up one behind the other when they could go no farther. Then the lead vehicle turned through a ninety-degree angle to face the river. With exemplary precision, the other three followed suit. When all four were in line, they moved together down to the water's edge, then plowed in.

It was a cloudy night. The progress of the Pandas downstream was virtually unnoticeable. The only thing a keen-eyed observer might have detected was the small waves made by the periscopes, which the drivers raised for amphibious operations. McGrath, from inside the hull, watched the flowmeters. He was surprised to notice that the volume of the Ussuri was greater than they had estimated. They would indeed have to recalculate some of the sums. This might have important consequences for the engineering side of the operation.

After twenty minutes of steady progress down the river, they could feel the cutback in the amphibian's engine. They sensed the turn to starboard. McGrath nodded to Silcott. "This is it. We're going ashore." He felt the tension in his stomach as he waited for the unmistakable sensation of water cascading off the hull of the surfacing vehicle and for the first sight of the bank through the periscope.

"If they're going to get us, this is their chance," he said to Silcott. "Another ten seconds and we'll be able to shoot back."

For Colonel Hsien Ming, the Chinese force commander, it was an equally tense moment. Earlier that evening, at the small airbase of Hu-Pei North, he had gathered his men for a final briefing session, taking them step by step through the details of the operation. "As far as you're concerned," he began, "this is just a routine patrol across the river. You've done it before and you'll do it again. We'll be taking four Pandas, which, as you can see, are decorated with the insignia of the Soviet Army 16th Khabarovsk Division and in every way resemble Soviet armor. We shall be maintaining radio silence throughout unless we are engaged by hostile fire, in which case I shall give commands in the usual way. Tonight's mission," he continued, "is not a strike operation. We have no wish to hit and no wish to wound. It is a reconnaissance probe into territory that the Soviet revisionists are at the moment illegally occupying." He went on to tell his men what he knew of the operation, but he himself had little inkling of the true purpose. His instructions had been to mount a border patrol involving four of the new Pandas, three of which would contain the usual complement of men and equipment, while the fourth would have no troops apart from the driver and the commander. The troop compartment would be occupied instead by a team of "experts." A certain amount of "special" equipment would be carried on the fourth Panda.

As far as the route of the patrol was concerned, he had received instructions that he was to carry out to the letter. They were to take to the water at Ch'i-li-pi. They would then turn downstream, hugging the Chinese bank, and enter the canyon. They would travel at periscope depth without lights. Three quarters of the way through the canyon they would turn right and aim for the Soviet shore. He went on to indicate the manner in which they would breach Soviet territory, the details of the reconnaissance itself, and, finally, the tactics for the return journey.

"As far as we know, there are no permanent Soviet defenses along this stretch of the river. Because there are no disputed islands lying midstream, this is not one of the areas of confrontation. If we run into a border patrol, the likelihood is that we shall be recognized and respected as Soviet armor on exercise." The colonel felt fairly confident in saying this. He knew from intelligence reports that the command structure in the Soviet Siberian Army left much to be desired and that, as often as not, confusion was the order of the day. This was especially true in the border areas where the KGB had a virtually autonomous role alongside, and sometimes in apparent contradiction to, the military.

"If it comes to a firefight, and frankly this is something I don't anticipate, I am sure we shall be more than a match for anyone we may come across."

Colonel Hsien Ming refrained from repeating in his general briefing the private instructions he had given to each of the three Panda commanders who were to act as escorts to the fourth vehicle. "In the event of a firefight," he had told them, "your first responsibility is to ensure the safe withdrawal of the 'special duty' Panda. If such safe withdrawal seems impossible, your duty is to ensure total destruction of that Panda, *including all personnel contained therein*. Total destruction. You are to ignore other targets until such time as this goal has been achieved."

He had instructed them that both the main gun and the Anshan missile launcher were to be used for this task and told them that to achieve the most rapid and complete obliteration of the 'special duty' Panda they should aim at the rear doors. These doors were made of relatively thin armor plate, and each contained 150 liters of fuel linked by rubber hose to the engine. The resulting conflagration would engulf the Panda itself, the occupants of the troop compartment, and their equipment. He did not think that any of the occupants would have time to escape through the access hatches, but if they did they were to be ruthlessly cut down with machine-gun fire and their bodies either recovered or destroyed beyond recognition. He stressed that no material from the special Panda was to be left behind.

Wilbur Silcott felt the Panda rise from the water. His heart pounding, he waited for the sound of gunfire. But there were no shouts on the other side, no rifle shots, no crash of artillery. The four Pandas emerged dripping, the tracks tilted at an angle approaching the maximum slope of thirty degrees as they hauled themselves up the far bank. They paused to regroup. The special Panda took the lead in an arrowhead formation, an escort vehicle on either side and one bringing up the rear.

Silcott's fear lessened as he realized they were not under fire. It was up to him now to take control and guide them to the best area for digging. He shakily switched on the radioactivity counter. The needle showed nothing at first. They were still too far from the edges of the deposit. But as the Panda moved forward the needle suddenly flipped into a vertical position.

"Hey!" Silcott shouted. "Take a look at this." The others pushed alongside him to see the dial.

Silcott wanted to find the very center of the deposit, the core area. Talking to the driver through the intercom, he used the red counter to guide the Panda forward. He tried to keep the needle on a maximum reading. If it dropped he asked for course corrections until he had recaptured the line. "Hotter!" he called. "Colder." Fu Pu-po, interpreting for him, told the driver what to do.

After five minutes they began to climb slightly; they breasted a slight incline and, as they reached the top, the needle suddenly swung almost off the dial. "Hold it!" Silcott called.

The escort vehicles immediately took up defensive positions. Every soldier was at his periscope. Every gun was trained outward, making a 360-degree field of fire. The three scientists, already wearing the special clothing that could protect them from the toxic plutonium, hooked up the oxygen equipment and screwed on their helmets.

Silcott came out of the hatch first, moving clumsily like a lunar astronaut. He was followed by Fu Pu-po and McGrath. They set up the drilling equipment and got it going, twisting down into the rocky soil. They dug outward from the vehicles, along the radials and at carefully spaced intervals, filling containers that had been clipped to the deck of their Panda. Each container was labeled with the co-ordinates of the spot from which its contents had been taken.

Silcott was sweating, partly from the labor and partly from fear. The wind had come up and there was a break in the clouds that had obscured the moon. "Hell and damnation!" Silcott muttered. Though his suit and helmet were both in camouflage colors, he felt conspicuous. He wished it was all over and that he was safely back home.

Suddenly he caught the glimmer of a light, on the other side of the spur, and he froze motionless, one hand on the drill. The others noticed it too. They stopped their work and stood poised as if for flight.

A few minutes passed and nothing happened—no more flashes of light, no movement, no sound. The hulls of the escort vehicles, lying low and sinister around them, guns poised, were reassuring. They concluded that they had seen nothing more than a trick of the moon, hitting the water through the clouds.

It took them over an hour to finish their work at the first site. Once they had filled the canisters, they stored them on the Panda. Then they climbed back in the same order that they had come out, Silcott first, then Fu Pu-po, then McGrath.

McGrath was halfway down the hatch when he saw the Soviet tank come out of the trees. "Quick," he hissed to Silcott, "pass me the cap and jacket."

In seconds, McGrath put on the Cossack fur helmet of a Soviet tank captain and the tunic to go with it. He thanked his lucky stars that they had come prepared. As the Soviet tank spotted them and switched on its searchlight, McGrath pressed the switch on the loudspeaker and broke into a stream of fluent Russian. "You lumbering idiots," he cried. "*Muzhiks!* Peasants! What the hell do you think you're doing? This is a special patrol of the 16th Khabarovsk Division, and we are not meant to be interfered with. Get that light out!"

McGrath saw the main gun on the Soviet tank swing in his direction. He waited, holding his breath.

Colonel Hsien Ming did not wait. His orders had been given by Marshal Lu himself. "Destroy the lead vehicle. Obliterate it entirely." He prepared to give the order to fire.

Suddenly the light went out. There was an interminable moment of silence. Then came an answering shout from the Soviet tank. "Keep your shirt on, comrade. We're not trying to interfere. We just saw some movement down here, and we came over to take a look."

McGrath, vastly relieved, kept the anger in his voice. "Well, clear out now!" he called. "Leave us alone." The Soviet tank rumbled back into the trees the way it had come.

McGrath ducked down through the hatch. "Close call." He removed the fur cap and wiped the sweat off his forehead. "I'd forgotten I knew how to curse in Russian!"

The two other men were shaking with fear as he looked at them. "Well," he said, "what do we do now? Do we go on and run the risk of that guy out there coming back with a couple of his friends—in which case we might have to shoot it out? Or do we call it a day and head for home? I can't decide that question. You two gentlemen are the geologists. You have to tell me if you have enough information or if you need more."

Silcott and Fu Pu-po held a rapid consultation. Silcott looked up at McGrath: "Ideally, we'd have liked to establish how far the deposit extends southward. But we think it's too risky. We could jeopardize the whole thing. As it is, we feel we've got enough to go on. Plenty enough. We think we should head for home now."

McGrath looked at him hard, wondering if they should go

ahead and try to get *all* the information they might need. "It's your decision," he said finally. He picked up the intercom and spoke to Hsien Ming. "Colonel, we think we ought to get back now. Over."

Hsien Ming acknowledged the message. He didn't want to get into a firefight, and he was glad he hadn't had to give the order to fire on the fourth Panda. The tall American was certainly an unusual man.

The gray light of dawn was showing over the still-sleeping village of Ch'i-li-pi when the first Panda pulled itself up the bank on the return trip. An old man standing outside his hut shook his head in disbelief as first one, then another, and then two more armored vehicles raced along the path toward him. He saw the Soviet markings. The Pandas did not stop. They clattered on through and by the time the other villagers had roused themselves to find out what the fuss was about, nothing remained to be seen. The "Soviet tanks" had vanished as suddenly as they had appeared.

12

The car came for them at dusk and drove them north into the hills.

"We're headed for the tombs!" McGrath exclaimed after half an hour.

"What tombs?" Silcott asked, happily resuming the role of tourist.

"The Ming tombs. This is the beginning of the famous Avenue of the Stone Statues." In the darkness they could just make out the gigantic animal statues they were passing at regular intervals. "The statues guard the tombs. There's a progression. First a kneeling camel, then a standing camel; a kneeling elephant, then a standing elephant. Now look—a rhinoceros. A unicorn. Then we move on to people. That one is the statue of the mandarin, a precursor of the Emperor."

The car slowed while McGrath told them some history. "There are thirteen tombs altogether, for the thirteen Ming Emperors. The largest and best is the sepulcher of Tchangling— that's where they put the remains of Emperor Tchengtsou." During the Ming Dynasty the Chinese Empire grew a hell of a lot. Except for a little while under the Manchus, it never got that big again. In the days when Tchengtsou sat on the perfumed throne, you can bet there was never any question of a

Russian presence in Manchuria or a Russian port on the Pacific. Wouldn't it be nice if tonight, right here among the spirits of the old Emperors, we made a decision to put things back the way they used to be? Territorially, of course, the gain would be small. But that plutonium up there has got to be worth a million times more than the treasures of Ming."

The road narrowed. They were up in the hills now. "These higher tombs have never been excavated, as far as I know," McGrath said. "I wonder where we're going."

He leaned forward and spoke in Chinese to the driver, who shook his head, and without taking his eyes from the road, muttered a few words in reply.

"He won't say. I guess we'll have to wait and see."

They went on climbing. The road described a series of sharp hairpin bends before it finally ended. They got out and looked down at the plain below. In the distance, the city of Peking gave off a faint glow. The evening was chilly and a fresh wind blew. They saw that they were standing on a huge mound, the size of a football field.

"Is this one of the tombs?" Silcott was curious.

"I think it must be. It's probably Tailing's or Kangling's. The earlier the Emperor, the higher up the hill he was buried. Or it may be a tomb we know nothing about."

"The tomb of the Unknown Emperor?" They laughed, and felt better.

They followed the driver across the top of the mound to a flight of stone steps in the very center. He showed the way down with a flashlight. McGrath counted sixteen steps in all before they came to a blank wall guarded by a sentry. The driver pressed the edge of one of the great stone blocks that formed the doorway. The massive granite face slid aside. Inside was a corridor, bright with lights, which led another twenty yards into the heart of the tomb. At the end of the corridor was another blank wall and another sentry. This time their guide took a key from his pocket and inserted it into a lock on one side. This wall too slid open. They stepped forward and found themselves in a stainless-steel elevator with a thick padded carpet and a little electric fan whirring away in the corner. Silcott, who had an eye for this kind of detail, was comforted by a small plaque on the wall of the car that read, MANUFACTURED BY OTIS ELEVATOR COMPANY.

They had no means of telling how far they descended into the bowels of the earth. They could not judge the rate of descent, and there were no intermediate floors. When the elevator came to a stop, the doors opened onto a cavernous vault. It still retained the geometric angles and the cold marble surfaces on which the sarcophagi of the Emperors had once been laid. But the vast chamber had been transformed into a twentieth-century boardroom, complete with green baize table, paper, sharpened pencils, glasses of water, name plates, microphones, and even a chairman's gavel.

Chairman Yang looked up as he heard them arrive.

"Hello. We've been expecting you. Sit down." He pointed to the table and the name plates.

McGrath was relieved to see that Ricker was already there. "So you made it?" He slipped into the seat next to the Energy Secretary.

"Yeah. I got them to lay on one of their Li 129 supersonic fighters to bring me back from Lhasa—journey time, ninety minutes. They were glad to show it off. That's some plane!"

"And Chung?"

"Chung's coming back on our Boeing, with everybody else, at a slow and even pace. I told 'em not to hurry!"

"What if you're still here when he gets back?"

"I won't be. I'm flying out as soon as this meeting's over." He leaned across to whisper to McGrath. "I hear you did a great job up there, John. Apparently you speak Russian like a native!"

Chairman Yang had given the newcomers long enough to settle down. "Comrades!" He rapped his gavel and waited for the Americans to put on their earphones. McGrath looked over toward the interpreter's booth and caught the eye of Li Lu-yan. He smiled in her direction and was rewarded when she waved and smiled back.

"Comrades," Chairman Yang repeated, "we meet today in the headquarters of the Politburo. These premises were originally prepared to help the Chinese leadership serve their people in the event of hostilities involving one or more of the hegemonistic superpowers. This room is in the tomb of Yung Lo, one of the earliest of the Ming Emperors and a great warrior. You are the first foreigners to have visited these headquarters."

He paused to make sure the Americans could follow him on their earphones. McGrath adjusted the volume control on his headset and decided that, after all, he would listen to the translation. He liked tuning in to the lilting tones of Li Lu-yan, and besides, Chairman Yang was speaking a little fast for him.

"You Americans, I know," Yang continued, "have your own command posts—the Situation Room in the White House, your underground Control Center in Colorado, SACEUR in Belgium. We Chinese are also prepared."

His opening remarks concluded, Chairman Yang turned to Marshal Lu, who sat chain-smoking on his immediate right.

"Marshal Lu, I think it is time to tell us all about the very significant activity that recently took place."

Marshal Lu, looking as crumpled as ever, took them through the whole story of the deposit, step by step. When he had finished his preliminary account, it fell to Fu Pu-po to explain the details of the reconnaissance expedition that they had conducted across the Ussuri. "So you see," he concluded, "that in addition to the results from the scintillation detector that were already available, we have now been able to analyze—by mass spectography and other techniques—actual rock samples from the deposit area. These samples confirm the presence in the area of a very large concentration of plutonium and an almost equally large concentration of Uranium 235!"

There was an audible stir in the room.

"Gentlemen," Yang called for silence. "I am once more going to give the floor to Marshal Lu so that he can outline to you certain propositions that the Politburo may wish to consider at this time."

"With your permission, Mr. Chairman," Lu replied, "I'd like to ask my old friend John McGrath to take over at this point."

McGrath took his time. There was no point in rushing things. He wanted to be sure his audience had a complete and unhurried understanding of what he was proposing. "Thank you, Mr.

Chairman." He took out his pipe and propped it carefully in the ashtray.

"Marshal Lu," he addressed his old friend, "I have often heard you quote the precepts of Sun Tzu. Will you permit me in turn to quote one of our own sages? The prophet Isaiah writes: 'And he shall judge among the nations, and shall rebuke many people: and they shall beat their swords into plowshares, and their spears into pruninghooks: nation shall not lift up sword against nation, neither shall they learn war anymore.'

"In February 1957," he told his now puzzled audience, "I was present at a secret meeting at the Lawrence Radiation Laboratory in Livermore, California. It was there that the Plowshare project—named after Isaiah's famous prophecy—was born. Plowshare was the idea of using nuclear explosions for peaceful or nonmilitary purposes. Nuclear explosives originally grew entirely from military requirements, but scientists were also interested in the possible peaceful uses of the great energy available in the atomic nucleus. The Livermore meeting, and the report that resulted from that meeting, was the first concrete expression of this concern. Lights, please!"

As the lights dimmed, the first slide was projected onto the screen. "In 1962," McGrath continued, "the first nuclear device designed specifically for the Plowshare program was fired at the Nevada Test Site in the United States with a yield of 100 kilotons. This picture shows the spectacular Sedan Crater, 370 meters across and 100 meters deep. It gives a very clear idea of the massive power we are dealing with.

"The cratering obtained in early weapons tests," he went on, "led to the Plowshare program's emphasis on the excavation capability of nuclear explosions. Buggy, for example, a Plowshare experiment conducted in Nevada in 1968, used a row of five 1.1-kiloton nuclear charges buried 41 meters deep and 46 meters apart to produce a ditch 260 meters long, 75 meters wide, and 20 meters deep.

"Here you see"—McGrath switched to the next slide—"an aerial photomontage of a crater-lip dam in the Soviet Union that has been excavated by a nuclear explosion with a yield of over 100 kilotons. This Soviet application, called 1004, was designed to block the river to the left. You can see from the picture that this is precisely what has happened. The lip of the crater has formed a barrier, and an inner reservoir has formed inside the crater itself. In fact, it is holding back something like 7,000,000 cubic feet of water.

"I might add," McGrath continued, "that in the Soviet Union the Plowshare concept has been taken very far indeed. At the present time, as part of their project to replenish the Caspian Sea, whose level has dropped significantly in the last 35 years, the Soviets are planning to use nuclear explosions to excavate a canal *112 kilometers long.* Conventional explosions and ground removal would take 15 to 20 years and would therefore be impractical. There has also been talk about the use of nuclear explosives to excavate a new route across Central America to supersede the Panama Canal, as well as a possible canal across the Kra Isthmus in southern Thailand. Lights, please."

McGrath let the animated whisperings die down and waited for questions.

Chairman Yang spoke first, an unmistakable note of incredulity in his voice. "As I understand it, what you are proposing is a Plowshare-type operation, using nuclear explosives, to divert the Ussuri River! Is that correct?"

There was a gasp of surprise in the room as those present began to grasp the magnitude and daring of the concept McGrath had advanced.

"That is correct, sir," McGrath replied quietly. "I am perfectly convinced, from the experience that has been acquired both in the United States and in other countries, that such an operation is both feasible and realistic. A nuclear device exploded underground, beneath the main channel of the river, could achieve a cratering effect like that which occurred in the Soviet 1004 project, which would effectively block off the river."

"What would happen then?"

McGrath took a deep breath. He didn't want the discussion to become too technical. They could go into details at a working-group level later. "To put it in crude terms, we have to make such a large obstruction in the course of the river that the river, as it were, gives up the attempt to flow that way and finds some other route."

"How can you do that?"

"Immediately after the explosion, the crater will be formed. The size of the crater, other things being equal, will depend on the magnitude of the explosion."

"You mean a 20-kiloton explosion will cause a larger crater than a 10-kiloton explosion?"

"Exactly. The problem is how long the damming effect will last. In our case, for example, it's of no use to obtain a temporary blockage of the Ussuri River. We need to achieve a permanent diversion."

Leaving his seat, he went to a table on which a large-scale relief model of the deposit area had been placed. "It is clear from the contours of this model that a cratering operation taking place more or less at the beginning of the canyon would cause the water to back up here, beyond the village of Ch'i-li-pi, until eventually it found its way around to the east and joined up with the Bikin, which would then take over as the main stream of the Ussuri."

"How large an explosion would you need to obtain such a crater?" asked Chairman Yang, continuing his cross-examination.

"We don't have final figures on that yet," McGrath replied. "The size of the crater itself is only one of the factors to be considered. We have to look at the scourability and permeability of the fill material as well. They're running new data on flow and sedimentation rates through the computer in Washington at the present time." He looked at his watch. "We hope the results of the new computations will come through any moment now. Arrangements have been made at our embassy in Peking to get the findings to us here by way of your offices.

"A dam is only good as long as it lasts. If water starts seeping through it, or under it, or if it builds up behind so much that it flows over the top of the wall itself, then all your effort is for nothing. The dam will wash away and you'll be back to square one."

Out of the corner of his eye, McGrath noticed a Chinese official come up to Silcott and hand him a plain buff envelope. Silcott glanced at the contents before he pushed it across the table to McGrath.

"Excuse me," McGrath looked quickly at the message. Still holding the paper in his hand he said rather formally:

"Chairman Yang, Secretary Ricker, through on-line transmission via satellite, I have just received a first set of calculations, based on corrected data, from our hydraulic computer in the United States. May I inform the meeting at this time of the results?"

"Go ahead, Mr. McGrath."

Ricker echoed Yang's words. "Go ahead, John. This is your baby."

McGrath could sense the tension in the room. He replied carefully so as not to mislead them. "You've got to remember," he said, "that this is an unorthodox calculation because we have to dam the whole width of the river at one go. We are confronted here with an all-or-nothing situation. The massive obstruction we need has to be created literally from one minute to the next, and when it is in place it has to be capable of withstanding the full force of the water at least until such time as the diversion has been satisfactorily assured."

He was being long-winded and he knew it, but he wanted to prepare them for what was coming. "Gentlemen, in order to achieve a dam or fill unit of appropriate weight and dimension, our people have assumed that cratering by nuclear explosion will be necessary. In order to achieve a crater that will throw up a dam with the required characteristics, they have calculated that a nuclear underground explosion in the order of 150 kilotons is called for! I should stress that this is only a first runthrough. We'll get more refined calculations later."

There was dead silence in the vault.

"Hiroshima times seven."

"Yes, sir. I suppose you could call it that."

The withering sarcasm of Comrade Yeh En-wen's voice broke the silence. "We are listening to a fool. Does Mr. McGrath suppose that the Soviets will for one minute admit an artificially engineered change in the international frontier? Does he not know that it is an elementary principle of international law that a de facto international frontier will change with a change of a river only if that change has itself been the result of *natural* causes?"

Chairman Yang raised his eyebrows. "What do you have to say to that?"

McGrath looked at them with wide-eyed innocence.

"Oh, but I *am* talking about natural causes. An earthquake *is* a natural cause. Let's look at the facts," he continued, before they had time to interrupt him. "You would agree, wouldn't you," he turned to Fu Pu-po, "that in the last few years we have seen increased seismic activity? Scientists are speculating that the world may be returning to the active conditions that prevailed between 1890 and 1910, which included the great San Francisco earthquake of 1906."

Fu Pu-po nodded in agreement.

"In fact," McGrath continued, "every year there are about fifty thousand earthquakes of sufficient size to be felt or noticed without the aid of instruments. Of these, about one hundred are large enough to produce substantial destruction if their centers are near areas of habitation."

He walked over to the world map that was attached to one of the walls. "Almost no area of the earth is entirely free of earthquakes. However, in recent times the great majority of earthquakes have occurred in well-defined regions. There are two principal active centers: a rather narrow belt extending around the margins of the Pacific Ocean, and a wedge-shaped area with its broad base in China, which crosses southern Asia, Asia Minor, and the Mediterranean, and has its point off the coast of Portugal. Within China, it is in the northeastern area—here—that we have recorded most earthquake activity. If we aggregate all the shocks in China over the last twenty years, we find that the province of Manchuria, where the deposit is located, has the most."

McGrath looked around. "Our plan is this: China will tell the world that she is expecting a major earthquake in the northeastern area of the country. Chinese scientists, like Dr. Fu Pu-po, will put their necks on the line and predict the actual time this earthquake will occur. After all, they predicted the Peking earthquake in 1976. There's no reason why they shouldn't do it again. Relief units will move into the area. That is both normal and understandable. At the appropriate moment we explode the bomb underground, the whole world takes it for the anticipated earthquake and marvels at the brilliance of the Chinese seismologists who predicted it so accurately. If all goes according to plan, the Ussuri is diverted. Chinese troops—engaged, of course, on purely humanitarian tasks—find themselves holding a new international frontier that is both legally and militarily defensible."

He was carried away by the beauty of his own scheme. "A winner, gentlemen, don't you agree?"

A buzz of conversation filled the room, its tone affirmative. Chairman Yang smiled, signaling his appreciation.

Marshal Lu grinned at McGrath. "You never told me about the earthquake, you rascal," he said in Chinese.

"I like to keep a few surprises up my sleeve," McGrath replied.

Fu Pu-po raised his hand and asked to speak. There was a tense, worried expression on his face. Something clearly wasn't right. He addressed himself directly to McGrath.

"You say you need an underground nuclear explosion of 150 kilotons?"

"Correct. Is that a problem?" For the first time that evening, McGrath looked anxious.

"Yes, it's a problem. Anything over 100 kilotons and you're within the limits of detectability, given the state of the art at the present time! I would like to explain this fully. With your permission, may I have half an hour or so to prepare? I am afraid it has taken me by surprise."

Chairman Yang looked around the room. "All right. We'll take a half-hour break."

Three quarters of an hour later, they took their seats, ready to absorb a new set of facts in what was already becoming a rather complicated equation.

Fu Pu-po went to a blackboard and pinned up a large piece of paper with a pattern of squiggly lines. "What you see here is a seismogram that was made in the Peking Geophysical Institute at the time of the Great Tangshan earthquake."

He pointed to different sections of the paper. "You will see from the chart that not all the waves reached the recording instrument at the same time. First came the primary, 'push-pull,' or 'P' waves." He indicated the first set of squiggles on the paper. "After some interval of time, another set of waves was recorded; these were secondary, 'shear,' or 'S' waves, which move from side to side. Last of all were surface waves, which move the instrument up and down. The P waves arrive first because they travel faster through the earth, about 1.7 times as fast as the S waves."

He had been speaking rather slowly at the beginning. When he saw that they understood, he continued more rapidly, emphasizing the key points with quick jabs of his forefinger. "In many respects an underground nuclear explosion resembles an earthquake. A small nuclear explosion equivalent to about 3 kilotons of TNT produces, under normal circumstances, an earthquake of magnitude 4 on the Richter Scale. This is a relatively minor shock and there are perhaps 10,000 natural quakes that powerful every year. However, a nuclear blast of 100 to 200 kilotons produces a magnitude-6 shock, of which probably no more than 100 occur naturally each year. From 600 to 2,000 kilotons of nuclear explosive produces a magnitude-7 quake, equal to some of the strongest natural occurrences.

"Mr. McGrath, you say you need an explosion of at least 150 kilotons. That means we are talking about a pretty sizable shock—not a supershock, I agree, but not a baby either. That 'pretty sizable' shock is going to be picked up on the World Wide Standardized Seismograph Network. And it is going to be picked up in the Soviet Union, which, even though it is not a participant in WWSSN, has its own monitoring network. Precisely because it *is* a big shock, the seismograms will be analyzed very carefully. People will look at the P waves and the S waves, and compute travel times to determine location and magnitude.

"What is more," he continued, "there is one overwhelmingly important reason why these seismograms are going to be analyzed and inspected and scrutinized so carefully, and that is because the idea of disguising an underground nuclear explosion as an earthquake is by no means a new one. The reason it took the Americans and the Soviets so long to agree on a test-ban treaty in the 1960s was largely because neither side could figure out how to police underground nuclear tests and to distinguish earthquakes from underground detonations that were meant to be banned."

He looked around the room. "In fact, you will all remember that in the first test-ban treaty, they solved the problem by leaving out underground tests altogether. The issue was just too complicated, so in the end the negotiators decided to duck it entirely."

"What's the problem then?" McGrath asked. "If there's no means of telling the two apart, why should we worry? That is precisely what we want."

Fu Pu-po smiled. "If this were still the sixties, I would agree with you. But science does not stand still. The 'state of the art,' as I put it, has evolved, and the limits of detectability must be drawn somewhat narrower now than in the past."

"Specifically?" McGrath did not like to see his brainchild come under attack.

Fu Pu-po turned to Chairman Yang. "May I take up a few more minutes of your time? I believe that this discussion is in fact quite crucial."

Yang nodded.

"Very well." Fu Pu-po was pleased. It was not every day that a seismologist had the chance to address the Politburo on his own subject. "A moment ago I mentioned that an earthquake produces surface waves as well as P and S waves. Recent calculations indicate that the amplitude of the surface waves generated by explosions should be an order of magnitude less than that of natural earthquakes of the same body-wave magnitude. I am going to show a slide to demonstrate the point. Lights, please."

Fu Pu-po projected a scattergram onto the screen. "This is a chart of surface-wave magnitudes compared with body-wave magnitudes for North American explosions and earthquakes. You will note that the two types of disturbance follow separate trends! The wave magnitude of the explosions falls below that of the earthquakes. This is a definite discriminant. Frankly, gentlemen, it seems impossible that a 150-kiloton explosion that will produce a seismic yield in excess of 4 on the Richter Scale will *not* be detected by our Soviet friends or, indeed, by anyone else who, literally, cares to keep his ear to the ground."

Yeh En-wen again interrupted the meeting. "Mr. Chairman," he said with intense irritation, "we are obviously wasting our time. It was clear from the outset that the idea was too fanciful and farfetched to work, but I never suspected that the flaw would be quite so glaring. If the Soviets can identify the diversion of the Ussuri as being due to a nuclear explosion instead of a natural earthquake, and if that analysis is confirmed independently by a hundred seismographic stations across the globe, where do we stand?" He pointed an accusing finger across the table at the Americans. "Chairman! Fellow Members of the Emergency Planning Committee of the Politburo! You are being led into a trap by these men, and you must resist! Clearly it is their intention to cause a war between China and the Soviet Union, a war in which the only winner will be the United States of America!"

Chairman Yang was visibly upset. He had gone out of his way to show himself favorably disposed to the American proposal, and now he looked like a fool. "Mr. Ricker," he began icily, "you have heard what Fu has to say about your computer calculations. I wonder at this point whether you have any comments to make?"

Ricker's anger was obvious. McGrath heard him swear under his breath. "Why didn't those bastards back home warn us we'd run into a 'limits of detectability' problem? What the hell do they think they're playing at?"

The Americans went into a huddle.

"Gentlemen!" Yang once again rapped the table. "The American delegation is 'caucusing.' I believe that is the right word? We will break for five minutes."

When they resumed, ten minutes later, Ricker looked more composed. "Thank you for giving us a little time, Mr. Chairman. Let me say straightaway that we agree with Dr. Fu Pu-po's evaluation." Silcott nodded his confirmation. "We agree that under *normal* circumstances an explosion of 150 kilotons will produce a seismic yield that is well within the limits of detectability—that is to say, one that can be clearly identified as a nuclear explosion and not an earthquake.

"However, we are not necessarily talking about 'normal circumstances.' "

"Oh?" Chairman Yang was again interested.

"Let me explain." Ricker leaned forward and fixed them with a steely glare. "When I say 'normal circumstances,' I am speaking about the conventional emplacement of the nuclear explosive. But in fact the energy of a subterranean explosion can be drastically decoupled* from the surrounding rock by firing it in a big hole. This is just the opposite of increasing the efficiency of seismic-wave generation by tamping rocks tightly around the explosive, or surrounding it with water."

He glanced quickly at the members of his team who sat beside him and behind.

"My people tell me that there are considerable engineering problems in excavating a large enough cavity to get the optimum decoupling factor for a big bomb. Maximum muffling of a 50-kiloton explosion at a depth of 1.2 kilometers would require a spherical cavity with a diameter equal to the height of the Great Pyramid of Cheops. And I agree that concealment of such mining activity and the dispersal of mined rock, given present-day satellite surveillance, would be very difficult. It might be especially difficult in a sensitive border area. However, we believe it could be done. Moreover, even if we achieve only a partial decoupling, we could reduce the seismic-wave strength by at least one order of magnitude."

Marshal Lu smiled across at McGrath. "Your idea, I suppose?"

McGrath shrugged. "Teamwork."

Lu laughed. "You love it, don't you? Dig one of the biggest

---

* To decouple a nuclear explosion is to absorb its shock. Here Ricker was saying that if the nuclear device were placed in a large cavity, the cavity would absorb much of the explosive shock.

holes in history. Hide the earth so no one knows what's happening. Plant a bomb. Bang! Divert a river! It's a game, isn't it?"

"More than a game. A challenge."

Chairman Yang interrupted. "This is a conference, not a dialogue."

He turned to Fu Pu-po. "Do you think this can be done? Are you satisfied that by exploding the bomb in an underground cavity the seismic yield will be reduced sufficiently for the nuclear detonation to remain undetected?"

There was a long pause. Once more the tension built up in the room. The Americans knew that much depended on Fu Pu-po's verdict. The geophysicist was a young man in a land where on the whole old men held sway. Yet it was clear that his professional judgment was respected by his colleagues and that the Chinese would never approve the operation if Fu Pu-po went against it.

When he finally spoke, he was equivocal. "I agree that a partial decoupling will help to reduce the seismic yield. But will it reduce the yield enough?" He consulted a piece of paper on which he had scribbled some calculations. "To achieve maximum muffling of a 50-kiloton explosion at a depth of 1.2 kilometers we would need to excavate, as Mr. Ricker put it, a spherical cavity the height of the Great Pyramid of Cheops. If we achieve only a partial muffling, the engineering exploits Mr. McGrath and his team will have to perform will be correspondingly less. But we must remember that we are not dealing with a 50-kiloton explosion, but with a 150-kiloton explosion. And we are using this explosion to achieve a surface crater. This means that we will not be able to go as deep as 1.2 kilometers if we are to attain our objective. Mr. Chairman, I respect the ingenuity of the proposal, but I do not believe that muffling by itself will bring us below the crucial magnitude limit on the Richter Scale."

"Mr. Secretary?" Chairman Yang raised an inquiring eyebrow. "I believe it is your serve!"

The use of the Ping-Pong metaphor brought a reluctant smile to Ricker's lips. "John," he turned to McGrath, "tell 'em the rest."

McGrath got up to unveil the last element in the package. "Gentlemen, the calculations we made to arrive at the 150-kiloton figure assumed no diversionary works. We planned just to let the river back up behind the dam until such time as the water forced itself into another channel around the back of the deposit area. That meant that the dam had to be a large one. But what happens," he asked, "if we assume some diversionary works, if we give the water a little assistance in its search for another channel?" He turned to the model and pointed to the ridge of land lying east of the Ussuri opposite the village of Ch'i-li-pi.

"What I am proposing," he said softly, "is that in addition to detonating a nuclear device underground to produce a crater to block the river, we also undertake a Buggy-type operation designed to carve a diversionary channel through this half-mile piece of rock."

"Buggy?" Yang had forgotten McGrath's earlier briefing.

"I mean a series of small nuclear charges, around the 1-kiloton range, used to excavate a trench that will draw off the water of the river the moment it begins to build up behind the dam. That way the dam can be considerably smaller—which means that we can reduce the size of the explosion to 100 kilotons or less and avoid the problem of detectability."

Fu Pu-po joined McGrath in front of the model. "Let me be absolutely clear about this. This diversion trench you're talking about is on Soviet territory, is that right? Entirely on Soviet territory?"

McGrath nodded. "Correct."

"You plan to use a series of 1-kiloton charges or so to create the trench. Is that correct too?"

"Yes."

"In the case of Buggy, the charges were placed at a depth of over 40 meters. Would you go to the same depth here?"

"More or less."

Chairman Yang suddenly interrupted. "How in the world do you imagine that you can plant a series of small nuclear charges on Soviet soil without being found out? Answer that first."

"It can be done," McGrath replied simply. "It can be done." Patiently he laid out his scheme, and then they argued it for an hour, and finally the engineering problems, as McGrath presented them, seemed intricate but not insuperable.

Yang called for a break before the final vote. When they got back to the table and resumed their seats, he turned first to Fu Pu-po. A yes vote from him would indicate that the plan was sound. After that the decision would be based on politics. Yang went around the table. The decision was unanimous: yes.

Both sides then agreed that McGrath would have supreme command as far as the operational phase was concerned. It was a unique tribute, a measure of the confidence the Chinese had in him. McGrath pressed the palms of his hands together, inclined his head slightly, and said in Chinese, "*Shye shye*. Thank you. I shall do my best to deserve your trust."

It was Ricker's turn to bring up the final business of the meeting. He read out the text of the "Secret Protocol" the Americans wanted to adopt at the same time as the far-ranging new Sino-American Economic and Cultural Treaty they had just negotiated.

When he had finished, Chairman Yang exclaimed: "Ah! So that is the quid pro quo! The United States is to have a 50 per cent share in exploiting the deposit! And if the operation fails? Is the treaty itself then null and void?"

"By no means. The only consequence will be that the Secret Protocol will not go into effect."

"You're taking a gamble, then, aren't you?"

"Some things are worth gambling for."

The Americans left the tombs the same way they had arrived; the Chinese obviously had an alternate exit. Cars were waiting for the Americans. Ricker said good-bye and shook hands with McGrath and Silcott. "I'm kind of sorry I'll be missing all the action. But I'll keep in touch. John, do a great job. You're running the show."

McGrath smiled in the darkness. "Don't worry, Mr. Secretary. I deserve a 'last hurrah'!"

Six hours after the secret meeting in the Ming tomb had ended, the American Boeing returned from Tibet.

Chung drove straight home. He made several telephone calls, and went out on the veranda to wait. Twenty minutes later, a courier arrived by bicycle. He handed over a small leather satchel hidden underneath a pile of fruit in the bicycle's basket. Chung took it into his private study and closed the door behind him. He removed the tapes from the satchel and quickly ran through the material on a play-back machine. Then he listened again, more carefully, to certain sections. Once or twice he uttered a short, sharp exclamation and sucked in his breath.

When he had heard enough he rewound the tapes, locked the machine away, and hid the recordings in a small wall safe. A hint of a smile appeared on Chung Feng's thin lips as he began to realize that going off to Tibet like that would probably turn out to be one of the most useful things he had ever done.

13

Ricker's plane landed at Dulles in midmorning, and he decided to go directly to the office. After his staff had welcomed him, his secretary took him aside. "Dr. Richmond called yesterday afternoon and said you should call her as soon as you could. She said it was important."

"Get her for me," he said and went into his office and shut the door.

"Ella," he said, when she came on the line, "how are you, darling?"

"Oh, Thaddeus, I'm so glad you're back. I loved those phone calls from China, it was so exciting, but I am glad you're back."

"Are you all right? I got a message there was something important."

"There is, I'm afraid. We really shouldn't talk about it on the phone. But you'll think I'm saying that just so I can see you sooner."

"That's okay with me. But what kind of thing is it?"

"Something's happened out here at Goddard you ought to know about. It's pretty delicate."

"Can it wait till this evening? I'm briefing the President and the rest of them this afternoon, and then I'm supposed to have dinner at the White House. But it won't be late. Is ten too late for you?"

"Never too late. That'll be fine. But don't come all the way out to Georgetown. I'll come in to you."

"I'll tell the doorman to let you in. You can bone up on my Matthew Arnold while you're waiting."

"Don't keep me waiting too long," she said fondly. "I've missed you very much."

After they had held each other and kissed and then embraced again, Ella pulled back a little and, a playful expression on her face, said: " 'The sea is calm tonight, the tide is full, the moon lies fair upon the straits. . . .' "

" 'Dover Beach'—isn't it a great poem?"

"It's a beautiful poem. But I only had time for a couple of stanzas. You were too punctual." She kissed him again, then started to undo his tie.

"What were you going to tell me?" he asked. "What's the problem out at Goddard?"

She looked suddenly dejected. "Yes, well, that . . . Okay, I'd better tell you. One of my team is a program analyst named Shirley Lewis. She's pretty—a sexy body if you like that kind of thing—and she tends to get herself into situations. She has a habit of picking up undesirable men of one kind or another and then getting let down with a bad bump. Sometimes I've had to pick up the pieces, and I'm happy to do it. After all, I'm almost old enough to be her mother."

"Call it mature," Thaddeus said. "It sounds better."

"I came across her sobbing her heart out in the john. So I sat down with her and asked her what the problem was, and bit by bit the story came out. Now here's the bad part, Thaddeus. You won't like it."

"I'm listening."

"It turned out," Ella continued, "that she'd been dating a Brazilian diplomat, a fellow called Roberto Delgado. He works at the Brazilian embassy. How they first met up, I've no idea. She said that Delgado had just jilted her and that she was feeling awful about it. So I asked her why the hell she always picks bastards and said she never should have chosen a Latin diplomat because all that meant was fast cars and easy sex and was that what she really wanted?"

"You really put it to her, didn't you?"

"Yes, I guess I did. To cut a long story short—because it took us about four cups of coffee to get this far—I told her I thought she was well rid of Roberto Delgado and why didn't she forget all about it and get back to work?"

"And?"

"At this point she broke into a fit of hysterics. She said Delgado had been threatening her. She was scared stiff of him, and she didn't know what to do! She finally admitted that she'd told Delgado about her work with LANDSAT, told him about the thermal anomaly and, as a result, he'd been putting enormous pressure on her."

"What for?"

"She said he kept asking her which side of the river the blob was."

"And what did she say?"

"She told me she told him she couldn't remember. She said she'd only had a quick look before I whisked her off and took things over myself."

"And what do you think she really told him?"

Ella thought for a moment. "I'm not 100 per cent sure, but I believe she's telling the truth."

"Why?"

"Apparently Delgado has been after her for the tapes as well. That's what precipitated the crisis. She says she told him she couldn't get at the tapes, that they weren't public domain, and in any case they'd been removed from the Goddard archives because she'd checked. He didn't believe her, and that was when he threatened to beat her up. That's about all. I thought you ought to know."

"Dammit, that's too much of a coincidence! A Brazilian diplomat meets your girl; a Brazilian consulting firm requests LANDSAT data. Hell and damnation!"

He poured himself a large brandy from a decanter on the sideboard and sat down on the sofa with the glass in his hand. For two or three minutes there was silence in the room. When Thaddeus finally spoke, there was a decisive note in his voice.

"You may be right in thinking that the Brazilians don't know which side of the river the thermal anomaly is on. Maybe Shirley Lewis, or whatever her name is, didn't tell them. And maybe, as you say, you can't read that kind of information from the photographs alone. You have to have access to the tapes as well, and the Brazilians don't have that access. Nevertheless, we have to assume the Brazilians know something and that from now on our life is going to be a bit more complicated than we thought. Agreed?"

"Agreed. What are you going to do about it?"

"The first thing I'm going to do is to make sure that that son-of-a-bitch Delgado leaves the country with his tail between his legs as soon as possible." He reached for the phone, then withdrew his hand. "It can wait until morning." He drank from his glass. "You've taken the girl off secret work? She ought to be moved out of Goddard altogether."

"I've taken her off secret work, but I can't get her transferred for now, I don't think, because then there might have to be a hearing, and this is the wrong time for that."

"Absolutely. Let's hold this thing tight."

"Ed Mobley knows, and he's got her off in a totally risk-free operation. No problem."

Thaddeus sighed. "Oh God, I hope nothing bad comes out of this. There's so much depending on everything going just right."

He told her about China and then took her to bed, and they fell asleep in each other's arms.

14

Because of the equipment—a whole freight-carful—McGrath took the train to Manchuria instead of flying. The Peking railway station was decorated with huge pictures of the leaders of the Revolution—Marx, Engels, Lenin, Stalin, Mao Tse-tung, and Yang—and with gigantic posters: LONG LIVE CHAIRMAN YANG! LONG LIVE THE CHINESE COMMUNIST PARTY! LONG LIVE THE GLORIOUS UNITY OF THE PEOPLES OF THE WORLD! Crowds thronged the concourse and loudspeakers blared announcements.

A special car was waiting for him in a deserted part of the station. After all the equipment had been loaded and McGrath himself was safely aboard, it was joined up to the train. The doors at either end of the car were locked, effectively sealing him off from the other passengers. Were they trying to keep the Chinese from seeing him, McGrath wondered? Or were they trying to keep him from seeing the Chinese?

At exactly eight o'clock, the train pulled out of Peking. It gathered speed and rolled northward into the night. McGrath was alone in a large compartment. The bed was made up with clean linen; an electric heater hummed in the ceiling; a thermos of hot water stood on the table; and the tea sat waiting to be made.

This was a special occasion, though, and called for Scotch. He took a bottle from his case. As he was about to pour, he heard a knock at the door. Looking up, he saw Li Lu-yan and a porter waiting for permission to let her in. He smiled with surprise and pleasure. "Come in. I had no idea you were on this train. Why are you here?"

"I'm your official interpreter," she answered. "You may have some trouble up there in the border area since they speak a different dialect. They sent me along to help."

McGrath wondered momentarily how much she knew, but then he remembered. Everything. She had been in the interpreter's booth throughout the meeting in the Ming tomb. "I'm glad you're going to be up there with me."

He poured his drink and fixed tea for her. They sat together talking, listening to the clatter of the wheels. McGrath spoke such good Chinese and was so at home in the country—it made her comfortable and less aware of the difference in their ages.

"Did you know," he asked, "that the Great Wall of China is the only man-made feature of earth that can be detected by someone standing on the moon?"

She hadn't known but she could believe it. "After all, it is called the Ten Thousand Li Wall. Actually it is twelve thousand li long."

"Then why is it called the Ten Thousand Li Wall?"

She gave him a mischievous grin. "Because, in the old days, thousands of years ago, soon after the wall was built, a huge dragon curled up one night against it and went to sleep. The next morning they discovered that the weight of the dragon's body had pushed a great bulge in the wall, making it two thousand li longer."

He laughed out loud.

"I'll tell you another story, if you like," she said.

"Please do."

"Long ago," she began, "during the reign of King Hsuan of the Chou Dynasty, a child medium appeared who strode around in a trance saying, 'Mulberry bows and wicker quivers, these

will bring about the downfall of China!' Now, the King made in-
quiries, and he discovered that there was only one couple in all
his kingdom who made mulberry bows with wicker quivers, so
he ordered them to be killed. But the couple learned of his plan
in the nick of time and fled to the West. On the way there, they
found an abandoned baby girl and adopted her."

McGrath listened, entranced by the way she told the story,
her head bobbing to make a point, her small white hands flut-
tering like birds before her face.

"This girl's name was Pao Ssu," Li Lu-yan continued. "She
grew up to be very beautiful and in due course was shipped off
to the royal harem. I'm afraid in those days," she added paren-
thetically, "the emancipation of women had not yet taken place
in China. The King, seeing how beautiful she was, became in-
fatuated with her. But there was a problem. Pao Ssu never
laughed. Nothing could make her laugh. In despair, the King
offered a thousand measures of gold to anyone who could make
Pao Ssu laugh."

"Did he try tickling her toes?"

Li ignored this. "The chief minister thought of a scheme.
He lit the beacon on one of the watchtowers on the wall, and
the light flashed from one hilltop to another, across the whole
breadth of China. Fire on the wall, you see, was the emergency
signal that the capital was being attacked. It meant that the
people should rush to the aid of the city. All the warlords from
the provinces, seeing the beacon fire, came to the defense of
their King. When they reached the capital they learned that
there wasn't any danger after all."

"A kind of April Fool?"

"April Fool?"

"A trick. A joke."

"Yes. Exactly." She nodded her agreement. "When Pao Ssu
saw them all assembled with no one to fight, she burst out
laughing."

"So the chief minister received his thousand measures of
gold?"

"Yes, he did. But she had caused the destruction of the Chou

Dynasty, because shortly afterward there was a real emergency. The beacon fire was lit, but the warlords ignored it and the city fell!"

The train thundered on. McGrath finished his drink and poured another. Li had another cup of tea. She asked about his experience on the Long March and his recollections of her father. "He was a great general, wasn't he?"

"He is still a great general. Only now he is fighting a different battle, a political battle. Your father, Li, has a certain vision of China's future, but that vision is not necessarily shared by his colleagues. It is not shared by Chung Feng, for example."

He saw her start at the mention of Chung's name, and assumed she had discussed him with her father. "As your father knows, China needs advanced technology from the West. Chung won't accept that. He thinks he can keep the Revolution pure by refusing to deal with the West at all. It's an impossible ideal.

"But I don't want to talk about politics. Tell me, you must be nearer thirty years old than twenty. Why aren't you married yet?"

"I haven't met the right man. Not yet."

The train pulled into a station. There was a clatter of passengers getting on and off. As they pulled out again, music came over the train's loudspeaker system.

"What's that tune?" McGrath asked.

Li Lu-yan was amazed. "It's the 'Internationale'! You must know it."

"Yes, of course. I thought I recognized the melody. But I don't know the words."

"Shall I teach you?" she asked eagerly. "Shall I teach you the words of the Communist 'Internationale'?"

"Why not?" he replied, deciding to ignore the incongruity of a U.S. colonel's being taught the words to the Communist anthem by an attractive Chinese interpreter.

So she began:

> Arise ye prisoners of starvation,
> Arise ye wretched of the earth,

For justice thunders condemnation,
A better world's in birth.

She turned away from him as she felt the tears in her eyes.
"Why are you crying, Li?"

"I'm just crying. That's all. We're allowed to cry in China, you
know." She looked sternly at him, a little prim now, almost like
a schoolteacher. "You had better repeat the words, to make sure
you've learned them properly."

He repeated them after her, and she corrected his mistakes.
When he had the first four lines by heart, she taught him the
next four.

No more tradition's chain shall bind us,
Arise ye slaves no more in thrall,
The earth shall rise on new foundations,
We have been not, we shall be all.

They came to the chorus. He learned the words first and then
sang it with her, his deep bass voice accompanying her sweet
soprano.

'Tis the final conflict,
Let each stand in his place,
The Internationale shall be the human race.

Suddenly McGrath found that there were tears in his eyes as
well. Behind the tears, for no good reason he could think of, he
had a vision of his two golden Labradors wagging their tails on
the porch of his Virginia farm as he came home at the end of a
long day.

Kao Pin-ying and Hsueh Si-chun were at work early. They
had positioned their boats in a circle and, with the help of three
other members of the Ch'i-li-pi Fisheries Production Team,
were now pulling up the nets, hand over hand, arm over arm. In
the dawn light the great river shone with an oily blackness,
broken by flashes of silver as fish tried to leap back over the
mesh. As the boats drew closer together, the men shouted to
each other. Inside the circle, the fish thrashed and struggled.

"It is a good catch, comrade," Kao yelled.

The boats were almost touching.

"Now!" shouted Kao. They heaved together and the catch slithered aboard. Then they pushed the writhing and twitching mass into the holding area amidships. Kao and Hsueh immediately sorted the fish and threw back the little ones. They piled their nets on the sterns of the boats and headed for home. They reached the village just as the first rays of the sun hit the rooftops.

A Chinese Army jeep, with a red cross painted on its hood, arrived at exactly the same time. Colonel Hsien Ming sat in the front seat beside the driver. Behind him was a tall Occidental man and a young Chinese woman. Kao and Hsueh unloaded their catch onto a handcart and began to trundle it up the path to the village. They watched the strangers get out of the jeep, sniff the dawn air, and walk toward the commune headquarters.

"Who are they, I wonder?" Kao remarked. Strangers seldom came to the tranquil village of Ch'i-li-pi. The biggest event in recent history had been when Hsueh found a forty-pound carp in his net and almost fell into the water trying to get the fish aboard.

Loudspeakers began to blare: "All commune members, young and old, are required to attend a democratic meeting at twelve noon today in the commune meeting room. A matter of great importance will be discussed."

The village buzzed with speculation all morning, while the new arrivals remained closeted with the village authorities. Some suspected that the presence of the Chinese Army jeep might be related to the mysterious appearance, not so many days earlier, of the "Soviet tanks." But no one could discover a link between the two events.

At midday the commune meeting room began to fill up. It was a large hall, big enough to hold the entire population of Ch'i-li-pi, about six hundred people. The building was of simple brick with a rough earth floor. Its construction had taken two years. Every commune member had contributed his or her free time to the work and each had provided what they could by way of materials. The rest had been supplied by the Revolutionary

Committee of Ch'i-li-pi. Inside, the walls were decorated with slogans and portraits. The chairs were made of plain, unvarnished wood. At the far end there was a dais on which a long, low table had been placed. The eight elected members of the Ch'i-li-pi Revolutionary Committee were already seated there.

Feng Cheng-yeh had been chairman of the committee for the past three years. He was a man in his forties, with a smooth face and a relaxed, restful look in his eyes. He handled the strenuous job of running the commune with graceful ease, and the villagers had complete confidence in him. He called for order. The room fell silent. Surveying the rows of upturned faces in front of him, he felt a surge of love and gratitude. "Trust the people," Mao had said. If ever there was a time to trust the people, surely this was that time.

"Comrades," he began, "this is a great and solemn occasion in the history of Ch'i-li-pi. Today I wish to present to you three friends of our village, three good and warm friends!" He began with McGrath. It was difficult for him to pronounce the American's name, except in the Chinese manner. "This is Ma Ga't. Ma Ga't is a good friend of the Chinese people. He was on the Long March!"

The villagers broke into excited applause and stared awestruck at the American. To have among them a man who had participated in the making of history was a rare privilege! Certainly he deserved their respect.

McGrath acknowledged the applause and replied with a little speech in Chinese. It was not elegant Chinese; he had long ago learned that nothing succeeds like the vernacular. When he finished, the villagers doubled their applause. McGrath pressed the tips of his fingers together and bowed.

It was the young woman's turn next. Feng introduced Li as the famous daughter of a famous father. Once more, there was a stir of excitement. No one could have aroused greater interest than the offspring of Marshal Lu. As they clapped, Li rose to speak. She told the members of the Revolutionary Committee and the villagers of Ch'i-li-pi how honored she was to be there and how happy she was to be able to serve the revolution in however humble a capacity. "You can all see, of course, that Ma

Ga't does not need an interpreter!" The villagers laughed. "Nevertheless," she continued, "I shall do my best to be useful." In saying this she was, she knew, being too modest. McGrath's Chinese might suffice for everyday conversation, but this operation would involve a great deal of technical detail and many complex instructions. Without the services of a capable interpreter, McGrath would find the going difficult. The local dialect made her presence all the more necessary.

Colonel Hsien Ming was stiffer than the others, more formal both in his bearing and his speech. He explained that he was the link man with the Red Army for this operation. His task was to provide the necessary logistical and material support.

After the colonel sat down, Feng asked the obvious question: "This operation. Will you tell us about it now? The people are anxious to know."

Though Feng had not addressed anyone in particular, the whole room turned to McGrath. The American sat there puffing on his pipe, the image of calm authority.

"Yes, Feng." He took the pipe from his mouth and cradled the hot bowl in the palm of his hand. "Of course we will tell you what needs to be done. And we will ask for your help. For without your co-operation, without the co-operation of all the villagers of Ch'i-li-pi, we shall achieve nothing."

He looked around the room as he spoke, running his eyes over the rows of faces. It came to him how much of his life he had spent in villages and with village people. Today was not so different from a hundred similar occasions when men and women had gathered to hear him explain in words they could understand the purpose of some scheme that would change their lives. The head-office people, the people who raised the money and paid the contractors, called this aspect of his job "public relations." To McGrath it was human relations.

This project was different, though. It was bigger and more important. It also carried a burden of sadness. He could not tell them the project's real objective, nor could he tell them their village would be destroyed in attaining it. So he simply told them that, to ensure the safety and security of the Chinese People's Republic, it was imperative to undertake a major engineering exercise in the vicinity of the village.

McGrath looked around the room. "Has any one of you ever been to Peking? Put up your hands if you have."

Feng and two or three others thrust their hands in the air.

"Good." McGrath was pleased. At least some of them would know what he was talking about. He addressed Feng directly. "Have you seen the subway system in Peking?"

Feng nodded. "You mean the tunnels?"

"Exactly. I mean the tunnels. We are going to dig a tunnel like the one in Peking."

There was a gasp of surprise and quick conversation.

McGrath held up his hand. "Just a minute. Let me tell you where we are going to dig." The chatter subsided. "We are going to dig the tunnel under the river, into the Soviet Union!"

This time McGrath's upraised hand could not quell the villagers' excitement and incredulity. A tunnel into the Soviet Union! Who had ever heard of such a thing?

When they had at last quieted down, McGrath explained that this was to be a great secret. They would need to move several hundred thousand cubic feet of rock and earth within a very short space of time, but there must be no visible sign of any excavation. He reminded them that as a nation and as a people they had already demonstrated their expertise in this field. He referred again to the extraordinary complexities of the Peking subway system, whose construction had for years been a closely guarded secret—"and right in the middle of the city! Think of Vietnam too!" he continued. "Think of the bunkers and underground storage areas built with Chinese assistance along the Ho Chi Minh Trail, all of them constructed under conditions of total secrecy!"

They understood as he had known they would. He had produced a frame of reference for them and had related the present to the past. They would follow the examples he had given.

McGrath realized, though, that Feng was looking increasingly skeptical. McGrath turned to him. "What's the matter, Feng? You look worried."

Feng was concerned. "We are only six hundred persons in Ch'i-li-pi, Ma Ga't. Some of us are too old or too sick to dig. Some of us are too young. How can we hew out a tunnel all the way to the Soviet Union without help? You need an army, Ma Ga't, not just a village."

McGrath gave him a warm, confident smile. "Don't worry, Feng. I have brought a machine with me, a tunneling machine. It is the only one in China—indeed, the only one of its kind in the world. Chinese engineers devised it for use on the Peking subway. Now they have interrupted the work there to lend it to us. They call it a 'mechanical mole'!"

The villagers smiled and nodded at each other proudly. The great city of Peking had lent the tiny village of Ch'i-li-pi its mechanical mole. Work in the capital would be interrupted while the villagers got on with their own job. Wasn't that something?

"Tomorrow night," McGrath continued, "we will fetch the tunneling machine from the railhead. It will take all day to assemble it. The day after tomorrow we will begin to dig. If all goes well, we should be finished within two weeks."

McGrath's speech lasted some time. He described the various tasks. "We will need the young and strong for the heavy work, the not-so-strong for the light work. Some of you will have to work underground, some on the surface. There will be work for everyone, and you can vary your jobs if you like. What matters is that we finish on time."

After his explanation, there was a general debate. Feng let the discussion run its course. If he wanted their wholehearted co-operation, it was unwise to hurry them.

They did not understand what it was all about, and found it hard to grasp the significance of the operation. They did understand, though, that for reasons of high policy the village of Ch'i-li-pi had been selected for special service. This in itself was reason enough to give their full co-operation. There was no higher honor than to serve the state, and no more glorious future than to be asked to make sacrifices for it. They also assumed that the selection of Ch'i-li-pi augured the eventual arrival of an unusual reward. If they left their fields and nets to work for two weeks on a tunnel, they imagined that a benevolent state would make it up to them later.

At the end, when they were all agreed, Kao Pin-ying asked a last question: "Where will we start to dig?"

McGrath had already looked around the cavernous meeting room, noting its immense possibilities for concealment. He now saw the bare-earth floor and the chairs that could be so easily set aside. Of course, they would make a mess, he thought, but they could easily clear it up later. He concealed his sudden sorrow as he realized that for Ch'i-li-pi there would never be a "later." He pointed at the floor of the commune meeting room. "This is where we will begin."

McGrath spent the rest of the day walking around the village, getting to know the people. They were shy at first. They had never had a foreigner in their homes before and certainly not an American. But they were well disposed toward McGrath—after all, he had known Chairman Mao.

The first hut he came to belonged to Hsueh Si-chun. McGrath looked in the open doorway. Like so many of the peasant dwellings he had seen around the world, it was a one-room house. Hsueh sat in one corner mending his nets for tomorrow's fishing. In another corner his wife, Liu Hung, was preparing supper. Two children, both under six years old, squatted at her feet playing some kind of hopscotch on squares they had etched with twigs on the dirt floor.

Hsueh looked up as he saw McGrath's tall shadow fall across the doorway. Hsueh glanced at his wife. For all his bravado among his fellow fishermen—especially when they had caught the big carp—he relied very much on her advice and counsel. They were a very close couple. People in the village always spoke of them in one breath. Women, marrying their daughters off, encouraged them by reports of Liu Hung's matrimonial good fortune.

"Ask him in, of course." Liu Hung said sharply. "Don't just sit there doing nothing."

Hsueh jumped to his feet and cleared a coil of nets off a chair so McGrath could sit down, while his wife brought out the best cups and took the kettle off the stove to serve tea. McGrath meanwhile took his pipe out of his pocket and made a great play of lighting it. "Did you have a good day?" he asked, looking at the nets. "Is it a good river to fish in?"

"Oh yes, it is a good river, the Wusuli," Hsueh said, using the river's Chinese name, "a fine river."

"I'd like to come with you someday."

"Oh yes, we would like that very much," Hsueh was flattered.

An inquisitive crowd collected in the doorway of the hut. Hsueh saw his partner, Kao, standing outside, peering in, envying his friend's good luck at being the first villager visited by the tall American.

"Come on in, Kao," Hsueh called. "Ma Ga't is going to go fishing with us one day."

Kao came in and McGrath motioned for the others to come in too. He stayed for an hour, drinking tea, smoking his pipe, and talking to the villagers. "You know it's a big job we've got to do," he said. "It will be hard work."

Hsueh displayed the calluses on his hands from handling the nets day after day, month after month, year after year. "We are used to hard work in Ch'i-li-pi. Isn't that true, Liu?"

"Yes, it's true." Liu Hung spoke directly to McGrath for the first time. "You are a good man, Ma Ga't. We will trust you to look after us," she added with passion.

"Of course, I will look after all the people of the village," he said somewhat wistfully.

Toward evening, when he had seen and talked enough for one day, McGrath made his way to the guest house that had been set aside for him. It was a plain cottage with two bedrooms, a kitchen, and washing facilities. He was surprised to see Li Lu-yan at the stove in the kitchen.

"What are you doing here?"

"I'm staying here too. There's nowhere else. I hope you don't mind. In any case, I can cook the supper."

"That's wonderful. Really wonderful," he said, pleased.

They lingered over the meal, talking about her father.

"I loved that man," McGrath told her. "He practically adopted me when my parents were killed in an air raid."

"Tell me about that."

"They were out in the open together when the bomb hit them. My mother was accompanying my father on his medical rounds. She always did. Your father was wounded at the same time."

"I know. How did you finally get out of China?"

"It's a long story. I was interned by the Japanese in a camp in Burma up near Mandalay. I escaped and hid on a boat that took me down the Irrawaddy. Then I found a ship in Rangoon going to India."

"How did you manage to escape from the Japanese camp?"

"Six of us dug a tunnel under the fence. It was a pretty small one, nothing like the one we're going to dig here. But we squeezed through. I wasn't very large—I was only a boy. And the others weren't much more substantial. You don't get fat in a Japanese prisoner-of-war camp."

"I'll feed you well here, Ma Ga't," she promised. And they both laughed.

In bed that night McGrath reflected on the events of the long day. Well, they were on their way. Tomorrow, the hard work would begin. Would it really take them only two weeks to build the tunnel? What if the Panda expedition had excited Soviet suspicions? He began to drift off, and in the twilight world between sleeping and waking he thought he heard Li talking in the next room. When he finally slept he found that her face recurred in his dreams.

15

The Chinese authorities began to broadcast warnings of a possible earthquake. This provided a convenient cover for a certain amount of activity in the area—movement of Red Cross jeeps, for example. But they had to avoid any conspicuous concentration of vehicles. All unusual movements had to take place at night, and displacement of the terrain was forbidden, since telltale signs could be picked up by Soviet surveillance satellites.

The solution was to use the little single-track railway that ran up from Chihsi, the last town of any size, through Mi-Shan, Hsing-Kai, and Pao-Tung toward the border. The equipment they needed was brought in by night to an unloading point about five miles before the railway reached the river. Here a trail ran north, past the villages of Hut'ou and Tu-mu-ho to Ch'i-li-pi itself. It was at least thirty miles from the unloading point to the village. To avoid excessive wheelmarks they carried everything they could on their backs, working in relays, each team taking a five-mile stretch. The first night, they needed every fit person in the village.

The tunneling machine came in sixty crates of different shapes and sizes. Some of them a man could carry five miles. Others had to be put on handcarts. A party at the rear of the convoy brushed over the wheelmarks to erase them completely.

They also had to transport enough lining material, concrete Voussoir segments, to keep up with the first three days of excavation.

When they finished unloading, the train that had brought up the equipment returned empty to the yards at Chi-Hsi. When day dawned, it had to appear that no activity had taken place during the night. The presence of a train five miles from the river would certainly look suspicious.

When all the crates were in that meeting room, McGrath had the pieces laid out according to number on the earth floor. It took the entire day to assemble the mechanical mole. The village had recently been wired for electricity, and as it got dark they turned on the lights inside the building. As they were finishing up late at night, McGrath could not resist a feeling of pride as he looked over the work they'd done. They seemed interested, and so he described the functioning of the machine to them.

"Here you see," he said, pointing them out, "a series of rotating picks that cut concentric grooves in hard clay. They mutilate the rock face so that any material that does not fall away is easily scraped off by the following buckets. As the ground gets harder, the picks have to be narrower so that they will penetrate. We may begin with clay, but we'll soon be into rock. The mechanical mole can be fitted with different cutters according to the hardness of the rock. Each type of rock requires a unique combination of cutter configuration, thrust, and cutter-head torque for optimum boring, and each combination is efficient over only a small range of hardness."

The villagers did not understand it all, but they maintained an admiring silence as they contemplated the lines and structure of the mechanical mole.

Walking back through the silent streets of the village, with most of the inhabitants long since abed and the glow of the embers from fireside hearths dying away into the night, McGrath knew something of the feeling a general has on the eve of a great battle.

He reached the guest house, hoping Li would still be up. There was no light under the door of her room, however—she must be already asleep. He felt disappointed as he got ready for bed.

He surveyed the work from the meeting hall, which covered the entrance to the tunnel about three hundred yards from the riverbank. The first leg of the tunnel, running from the start to the bomb chamber, would be over nine hundred yards long. It was not simply a question of reaching the beginning of the defile. The tunnel had to be brought to midstream and it had to attain the desired depth. Once they got to the bomb chamber they would still have to take the tunnel on under the river and well into Soviet territory in order to lay the series of charges that would excavate the diversion trench. It was a huge job, even with the miraculous tunneling machine.

In the morning they dug up the floor of the hall so that the tunneling machine could start its run at the correct angle of attack. The cutters bit true and deep. They were lucky to have self-supporting ground right from the beginning. The "muck," as it was known in tunnelers' jargon, began to come back steadily along the tracks they laid behind the machine. By noon they had gone forty yards. McGrath decided to begin the work of lining the tunnel.

Late in the afternoon they hit hard rock and had to break for a change of the cutter heads. Feng came to him in the interval. "My people are unhappy, and they are tired. There is too much carrying."

"What! Tired already? They've only been at it for a day or so."

Feng was adamant. "They are tired. The first night they carried the machine. Today they helped with the tunneling and the lining. Tonight they will have to carry the spoil from the day back to the railhead, and tomorrow they will have a double load since, even at night, the machine does not stop."

"Hell! I thought we could rely on the manpower!"

"We are men." Feng's reply was quiet but firm. "We are not supermen."

McGrath knew he was beaten. "Give me some time to think about it."

A temporary office for him had been set up by blocking off a corner of the meeting room. Here McGrath had a desk, his maps, his basic textbooks, an electronic calculator, and other tools. The project communications center was also here—the field telephone that connected him directly to military headquarters in nearby Shenyang, and to Peking itself. If necessary, he could be switched through to Washington in a matter of seconds.

As the tunneling progressed, McGrath sat at his desk watching the spoil heap at the end of the hall grow larger and larger. He puffed at his pipe and once he got up to consult a large-scale map of the area. He sat down again, then got up to look at the relief model that had been used during the meeting at the Ming tomb. He ran his finger searchingly down the line of the river. A satisfied smile appeared on his face. He summoned Feng and Li. They came to his office and he gave them tea while he told them his proposed solution to the problem.

"What we are going to do is slurry it."

"Slurry* it?" Feng didn't understand the meaning of the term. Nor did Li, though she tried to translate it faithfully.

"Yes, slurry it," repeated McGrath. "We'll get a pulverizer and a mixer and set them at the end of the shed here."

"Where will you get the water?" Feng asked when he had understood the concept. "You will need a lot of it."

"From the river, of course."

"Then you will need a pipe."

"We will need two pipes. One to bring the water, the other to discharge the slurry. The outlet will be here." McGrath showed them on the model the discharge point he had selected. "Of course, there will be a discoloration in the river, but we cannot help that. In any case, the dispersion characteristics of the river are good. There will be some increase in turbidity but not much."

"Bravo." Feng clapped his hands, impressed and relieved.

The villagers carried in the mixer and the pulverizer as they

---

*To slurry is to move a solid—in this case, the spoil from the digging—by mixing it with a liquid, usually water, and pumping the liquid from one place to another.

had carried the mole before. They had to carry the pipe in sections too, assembling it with relative ease the next day. Once it was in place, they covered it with a layer of earth. The pump at the river end was a problem. After much reflection they decided that they would risk building a sort of blind, suitably camouflaged, of the type used by hunters, at the river's edge. Here one pump was installed. The disposition of the second pump was simple. A slurry pond, into which the mixer discharged its load, was dug in the floor of the commune hall. As fast as one pump brought up clean water, the other pump discharged foul.

"There may be some spoil, which for one reason or another we are unable to pulverize," McGrath informed them. "That'll have to be carried out by hand. I'm sorry about that. It's the best I can think of."

His apologies were unnecessary. Feng was well content with the results of his intervention.

That night McGrath and Li ate together again. She cooked a simple country dinner for them. It was the kind of food he liked best—boiled pork, rice, noodles, and bamboo shoots. After the meal they sat on either side of the stone hearth and talked far into the night.

Li wanted to know about American women. "Women's Liberation is very important in your country, isn't it?"

"Yes. It is important. I don't know enough about it. I've been retired, keeping to myself."

She was scornful. "Women are 'half of heaven,'" she said. "Women manned [he smiled at the malapropism] the 'March 8' fishing fleets; they pilot jet aircraft, drill for oil in Taching, build bridges in the forest areas, and work on live ultrahigh-tension power lines. In China men and women are equal. The broad masses of working women are emancipated and independent. Women are playing important roles in China's socialist revolution and socialist construction."

McGrath loved hearing her talk; he loved watching the mobile lines in her face, the delicate, almost dainty movements of her mouth as she spoke. But he still did not want to talk about politics, and he flattered her into talking about herself.

She told him of her childhood in Peking, about how her father had often been away from home on political or military business. She had gone on to speak of life when her mother died, of her time at school and university. "It was lonely at times. I had to work very hard. I was determined to succeed."

He was touched by the vision of little Li, effectively orphaned by her mother's death and her father's absences, working late into the night so as to make something of herself. He took her hand and then sat in silence.

After a time she stood up and disengaged her hand from his. "It is time to sleep," she said. When the light was out, she came and lay down next to him on the narrow bed. She was separated from him only by the thin, coarse coverlet; a blanket was pulled up over them both. He seemed to her overwhelmingly masculine, awesomely large, a solid rock of a man, yet at the same time tender. She seemed to him so small, so fragrant, almost like a child.

The next few days were among the happiest McGrath had ever known. He saw Li constantly. He felt himself falling in love with her, with a passion he had not imagined possible. He did not know whether she loved him. He felt only that fortune had smiled on him. In what he saw as the twilight of his days, he had found someone new and wonderful.

They walked in the fields together, hand in hand. The high summer sun shone for them, and warm breezes blew. Peasants working on plots of land sensed their happiness and smiled at them.

They talked and laughed, Li always trying good-naturedly to educate and convert him. "To increase agricultural production," she told him, "it is imperative to bring into full play the socialist initiative of our peasant masses."

McGrath looked out over a paddy field at a line of women working their way slowly toward them. Because they were bent double as they worked, their faces were obscured. The large coolie hats slung around their necks bounced each time they straightened up. "Li, you can do better than that. These are people, not political slogans. They aren't just units of production."

Sometimes they went down to the river and watched the swirl

of the water. Once, when the men had taken a break from tunneling, Li and McGrath went out in Hsueh's boat and helped him and Kao pull up the nets and haul the catch aboard. When the catch was in, Hsueh insisted on rowing them downstream to a little island in the river, an island covered with trees and shrubs and rich in birdsong.

"Stay here for an hour or two, Ma Ga't," Hsueh said. "You have been working too hard. You must be fresh and fit if we are to complete the tunnel in time."

McGrath took Hsueh's gnarled hand and shook it, feeling the calluses on the palm. He looked straight into the fisherman's dark, trusting eyes. "Thank you, Hsueh. We would like that. Come for us before evening, if you would."

So McGrath and Li lay together on the little island in the middle of the Ussuri River, away from all prying eyes.

"What do they think about us, the people of the village?" McGrath asked. "Do they think we are lovers?"

"I don't care what they think."

McGrath felt so happy here with Li. He realized how much he had lacked companionship, how alone he had been. Men weren't meant to live alone. He thought of his wife, knowing she would understand.

Li undressed him and took her own clothes off as well. They lay together under the green and gold of the trees, surrounded by lapping water.

In a lifetime of experience, he had never known lovemaking like it. How could she have learned the infinite, painstaking tenderness, the subtlety, the exquisite inventiveness that made their passion so sweet? The erotic had played a vital part in the artistic and cultural life of China for centuries. Now he was learning for himself what the word "erotic" really meant.

Once he cried out to her, "Stop. You'll kill me!" And then he realized that he didn't really mind. He wouldn't mind dying from this pleasure.

They rested. When he turned to her again, there were tears on her cheeks. "Li, you're crying again! Why are you crying?"

"I love you, Ma Ga't."

"I love you too. Is that a reason to cry?"

"Oh, Ma Ga't! You don't understand." She was sobbing now with real anguish, as though racked by some inner conflict.

"Tell me," McGrath said gently. "Perhaps I can help."

She didn't answer him. Instead she nestled deeper into his arms and they made love again, slowly, quietly, almost without moving, while the tears streamed down her face.

Toward evening, when they were waiting for the fishermen to return, Li said to him in a quiet voice: "There's a Soviet patrol on the far bank. I can see them through the trees. They must have binoculars. I caught a flash of the sun a moment ago as though it was being reflected in a glass."

Keeping well down, McGrath crept through the trees to the edge of the island. He parted the bushes and looked. "You're right. There is a Soviet patrol. It looks as if they're bivouacking for the night. Now what the hell do we do? If I'm seen in the boat, it's going to look strange to them. They'll never mistake me for a Chinese fisherman!"

"The island will shield you from view as we get on board the boat. Then you must lie on the bottom, among the nets."

When Hsueh arrived, McGrath lay down on his back and wondered which was worse—the Soviets across the river or the stench of a season's fishing. He wrinkled his nose in disgust and saw Li laughing down at him.

By the time they reached the village it was almost dark. McGrath was able to climb out from his hiding place without risk of being seen.

The mechanical mole reached the center of the river at the end of the fifth day. They had rigged up a line of lights along the tunnel, and McGrath walked the length of it to inspect, checking the lining as he went. The lining was crucial to prevent the danger of a cave-in, which could block the tunnel, or worse, allow flooding. If that happened, they might as well all give up and go home. McGrath had insisted on double thickness for the lining, even though it meant more work. He didn't want to take any chances. When the moment came to blast out the cavity for the nuclear bomb to be placed in, the tunnel would be under severe stresses, and only the lining could hold it intact.

When he returned to the surface, he was clearly pleased with the progress of the work.

Feng was waiting for him at the top.

"I think we should have a celebration tonight," McGrath said. "Your people deserve it. Tomorrow we'll start blasting."

Feng's face brightened. "That is a fine idea, Ma Ga't. The people are getting tired. A celebration is just what we need."

Shortly after sunset, music poured forth from the loud-speakers in the village square. Usually the music played in the predawn hours, meaning that it was time for collective gymnastics and calisthenics. Men and women, young and old, turned out to do exercises in time to political songs. Since they had started building the tunnel the villagers had been less enthusiastic about this ritual, but they went anyway, and McGrath made a habit of joining them. If old men of eighty, men who had already dreamed their dreams and seen their visions, could hop and skip around in the morning chill, so could he, and he felt himself fitter as a result.

The idea of a party brought the people out happily. A stage had been erected at one side of the square, and the villagers gathered in orderly rows in front of it. The privileged guests, McGrath and Li, were to sit in the front row.

There was a burst of clapping as McGrath arrived. He turned to face the crowd and clapped back. He had always liked the Chinese custom of the performers applauding the audience as well as the audience applauding the performers.

Feng sat next to McGrath. "First we will see an acrobatic and conjuring performance by the Ch'i-li-pi Revolutionary Acrobatic Team. Then there will be a little opera. And finally," he smiled mysteriously, "the schoolchildren will present a special play that they have invented themselves."

McGrath sat back to enjoy the evening. The martial music was replaced by a soft, lilting melody. A young girl ran swiftly onto the stage carrying a large Chinese bowl. The audience could see that it was empty. The girl, with a bow and a nod to the crowd, put a lid on it. Then she took the lid off, and, from the bowl's interior, began to remove an endless succession of objects—flowers, ducks, and smaller bowls filled with goldfish. There seemed to be no limit to the contents. With each treasure, the audience grew more excited.

The girl finally tilted the bowl to show the audience that there was nothing left inside it except a piece of red material. With an impassive expression, she began to pull on it. She pulled and pulled and still the material poured out of the bowl. She beckoned to the wings and another girl ran out to help her. The second girl pulled from the other end and they both ran about the stage still tugging away while the material streamed out behind them. They stopped at either end of the stage and gave one final pull, so that the last of the red cloth came out of the bowl and they were able to hang a banner between them.

"PEOPLE OF CH'I-LI-PI, UNITE TO WIN STILL GREATER VIC- TORY," Feng translated.

McGrath clapped as vigorously as anyone else in the crowd.

After the conjuring tricks, the acrobats came out. McGrath recognized familiar faces as they jumped, balanced on uptilted chairs, walked on their hands, and leaped to each other's shoulders. It was quite dark now in the square except for the lights that illuminated the performance. He reached for Li's hand. "Are you enjoying this?" he asked.

"Oh, very much. I would love to have been a dancer."

"Perhaps you still can be."

She smiled and shook her head. "I don't think so. I spend too much time on politics."

He was surprised to hear her say this. He had supposed she was dedicated to her profession. "Where do you stand?" he asked as they waited for the next item on the program. "Are you with the moderates or the radicals?"

She frowned. "Let's not talk, Ma Ga't. I want to watch."

Feng stood up to announce that, because of this special occasion, they were going to witness—for the third time that year—a performance of *Two Heroic Sisters of the Steppe*. There was much excitement and applause. "This is the villagers' favorite," Feng explained as he sat down.

The ballet began with a roll of drums. McGrath tried to watch but he was tired from lack of sleep and dozed off during most of it. When he woke, it was to the sound of applause. "Marvelous. Wonderful," he said, joining in.

Li looked at him skeptically. "You were asleep."

"Only for part of the time."

Feng climbed up onto the stage. "The last item in this evening's entertainment," he announced, "will be a play performed by the schoolchildren of Ch'i-li-pi. There are two main characters. I think you will recognize them."

There was a burst of laughter from the crowd. McGrath and Li exchanged puzzled glances. Everyone except them seemed to be in on the joke.

They clapped along with the others as a dozen or so neatly dressed schoolchildren took the stage. Half were boys and half were girls. McGrath admired the neat blue uniforms, the crisp white shirts, the red kerchiefs knotted about their necks as Li explained, "The schoolchildren are supposed to represent the villagers of Ch'i-li-pi."

"Ah!" McGrath nodded. "I understand." But he didn't really understand. In fact, he didn't understand what was going on at all.

"Now," Li continued, as a larger boy arrived and began to address the children, "Feng is giving a lecture."

The boy was speaking in a fast, high-pitched voice. The audience was laughing at his speech, but McGrath had difficulty making out the words. "What's he saying?"

Li began to blush as she realized what the play was all about. "He's saying that some very important people are about to arrive and the villagers must do everything they can to make the visitors happy!"

The audience burst into fits of laughter as a still taller boy wearing a U.S. Army forage cap (Where did you get that hat? McGrath thought) strode commandingly onto the stage, followed—to the accompaniment of still more laughter—by a pretty little mincing girl who was clearly meant to represent Li.

McGrath looked over and saw that Li's blush had deepened still further. "Don't get upset, Li. They mean well. Sit back and enjoy it. We might learn something."

For the next ten minutes they watched a re-enactment of their time in Ch'i-li-pi. The children listened to their visitors' instructions. They pretended to be villagers running off to fetch the tunneling machine. They pretended to dig and cart away the spoil. The tall boy and pretty, mincing girl acted out to perfection the parts of McGrath and Li in the classic roles of hero and heroine.

"Who is the class-enemy, the baddie, I wonder?" McGrath asked.

"I wonder too." Li seemed puzzled. She wasn't sure how the little drama would end, but she was afraid it would end badly.

The tunnel was finished. The villagers rejoiced. The Army and the militia arrived to join in the festivities.

"So what happens to me?" McGrath asked. "Do I get the girl or do I just get the medal?"

There was a sudden accusing roll of drums. The heroine sprang back from the arms of the hero with a look of horror on her face. She indicated with outstretched arm the U.S. Army forage cap, which was still perched on his head. She denounced him as an agent of U.S. imperialism and a capitalist running dog.

McGrath was hurt and angry. This didn't sound like the new China, accepting of the West. This was radical ideology the kids probably didn't even understand. "Hell," he cried, "who put them up to that?"

He glanced at Li, but she had hidden her face in shame and embarrassment.

Feng jumped to his feet and shooed the party of schoolchildren off the stage, scolding them angrily. The murmuring audience clearly agreed with him. The children departed in some disorder.

Feng apologized to McGrath: "I don't know why they did that. I'm really sorry."

"Don't be sorry, Feng," McGrath laid a friendly hand on his shoulder. "They're only kids. They've been brought up to think of the United States as the enemy. I can take it. But I thought the reconciliation of China and America had pretty much brought an end to that kind of thing."

He walked home feeling a bit sad. Some of the magic had gone, along with his romantic illusions about the villagers and his importance to them. He thought they liked him and respected him, but he was also a symbol of a way of life they still distrusted. Or was something new in the wind? He was treading a delicate balance. He would have to be careful not to take a wrong step.

Li had gone on ahead of him in the confusion. When he reached the guest house the light was on in her room, but he decided not to go in. Something about Li's behavior during the play puzzled him. It was almost as if she knew that the schoolchildren might overstep the mark. He realized that, many times, he had seen Li talking to groups of the schoolchildren. Had she been talking politics? If so, whose side was she really on? She had ducked that question tonight.

He got into bed and fell asleep. Some time later he woke up with a start. Once before he had imagined he heard Li talking in a very low voice in the next room. This time he was sure. He was convinced there was no one in the room with her, but then why was she talking, and to whom?

The next morning the mechanical mole was backed halfway out of the tunnel, for this was the day they would blast out the cavity the bomb would rest in. He didn't want the mole damaged—it was irreplaceable. Once it was clear, he ordered all workers to the surface.

The cavity was important, as a means of decoupling the force of the nuclear explosion. But McGrath had changed his mind about how the cavity would be created. Instead of excavating it, he decided, he would make a cavity by setting off a nonnuclear percussion device, the explosion of which would compress the surrounding rock, leaving a neat, clean chamber with an arching vault, five hundred feet below ground. This way there would be none of the time-wasting drudgery of digging and then hauling out debris.

The danger was that if the percussion device misfired, they would be left without a bomb chamber. They would then have to decide whether to excavate the chamber manually or do without a decoupling cavity. The one alternative seemed a nearly impossible labor, and the other meant that the nuclear explosion would almost surely be detected by the Soviets. The percussion device had to work.

At 11 A.M. McGrath gave the order to fire. The ground shook from the force of the underground explosion. McGrath waited thirty seconds for the trembling to subside. Then he picked up his hard hat and a flashlamp and strode to the entrance of the tunnel.

"Okay. Let's go."

He could tell immediately that something was wrong. Then he smelled rock dust in the air. "Christ!" He started to run, crouching to keep from hitting his head on the roof of the tunnel. Feng and several men followed him. In less than half a mile they came to a wall of rubble.

"There's been a cave-in," McGrath said tersely. "The tunnel lining gave for some reason. We need diggers. Lots of them. Fast. Water's coming through the roof already. We've got to hurry or we'll have a flood." A thought struck him. "Where's the mole, Feng?"

"We left it in the tunnel."

"Where? Maybe the cave-in missed it."

But Feng was not interested in the tunneling machine. "Ma Ga't, there were men down here. Kao and Hsueh. I told them to stay. We thought it would save time."

"Feng! I told you to clear the tunnel!"

The sound of a long, low groan made him forget his anger. "Oh, my God. Somebody's trapped in there."

16

The diggers worked in relays, in two-hour shifts. They stopped the leak, but even if the trapped men would not drown, they couldn't hold out for long. Their groans reached the men as they worked. McGrath stayed underground during the entire operation. He kept up the pressure, showing an almost maniacal determination. He talked very little, giving commands in short, sharp sentences that expected, and received, immediate compliance.

They reached Kao on the second day. His legs were pinioned by rock and some ribs had been crushed, but he was still alive. As they worked toward him, inch by inch, McGrath tried to keep the fisherman's spirits up. He told him the story of Pao Ssu. "So you see, Kao, even Pao Ssu smiled in the end when the warlords from the provinces came to the Great Wall and found that it was all a hoax!"

Hours later, when Kao seemed about to give up, McGrath urgently tried to buoy him with a sense of purpose. Survival depended so much on sheer willpower—he had to keep the injured man alert and interested. If Kao lost the will to live, it would soon be over.

"Remember when we went fishing. The fish need you, Kao. Do you know what Chairman Mao said when someone asked him what was the oddest thing he had encountered on the Long March? Do you know what he said?"

Kao shook his head.

"Well, I'll tell you. Chairman Mao said that the oddest thing he had encountered on the Long March was the fish. He said: 'We came to places where so few people had been before that if you waded into the river, the fish would leap into your hands!' "

He saw the man stir. A hint of a smile mingled with the pain. "I'd like to fish in a river like that!"

"You will, Kao. You will. Just as soon as we get you out of here."

They got to him in time. McGrath administered first aid on the spot as best he could, giving him a shot of morphine for the pain and making a rough bandage for his ribs. Then they laid him on a stretcher and hauled him back along the tracks to the surface.

When they reached Hsueh, he was already dead. His head had been crushed by the rock. Death must have been instantaneous. McGrath thought of him spreading his nets on the wide river, the water glinting with silver as the fish jumped in the morning sun.

McGrath walked behind the cart that carried Hsueh's body to the surface. He hadn't slept; he hadn't even seen the sun in almost forty-eight hours. He was covered with dirt and dust. He wanted a bath and a shave and a glass of Scotch, but first those who mourned had to be comforted and those who doubted had to be reassured.

McGrath was weary with sorrow and guilt. He was to blame for Hsueh's death. The final responsibility was his. How could he reassure them when he felt his own failing so strongly? He was even beginning to doubt his professional judgment—he had obviously miscalculated the impact of the blast on the double-thickness tunnel lining. He didn't understand what had gone wrong.

He came out of the tunnel stooped and diminished by death. The villagers were waiting at the top. They had been waiting for two days. When Liu Hung saw that her husband was dead, she broke from the crowd and threw herself on the body. McGrath stood aside, his head bowed, his hard hat in his hand.

Liu Hung suddenly turned and looked at McGrath with hatred in her eyes. "We thought we could trust you," she said, "and this is what you have done!"

McGrath could only shake his head. "I am sorry, I am truly sorry."

It was not enough. The villagers of Ch'i-li-pi were angry and scared. A low, threatening rumble ran through the crowd. They had all known and liked Hsueh Si-chun. Now his children, who had played with their children, would be fatherless. His parents, who had grown old with their parents, would be without a son to care for them in their old age. Who was this foreigner who had come into their village bringing disaster? What authority did he have to push them day and night to the brink of exhaustion and beyond? Perhaps Americans were the enemy after all. Maybe the schoolchildren had been right to denounce him. Fists were raised threateningly. The front row, pushed forward by the pressure from the rear, closed in on McGrath as he stood, still blinking in the bright light.

He recognized the danger signals. He had faced angry mobs before. He looked at the faces of the villagers and saw that while some were sullen and indifferent, others were marked with passionate hostility.

He held up his hand in an attempt to reason with them, speaking their own language. "It was an accident," he pleaded, "a sad and very unfortunate accident. I will find out the reason. There will be compensation. Liu Hung will be taken care of."

The crowd did not listen. They were angrier and louder. They kept moving in, forcing McGrath backward into the mouth of the tunnel. He tried to move away, knowing that, if they got him in there, he would not escape.

The first clod of earth took him full in the face. He gasped in shock. Who had thrown it? "Hey! That will do!" he yelled, frightened. "That's enough! Cut it out!"

Next time it was a stone—not a big one, but it caught him on the cheekbone, cutting the flesh. McGrath could feel the blood.

He looked up. Some of the crowd had found a pile of rubble and were picking up stones and rocks. Damn it. Feng had gone with Kao to the doctor. The villagers would have listened to him.

Another rock, a large one, hit him in the chest. He staggered and fell to his knees. He saw the crowd come closer. As he tried to get up, he was hit again, on the side of the head.

"Stop it. Stop it." He heard a woman's enraged voice. "What are you doing?" He heard rocks drop harmlessly to the ground. "This man is our guest. He is a friend of my father, Marshal Lu, a friend of the Chinese people. He walked on the Long March!" They fell silent and began to back away sheepishly.

McGrath crawled forward from the mouth of the tunnel. He was dizzy, and blood streamed from the cuts on his face. Li helped him up.

"You should be ashamed," she went on. "Ma Ga't has worked for two days to rescue these men. Ask Kao who saved his life!"

The crowd slowly dispersed. McGrath gave Li's hand a firm squeeze.

"Thank you. You came just in time. I think they might have killed me."

She followed him in to his office. He fell into a chair, while she brought a bowl of water to wash his wounds.

"Li," he said as she sponged his face, "I took a look at the tunneling machine before I came up. I'm afraid it was damaged in the cave-in. Even if we can repair it, it'll take at least two days."

17

Wilbur Silcott returned to Washington facing one major task—
to verify the calculations they had done so hurriedly at the Ming
tombs. They had to be sure 100 kilotons was the right size explosion. Silcott looked over the figures, visited the hydraulic model,
and examined the computer program in detail. After checking
and double-checking, he concluded that they had been overly
optimistic.

He called Thaddeus Ricker at his office. "We have a problem.
We've been working on the basis of 100 kilotons, believing—
and the Chinese agreed with us—that as long as we could keep
the bang to 100 kilotons or less, we could pass off the nuclear
explosion as an earthquake."

"What's the matter now?" Ricker sounded worried.

"The trouble is," Silcott explained, "that the flow and sedimentation rates we used seem to be too low. If we up the flow
rate, the dam the explosion creates in the river will have to
withstand more water pressure than we thought. If we up the
sedimentation rate, the dam will silt up quicker."

"What does it all add up to?"

"It means we're going to need a bigger bang!"

"Damn! How much bigger?"

"One hundred ten or 120 kilotons. Something of that magnitude."

"And that would bring us within the limits of detectability again?"

"I'm afraid so."

"Do you have any ideas?" Ricker asked, resigned to dealing with yet another problem.

Silcott paused. "Well, actually, I do. It's rather complex but I think it could work."

"Can you tell me now? Over the phone?"

"I'd prefer to meet. I could come into town."

"No. I'll come out to your office. Just say my visit is informal."

When Ricker showed up, Silcott was ready to explain his plan in complete detail. He handed Ricker a piece of paper. "That's a seismogram from the Jamestown seismograph showing waves recorded on November 24, 1971. The traces are fifteen minutes apart. You can see that two earthquakes are shown in the early part of the record. While the P, or body waves, are still arriving from the second quake, the ground begins to shake from an underground nuclear explosion at the Nevada Test Site."

Ricker studied the squiggly lines on the seismogram carefully. He could easily detect the onset of the two earthquakes. The lines skidded from side to side in a frenzy of activity. It was much more difficult to detect the underground explosion.

Ricker pushed the paper back across the table. "It seems that the waves from the second earthquake are still strong enough, two minutes after its occurrence, to mask the nuclear explosion. Is that right?"

Silcott shook his head. "No, I wouldn't put it like that. If you look carefully at the seismogram you can certainly see that something else has happened besides the second earthquake. There's a general thickening of the later lines, which indicates that there has been another event of some kind occurring virtually simultaneously with the second earthquake. What you can't tell from the seismogram is that this other event was an underground nuclear explosion! In fact, going on the evidence of this chart, if we didn't know that an underground nuclear explosion took place at the Nevada Test Site on November 24, 1971, at precisely that time, the natural assumption would be that there had been a third earthquake, or an aftershock, perhaps, which the seismogram picked up and recorded."

Ricker whistled with enthusiasm as he pondered the seismogram again. "You're suggesting, aren't you, that we wait until an actual earthquake occurs and then immediately fire the underground device. As I understand it, seismic waves recorded at more distant stations would be a mixture of waves from the natural and the artificial seismic sources, and would be difficult if not impossible to tell apart. The waves produced by the bomb would seem part of the natural aftershock sequence. Is that right?"

Silcott smiled. "You learn fast, Thaddeus, don't you?"

Ricker smiled back. "I'm just good at jargon. Half of any job is learning how to master the jargon. Well, am I right?"

"Correct," Silcott nodded.

"But that means we'll be standing around for God knows how long waiting for a natural earthquake to occur over there. It might be months or even years."

"Actually, no. The success of this particular evasion ploy does not depend on local seismicity. The earthquake doesn't have to be in the region where you want to set off the explosion. The beauty of this scheme is that you can use a natural earthquake happening anywhere in the world to mask your underground explosion, provided that that earthquake has the right characteristics."

"Sorry, you've lost me."

"Well, it depends on the magnitude and location of the natural earthquake, and also on the magnitude and location of the event you're trying to hide. In this case, we hope that the cavity-decoupling operation will reduce the seismic yield to around the 4-magnitude mark. I've calculated that, after making the worst possible assumptions for distance—that is, assuming that the monitoring station is relatively near the event you wish to hide and relatively far away from the hiding event—we'd need an earthquake magnitude of 6.6 on the Richter Scale to mask a nuclear explosion of that magnitude."

"Six point six! That's a biggie, isn't it?"

"Sure it's a biggie. But it's not a San Francisco; it's not a Tangshan. In fact, there are about 30 earthquakes a year with a magnitude of 6.6. That's 30 hiding opportunities a year. On the average, one every 12 days. Of course, of those 30, some will be better than others. One may be bigger, or it may be better situated for our purposes.

"Take Iceland. Iceland lies at the edge of two tectonic plates* or, if you like, on the crack between them. Each time they move apart, which they do at a rate of between 1 and 20 centimeters a year, Iceland is the first to feel it. Now, in the last few days," he continued, "I've been getting a sheaf of reports from Iceland about increased volcanic and seismic activity. The strain is building up out there and a lot of us believe that quite soon something is going to give."

"You mean that some time soon there may be a biggie in Iceland?"

"Yes—that's what all the readings show. If they're correct, it would be very good news indeed. A sizable earthquake occurring in Iceland is precisely what we need. According to my calculations a quake right up there near the Soviet Union would have very favorable masking characteristics. It might, in fact, be an ideal opportunity."

"How soon might such an earthquake happen, Wilbur? What's the time factor?" A note of urgency sounded in Ricker's voice as he realized the time pressure they might be under.

"It's hard to tell from the reports. The people who write these things don't know what we want. They're not customer-specific." He looked inquiringly at Ricker. "But I thought I might take a couple of days off. I think it might be worth our while to visit Iceland and take a look at what's happening."

Ricker banged on the desk. "Damn it, Wilbur. You're not waiting for me to say 'yes,' are you? You ought to be up there already!"

---

* A tectonic plate is a vast piece of the earth's crust that moves as a unit, often grinding up against or pulling away from other plates. Earthquakes tend to occur where plates meet.

Sigmund Sigmundsson, the director of the Nordic Institute of Volcanology in Reykjavik, was a tall, courteous, fair-haired man. Silcott explained that he was a geologist by profession and that he was visiting Iceland as a tourist on a stopover to Europe. He said he had heard about the Institute's work and was particularly grateful to have this chance to visit with its director.

It was easy for Silcott to steer the conversation in the direction he wanted to take. Sigmundsson was pleased to be talking to an American colleague. "Yes," he said, "we have a seismographic net that covers the whole country. Information from outlying stations is relayed here to the Institute by radio signal or by telephone."

"I understand you're expecting Mount Katla, on the Mýrdalsjökull glacier, to erupt in the near future. Is that really so?"

"Ah, Katla!" Sigmundsson responded enthusiastically. "Something is happening there for sure. I believe it could be considerable. It's a perfect opportunity to predict and possibly control a major eruption. We've ringed the volcano with seismographs. We have trained the farmers—there are only a few of them in this inhospitable area—to read them. We have also installed tiltmeters, because changes in the tilt of the earth may give us some indication of an imminent volcano or earthquake. The problem is that Katla overlooks the main coast road. If it blows without warning a lot of people could lose their lives."

"Are you taking other precautions?" Silcott had a feeling that he had read somewhere in the literature that Iceland was beginning to experiment with unconventional methods of earthquake control.

Sigmundsson looked at him sharply. "How did you know?"

Silcott, diplomatically, didn't answer.

"Well, it doesn't matter," Sigmundsson said, shrugging. "People were bound to hear about it sooner or later. Frankly, we would prefer to have a controlled eruption than one that takes us by surprise, and so we've been using water injections. Our idea is that injection of large quantities of water could cause the rock to slip earlier than it would otherwise have done. Thus we may have some control over the timing of the slip and the resulting eruption. We have been pumping water into underground strata in the Katla area for the last ten days."

"How long will you continue?"

"We think at least ten more days. Of course, we'll keep a continual watch on the seismograph and tiltmeters. At the end of that period, we expect a slip and possibly an eruption. Certainly we intend to enter a state of emergency preparedness from that time."

Silcott swallowed hard. This information placed their operation in a whole new perspective. If they were to take advantage of the opportunity Iceland offered, seismologically speaking, for masking the nuclear explosion in Manchuria, everything—the cavity, the bomb, the diversion trench—had to be ready within ten days at the outside. If they missed this opportunity, it might be some time before another such perfect one came along.

Silcott brought the conversation back to casual discussion between colleagues. He didn't want to seem overly interested in the Katla phenomenon. They talked some and Silcott rose to leave. He took out his card. "If you're ever in the States, be sure to come see us at Reston. I'll look forward to it."

On the way back to his hotel, Silcott visited the nearby Iceland Historical Museum and spent some time studying Viking relics and other mementos of Eric the Red. He bought postcards and made his presence generally known. When he returned to the hotel, he prominently displayed a museum catalogue, indicating that his afternoon had been spent on innocent activities.

He flew back to Washington that evening, pleased to have a chance to think about the Ch'i-li-pi operation. He was uncomfortable with all this emphasis on speed. And he was uncomfortable talking to a colleague like Sigmundsson on what he felt were false pretenses. He was afraid that they might overlook something in their hurry, that proper scientific precautions were not being taken. For instance, that night in the Panda— and it had been his own fault. McGrath had wanted to go on, to finish the job. But he had said no. He had been satisfied with the data they already had and didn't want to run further risks.

Was that professional of him? Was it true that they had had enough evidence already?

He called Ricker from Dulles International Airport.

"Ten days?" Ricker responded. "Surely McGrath can be ready in ten days? I'll call and tell him to speed things up."

18

For once, McGrath didn't go to work early. Li wasn't around, so he ate alone and stayed in his hut, not sulking but brooding—about the future, about the operation, about his own viability as a leader. Feng had told him that the men wouldn't go back down. He knew they were scared, but they had also lost confidence in his leadership.

He had just finished his meal when a small boy ran up, panting. "Ma Ga't, there is a telephone call for you. In the meeting hall."

Three minutes later he picked up the green telephone on his desk. "McGrath speaking."

"This is Washington calling. I'll put Mr. Ricker on the line."

"John? Is that you? How are things going out there? Are you on schedule?" Ricker's voice was full of its usual energy and optimism.

McGrath looked out the open end of the hall. He gazed down the street where a cart, carrying a body draped in rough cloth, was being trundled across the village square. He recognized Liu Hung in the party of mourners. He thought he might tell Ricker about the cave-in, but no, damn it all, he was the man in charge. He was either in control of the situation or he wasn't. Unless he actually needed Ricker's help there was no point in bothering him. "Things are going fine. We had a little local difficulty. The tunneling machine has suffered some minor damage but I can fix it in a day or two."

"Two days! You can't lose two days! Not now. Listen, we're into a whole new ball game on the timing of this thing."

When Ricker had finished, the sweat was pouring off McGrath's face. "You mean we've got ten days at the outside to finish the job? Ten days to dig another thousand yards of tunnel. That's one hundred yards a day! And then we've got to install the bomb in the cavity chamber. It can't be done, Thaddeus. There's just not enough time. We've still got to repair the machine."

McGrath walked down to the mouth of the tunnel. The lights were working again, but there was no sign of life or movement. There was no roar of machinery from the work face; no clatter of buckets as the muck came back along the conveyor belt; no hacking and spitting as the men of the village cleared their lungs of dust and dirt. The great project had ground to a halt.

Feeling dejected and anxious, McGrath began the long walk toward the bomb chamber. He could at least take comfort from the perfect cavity created by the percussion device. As he walked he inspected the lining. Why the hell had it cracked? What had gone wrong? The roof of the tunnel where the cave-in occurred had been repaired in a makeshift manner. McGrath switched on his flashlight and suddenly he had the answer. Someone had been cheating. Instead of double-thickness lining, only single thickness had been used. No wonder the roof had cracked beneath the shock waves of the blast.

A rapid survey of the next three hundred yards revealed that there were several places where only single-thickness segments had been installed. Goddamn them all! How did they think they could get away with it? He was suddenly puzzled. Where were the spare segments? He had worked out precisely the amount of lining they would need. He knew how much had been dispatched to the railhead and unloaded. In theory they should have used it all. So what had happened to the rest?

He broke into a run, sped back up the tunnel, tossed his hard hat onto his desk, and leaped into his jeep. As he roared through the village square he passed Feng, who was returning from the funeral.

"Jump in," McGrath cried.

Feng was startled but did as he was told.

"I suppose you knew about it!" McGrath shouted above the roar of the engine. They were driving at breakneck speed down the little track toward Tu-mo-ho and Hut'ou. Changing gear savagely as they bounced over the hard earth, swinging the wheel from side to side as he avoided rocks and boulders, Mc-Grath was able to give vent to his rage and frustration.

"Knew about what?" Feng seemed genuinely amazed.

"Knew that your people were cheating on the lining. That's why we had the cave-in. Because they used one thickness instead of two. That's why Hsueh Si-chun died."

"Oh my God! I didn't know!" Feng was shocked, but he still felt loyal to his fellow villagers. "My people were tired, Ma Ga't, from the digging and carrying. Perhaps they thought it wouldn't matter."

Fuming, McGrath drove on. He was mad at the villagers but also at himself. He should have watched them more carefully. Had he asked too much of Feng and his people? Well, they would all pay the price. Hsueh Si-chun had already paid it.

Just before Hut'ou, McGrath saw what he was looking for. He turned the jeep off the track and jammed on the brakes. "Look! There's the lining that should have been used in the tunnel. That's what they did with it."

Feng grimly examined the pile of concrete segments that had been dumped at the side of the track. "They didn't even bother to conceal them," he said sadly. "At least they might have done that."

They drove back in silence. As they neared the meeting house, McGrath said, "Call a meeting. I want everyone in the village square half an hour from now. I want to talk to them. In the meantime, I've got a phone call to make."

He got through to Ricker at his private number. "Thaddeus, this is urgent. I need you to check something out. There's been a mixup here and some of the tunnel lining has been left behind at the railhead. Will you check and see whether it shows up on satellite photographs of the area? My guess is that the pile has been there three or four days. We may be lucky. There's been a good deal of cloud cover around and so the evidence may have been obscured. But I'd like your people to verify."

Twenty minutes later, Ricker called back. "Rotten luck, John. We just looked at the latest batch of satellite photographs and that pile of lining sticks out like a sore thumb! Damn it, that means the Soviet satellites may have picked this up as well. If they already suspect something fishy they'll be looking at those photographs with a magnifying glass."

"Exactly," McGrath answered. He put the phone down.

The dais was still in place from the "celebration." McGrath stepped up, treading heavily on the wooden planks. His foot hit a soft woolen object. It was the U.S. Army forage cap, obviously discarded in the general confusion of the play's ending. McGrath reached down for it, held it up for the people to see, and thrust it on his head.

He didn't shout. Feng had already chastised them. Instead he used the occasion to express his sorrow for the death of one of their people and to apologize for not making it clear just how important this operation was. When it was clear that they were getting away with a mild scolding instead of being reported to Peking for collective punishment, McGrath let them know the price of his leniency. "Now we're going to make up for lost time. We're going to make up for the death of Hsueh Si-chun and for Kao Pin-ying's broken leg. And we're going to get that tunnel finished in ten days.

"As for the Soviets, they may already have spotted that pile of linings. Tonight a party will go out and get what you left behind, and we'll line the tunnel the way it was meant to be lined. After that, you'll be extra careful. There's a spy in the sky and that spy can see every movement you make."

When they had gotten the point he let them go. He watched them leave the square, and stepped down from the dais with a tremendous sense of relief. He could feel that they trusted him again. Success was possible.

The next day, after a night of very little sleep, McGrath repaired the drive pinion, but the tunneling machine was still prone to accidents. A cutter head broke and had to be changed. The conveyor boom, which shunted out the rock and rubble, had to be repaired. As they went farther in, they had to stop while new and more efficient air pumps were installed to improve the tunnel's ventilation system.

There was also a new problem, one they had not encountered on the Chinese side of the river. Monitoring the spoil continually, McGrath was concerned to note that the measured levels of radioactivity mounted steadily the farther they dug under Soviet territory. He insisted on protective masks and clothing for the people working on that side of the river, and required frequent changes of shift to avoid any danger of overexposure. This, too, was a brake on progress.

On the fourth of the ten days that were left to them, McGrath went down to the work face with Feng. They stood behind the machine while it shuddered and scraped its way forward. "It's not going quickly enough, Feng," McGrath said. "We're only making fifty or sixty yards a day. We need to double that, considering how much time we've lost." But how the hell could they speed things up? They were tunneling through solid rock—about 7 on the 1-to-10 hardness scale—and it just didn't seem possible to go any faster. He watched the great machine grinding away. Even through the necessary ear mufflers the noise was devastating.

"Turn it off a minute!" he shouted. "I want to think."

The men on the face were grateful for the unexpected silence. The little group standing by the machine watched McGrath's frown of concentration. "The problem, as I see it," he said, "is basically one of thrust. The cutters can cut the rock, all right, and the scrapers can clear it away, but we're not getting enough bite because the machine isn't generating enough forward thrust."

"What do you mean?" Feng asked.

"The thrust applied to the cutters is obtained by the machine pushing backward against the sides of the tunnel already dug.

The force that can be exerted depends on the firmness of the rock. Right now the rock is no longer in its natural state of high compression, so it's not firm enough to give the greatest force."

He walked to one side to study the front of the machine. Then he looked up excitedly. "Hey! I've got an idea. Look, Feng. Let's say we were able to drill a hole, just a few inches in diameter, *ahead* of the main boring machine. We could do that by installing a triple cutter on the front end of the nose. Then we could slide a collar along the nose as far forward as it will go and expand it so that it grips evenly all around the hole. That would temporarily restore the rock to its natural state of high compression. The collar will provide an almost unbreakable grip. As well as pushing itself forward in the conventional way, the machine will be able to *pull* itself forward. I bet we could produce a forward pull that would thrust the cutters against the tunnel face with a force of about 350 tons. And the self-centering action would improve the steering!" He banged a clenched fist into the palm of his hand. "By Jove! I think we've got it! If it works we'll improve our performance 200 or 300 per cent!"

Half a day later, they started up the machine again. Immediately it leaped against the tunnel face and chewed through the rock. The conveyor belt could barely keep pace with the flow of material. McGrath was delighted. "Feng," he said, "I'm going to patent that trick when I get back to the United States. It could make me a million or two."

Feng looked at him askance. He wasn't quite sure what a patent was, but making a million or two certainly had a capitalist ring to it.

At the end of Day Nine, the machinery was finally silenced. The car, laden with rock and rubble, had been shunted back up the tracks for the last time. The pulverizer had ground its last load. The lights still shone brightly underground, but the tunnel was silent and empty.

In the late evening, McGrath left his hut and walked to the meeting hall. He moved with long, lanky strides, head held high, proud of having done a good job. One or two of the villagers were still outside, sitting on the steps of their homes and watching the last faint streaks of light disappear in the west. McGrath nodded at them and they smiled back! He felt good that he had regained their confidence and earned their respect.

He leaned down to pat a dog sniffing at his ankles. All the village dogs knew him now. He recognized Ping Chen's old mongrel and looked around to find the owner. Ping Chen was the village character. He often told the story of how one gray morning he had seen "Soviet tanks" come up out of the river, like sea monsters.

"Hello. Been out for one of your late walks?" McGrath asked.

"Yes. We went up the path beside the river as always. It's nice at night, but lovely in the daytime too. My dog and I like to take that path "

McGrath was fond of Ping Chen, and stayed talking to him for quite a while. At last the old man went inside, taking care not to trip over the doorstep.

The lights were on in the meeting room when McGrath reached it.

"Ni-haw," the guard greeted him.

"Ni-haw!" McGrath replied. "Good evening."

McGrath picked up his hard hat and went down into the tunnel. As he walked along it, making a final check on the lining and the air ducts, inspecting the roof for any hint of water, patting the walls from time to time, he could not help feeling satisfied.

He came to the slight curve in the tunnel just before it reached the bomb chamber. As he rounded the corner, he was startled to see that someone was in there. The guard had said nothing to him about another visitor. Who could it be, and why?

"Li Lu-yan! What are you doing here?" he cried, uneasy at having been surprised like that.

"Oh, Ma Ga't. I am so glad to see you. Now that all the work is finished, I wanted to come and look." She clapped her hands excitedly.

Her voice echoed in the chamber, reminding McGrath of her voice late at night, coming through the walls of her room. He hid his sudden nervousness under a light smile. "Now don't clap your hands like that. You might bring the roof down and you're not wearing a hard hat!"

He was only half joking. The vault that towered above them was not lined or supported. The shape of the roof itself sustained the pressure of the rock overhead. A sudden displacement could be caused by nothing more than the sound of a human voice.

Li Lu-yan moved toward him, turning up her face to his. "If I kiss you, is that permitted, or does that make too much noise too?"

McGrath looked at her. He looked into her wide, tragic eyes, dark as plums, at her soft lips, whose magic he had discovered at a time when he had thought such magic was gone forever. He took off his hat and placed it on her head. "Yes, kissing is permitted."

The next day, at first light, three Red Cross trucks drove into the village. In the first two were soldiers and technicians. The third backed up to the door of the meeting room. It carried blankets, food, and other emergency supplies. Under the blankets was the nuclear bomb. It was spherical, four feet in diameter, weighing a little over one hundred pounds—approximately one pound for every kiloton of yield. The detonators and the cladding added to its weight, so six soldiers were needed to lift the frame on which it rested onto the conveyor belt. McGrath, Feng, and Ming watched as it started down into the tunnel, but only McGrath followed it underground. Under the directions of the technicians it was placed at the center of the cavity. It looked somehow silly perched there, and it was hard even for McGrath to comprehend the lethal force contained within that shell.

Once it was properly installed, the technicians armed the device as well as the series of smaller charges that would carve out the diversion trench. When they finished, McGrath took one last look around. Then they went back up the tunnel. As he walked, McGrath remembered the line of poetry that had haunted him ever since the bomb had arrived. It came from the

Bhagavad-Gita. Krishna, trying to persuade the Prince to do his duty, says: "I am become death, the shatterer of worlds."

McGrath shivered. All of a sudden, he felt cold.

The people of Ch'i-li-pi thought their village was as old as the river. For centuries their ancestors had fished and grown crops, lived and died, in this place. Their parents and grandparents and great-grandparents were buried in the surrounding hills. The "soul" of the village—an amalgam of present and past, a sense of belonging, a quality that made Ch'i-li-pi a good place to live—depended on continuity, on this generation's relationship with earlier generations. So far the ancestors had smiled on Ch'i-li-pi.

But how would they feel now that their descendants were to be taken away, relocated? McGrath knew the people would worry about the ancestors, who couldn't move and would be left behind. He decided to stress the absolute inevitability of the earthquake. He reminded them that the science of predicting earthquakes had begun with the Chinese. "Remember the story of Chang Heng," he said, "who was one of the early scientists. Remember how Chang Heng constructed the first seismoscope? Chang Heng's machine looked like a huge decorated wine bottle. It was three feet in diameter and eight feet tall, made out of copper, carved and ornamented with many animals. Eight large dragon heads were spaced equally around the vessel. Each dragon held a ball in its mouth, and below the dragons were metal frogs, heads tipped back and mouths wide open to catch the balls if they dropped. Inside the copper vessel was a hinged rod with a weight at the bottom. When it swung far enough to one side it would strike a dragon head and dislodge the ball from its mouth.

"Now, many people maintained," continued McGrath, "that Chang Heng had produced an expensive and useless mechanism. But one day a ball dropped to the east and Chang Heng told the Emperor and his courtiers that a great earthquake had happened in the West. They laughed at him and didn't believe him. But several weeks later travelers came from the West and informed the Emperor that there had indeed been an earthquake. So Chang Heng was vindicated and the science of predicting earthquakes was born.

"Today, of course," he went on, "the instruments are more precise and communications are swifter. We believe the earthquake is going to happen within the next few days. If we are right in our predictions there will be certain signs detectable by instruments, such as foreshocks, or the release of gases from pressures in the earth. All the indications," he warned them gravely, "are that the village of Ch'i-li-pi will be at the very center of the shock. The Army relief units are already in position at Chihsi and Mi-Shan and Hulin and will be able to move rapidly to the affected area."

He also told them he could now reveal the reason for the tunnel. Believing that an earthquake would happen in the area of the village, and anxious to use this opportunity to improve their knowledge of the earth's geology, and particularly of the earth's interior, Chinese scientists had asked to have recording instruments installed deep underground in the very heart of the earthquake itself! If the earthquake happened and the village was destroyed, there would at least be some consolation in the knowledge that the instruments planted in the tunnel would be able to make a major contribution to science.

"And what will happen to the villagers of Ch'i-li-pi if the village is destroyed?" Feng asked.

McGrath smiled and patted the man's shoulder. "Good news! You will not have to move far. About ten miles altogether." He picked up a folder and waved it in his hand. "These are the plans for the new village of Ch'i-li-pi. It will be a fishing village just upstream of here. You will not have to change the pattern of your lives."

"Who will help us construct this new village?"

"You will receive much help," McGrath promised him solemnly. "The government has even promised concrete!"

Feng's eyes widened. Concrete! With concrete, all things were possible. With the promise of concrete, the villagers would have gone a hundred miles, a thousand miles, not a mere ten.

Then McGrath explained the logistics of the evacuation. The

villagers were warned that when the loudspeakers in the village square blared out the "Internationale," they were all to go to their predetermined positions, where they would wait for further instructions. They were told what possessions they could and could not carry. A maximum effort would be made to assure that no one was needlessly deprived of belongings he held dear, but no guarantees of total satisfaction could be made.

"How long will we have for the evacuation?" asked Feng.

McGrath shook his head. "I'm afraid we can't give you much time. About four hours from when we give the signal."

"Four hours, is that all?"

McGrath quietly shook his head. Then he stood up and faced the villagers. "Thank you all. I'm sorry for all the trouble and pain we have caused, but remember that you have done a great service for your country."

He turned to Feng and held out his hand. "Thank you for all you have done, Feng. No one could have done more."

Feng took the outstretched hand. "Thank you, Ma Ga't. I am very proud to have met you and to have worked with you."

McGrath turned his head away so that they should not see the tears in his eyes.

19

Jon Bödvarsson had lived all his life in the region of the Mýrdalsjökull glacier. At the beginning of autumn, he would take his dog to the edge of the icecap to bring the sheep down to the farm for the winter. In the tourist season—like many farmers he took in summer visitors to supplement his income—he took parties there on sure-footed Icelandic ponies. He knew the fauna and flora; he had seen the gyrfalcon and the huge white-tailed eagle. He counted seasons by the passage of migrant birds, such as pink-footed geese and harlequin ducks. He knew which lava fields had the best mosses and lichens, and he led his favorite visitors there.

One morning in high summer he rode his pony right onto the glacier itself for a special purpose. Besides farming, besides tourism, besides his interest in plants and wildlife, Jon Bödvarsson had another activity: He read seismographs. He had done it for fifteen years, ever since they first established the network around Katla. He had gone on a weekend course in the city, where he learned about the different waves and their varying characteristics.

Bödvarsson had three seismographs to visit on the glacier, each one the same distance from the spot where the dormant

Katla peaked beneath the ice. He rode along the contours, visiting first one, then another of the little huts in which the instruments were placed. That morning all three seismographs told the same story.

Katla was about to blow! Foreshocks of considerable magnitude had occurred within the last twenty-four hours. As he watched, the delicate instruments were registering tremors deep within the crust of the earth. Bödvarsson could sense them as he stood there, a low, rumbling motion. It was as though the whole world was beginning to shake. He looked over at the tilt-meter that had been set next to the third station and noticed with mounting alarm the colossal gap that had been made since his visit the previous day. Then he swung his leg over the saddle, turned his pony's head down the hill, and galloped for the farm.

Sigmund Sigmundsson, who monitored the information from his desk at the Nordic Institute, was not surprised. They had been pumping millions of gallons of water into the underground strata for the last three weeks, and he had been expecting the fault to move at any time. At noon, when the indications of subterranean activity were confirmed, he put out the red-alert signal. The coast road was immediately closed and other precautions taken.

The red alert was given at 9 A.M. local time. It was picked up by the USAF base at Keflavik, bounced down to NATO headquarters in Brussels, and then relayed to China via satellite. McGrath received it at his project headquarters in Ch'i-li-pi. He called for Feng, who switched on the tape machine.

The village was just settling down for the evening. Cows meandered in from the fields, and chickens clucked in the yards, waiting for scraps. The people had concluded that they would not have to leave until tomorrow and were peacefully spending their last night at home. Suddenly a shrill roar filled the air, as the loudspeakers began to play:

Arise ye prisoners of starvation,
Arise ye wretched of the earth.

The music thundered forth while the sun dropped in the west. The villagers came resignedly from their houses, leaving meals they had just begun and taking with them only the allowed possessions. They gathered quietly in the square, looking back at their homes for the last time. There were no tears, or much emotion of any kind. The villagers were ready.

Within half an hour the first Army trucks had arrived. Like the Red Cross truck that brought the bomb, these vehicles were on an explainable public mission, and so were not concealed. A last pass of a satellite before sunset might reveal to the Soviets the mustering of vehicles, but the truth would be obvious: The vehicles were engaged on a relief-and-evacuation operation.

Each family unit reported its members present and accounted for to the leader of its street committee. Those leaders came up to Feng as he stood beneath the loudspeakers with McGrath and Li beside him. The music ended and Feng began the roll call amid a silence broken only by the occasional squawk of a chicken or squeal of a pig.

"All present?" Feng asked each man.

"All present," they replied.

McGrath looked at the crowd, at each small group. He had come to love these men and women and felt himself privileged to have had this chance to get out in the field again. He liked dealing with real people—it had always been one of the pleasures of his work. Occasionally he caught the eye of a villager and nodded his head, both in greeting and farewell. He saw Kao Pin-ying on his crutches. They smiled to each other. He saw Hsueh's wife, waiting with her children to board the truck. She would not meet his eyes, but McGrath felt that, if he ever visited the new village of Ch'i-li-pi, he would not find her so implacable in her grief.

Suddenly McGrath frowned. He quickly scanned the crowd. Someone was missing—he knew it instinctively. Who was it? He turned to Feng. "Someone's missing."

Feng looked puzzled. "Everyone's here. Each family has been counted."

"It's old Ping Chen and his dog," McGrath cried. "He doesn't have a family. He lives by himself."

Feng gave rapid instructions and two men ran off up the street. They returned in five minutes.

"He's not in his house or anywhere nearby."

"Search the village."

They delayed the embarkation to search systematically, dividing the village up into squares and entering each house. Ping Chen was in none of them. McGrath thought of Ping Chen's nightly walks. He turned to Feng. "Go ahead with the evacuation. Don't wait for me. I think I know where he may be. I'm going to look for him." They did not try to dissuade him.

As he drove out of the square, he saw the people boarding the waiting trucks. His part in the operation was over. He knew that now everything could go on perfectly well without him. Li was going back, and he knew their affair would have to end. And so, his job done, he felt dispensable and therefore strong.

He had very little time. He had estimated four hours for the evacuation because he wanted to tell Feng something definite, but frankly there was no way of telling when the bomb would blow. The decision had long ago been made that the evacuation would take place if possible, but it was not a sine qua non of the operation. Nobody wanted unnecessary loss of life, but once they had linked the firing of the bomb to a seismic event happening elsewhere in the world, total safety could not be guaranteed. McGrath knew politicians, and when the stakes were this high, nobody was going to give the order to hold fire just because there were a few stray people in the danger zone.

Outside the village he paused, flicking the gear lever into neutral as he pondered which way to turn. If Ping Chen had walked west through the fields someone would have seen him and said so. If he had gone south, the convoy might pick him up anyway. Due east was the river. So McGrath rammed the jeep into gear and swung north along the track that led into the canyon. He seemed to remember Ping Chen saying he liked to walk up there.

He drove as far as he could, bouncing over boulders and crags as the steep path twisted and turned above the river. Soon it became impossible to drive any farther. He got out and looked back toward the village in time to see the last of the convoy pulling out of the square. He continued on foot. To his right, the cliffs fell away to the water. The last light of the sun caught the mountainous ground on the far side, but the river itself was already in shadow. McGrath looked at the hills on the other side, remembering the Panda incursion onto Soviet territory. How much did the Soviets know about what was happening? How much had they seen by satellite or by their surveillance from across the river?

McGrath shouted Ping Chen's name but was rewarded only by the startled rush of wings in the forest. Once a small deer leaped out from behind a tree and sprinted down the rocks toward the river, white tail bobbing. McGrath hoped that the small animal would have the sense to run and keep on running before its whole world crumbled. He kept up the search in the now darkening twilight, following the narrow path. The shadows and mist brought images to his mind, and thoughts of his wife, and Li. Another half hour and he decided it was time to turn back. The search was pointless. Ping Chen wouldn't have walked so far. He gave one last shout and heard his voice rebound among the rocks. No, there was no one. It was time to go.

Then he heard it, the barking of a dog, somewhere below him where the rocks made a semicircle jutting out over the river. McGrath ran downhill, jumping over boulders and kicking aside dead branches. The dog met him with hackles bristling but then recognized him and wagged its tail. McGrath found Ping Chen asleep, his mouth open and a peaceful look on his face. He watched the rise and fall of the old man's breathing and listened to his gentle snore for a moment. Then he shook him urgently by the shoulder.

"Wake up, Ping Chen. Hurry! We have to go quickly."

The old man was rudely startled awake. They went back as fast as they could, the dog leading them. Night had closed in and the forest was full of ominous noises. Two or three times McGrath heard the unmistakable howl of a wolf. He saw the jeep glinting in the brightening moonlight and ran the last few yards. He managed to turn the car around on the hill, then stepped on the gas, and roared back toward the village. The instinct for survival was now uppermost in his mind, and he was surprised how passionately he wanted to live.

Just as a series of beacon fires mounted on successive hilltops flashed the news of the fall of Troy from Asia Minor to the Peloponnese, so a series of electronic relays communicated the vital message from Iceland to China. Split seconds after the needle of the seismograph on the Mýrdalsjökull glacier pushed over the critical 6.6 mark, an electrical circuit was closed in the black control box that had been left behind in the meeting hall of the village of Ch'i-li-pi. Simultaneously, in the bomb cavity five hundred feet beneath the river, the total energy of the nuclear fission-fusion was released. In about ten-millionths of a second, the temperature near the explosion was raised to millions of degrees. The pressure jumped to thousands of times the pressure of the earth's atmosphere.

The concentrated energy of the 100-kiloton explosion vaporized the metal shell containing the bomb mechanism and the nuclear fuel. It vaporized the surmounting rock. A globe of incandescent gas, like the inside of a star, expanded in a fraction of a second to fill the bomb cavity. The cavity grew as the boiling rock vaporized from its surface while, all around, the rock was fractured by the force of the explosion.

As the first compressive seismic wave reached the surface above the white-hot cavity, the ground abruptly arched. The river became suddenly a seething mass, huge fragments of rock hurtling up through the water and into the air and the flow of water instantly converting into steam. For a few moments the narrow canyon became an inferno, a witches' cauldron, a place of unimaginable happenings. Primeval forces were unleashed, and powers that belonged more properly to gods than to men.

As the steam and boiling mist began to clear in the canyon, the three 1-kiloton charges that were destined to dig the diversion trench exploded in sequence. The "ripple" firing went exactly to plan. While the great earth wall formed in the canyon, blocking the flow of the river, so the trench opened up, ready, as the water level rose in the valley, to offer an outlet and thus relieve some of the overwhelming pressure on the dam itself.

McGrath was about half a mile south of Ch'i-li-pi when he felt the earth begin to shake. The jeep was picked up and flung off the road. McGrath watched it catapult through the air as he and Ping Chen were pitched forward to the ground. McGrath recovered consciousness aware of the severe pain of a broken leg. By the light of the moon shining fitfully through the clouds, he saw the twisted wreck of the jeep, and Ping Chen, his neck broken, lying beside it. McGrath also saw that he was on an island created by the flooding and that the water was rising slowly all around him. Good, he thought, the dam was holding. Everything must have gone all right. His calculations were correct. His current calculations, however, told him that he had about three hours before the water rose over the jeep. At that point he would probably drown, since with a broken leg he would be unable to swim.

He gingerly looked down to examine the leg. The break was below the knee. The flesh was torn and there was considerable bruising. He looked around for something to use as a bandage, and his eyes settled on Ping Chen. *"Dwe'y-bri chi,"* he said. "I'm sorry." Then he tore a strip from the bottom of Ping Chen's shirt and bound his leg up methodically. The essential thing was to keep calm and to respond to events in an orderly and controlled manner. He had plenty of time if he used it right.

It took him twenty minutes to get the radio to work. The water was lapping at the wheels of the jeep. McGrath felt the tension rise as he twisted the dials, searching for the right frequency. He had to do it by feel, because the whole face of the radio had been smashed in. Finally he heard static and a low hum.

"This is ANCHORMAN! This is ANCHORMAN! Can you read me? This is ANCHORMAN making a Mayday call. Can you read me? Over."

He strained to hear the voice of the Chinese operator from the base at Chihsi. "Come in ANCHORMAN. Come in ANCHORMAN. This is SAVAGE. We read you loud and clear."

McGrath gratefully gave his position and described what had happened. He spoke *en clair* because he had no other choice.

"Hang on there, Ma Ga't." He heard Colonel Ming's voice. "We're coming to get you. Twenty minutes from now, light flares to indicate your exact position."

McGrath replaced the mike. It sounded so simple. "Please light flares!" He tore up the rest of Ping Chen's shirt, and then, constrained by respect from taking his trousers as well, he tore up his own shirt. He dipped the rags in gas from one of the cans in the jeep, set them in a circle on the hood, and sat down to wait.

The clatter of a helicopter sounded overhead much sooner than he expected. He flicked on the radio. "Hello SAVAGE. This is ANCHORMAN. I hear you overhead and am lighting flares now."

There was silence on the other end, a crackle, and then an urgent voice. "ANCHORMAN. This is SAVAGE. We are still ten miles from your position. We are not overhead. Please explain your last message."

McGrath paused in the act of lighting the first flare. What was going on? He could plainly hear the noise of the helicopter getting steadily louder. Goddammit! The Soviets! The damn Soviets! They too would be mounting relief operations as a result of the earthquake. They would be using helicopters for sure, and one of them must have picked up his transmission. Hell! The last thing he needed was to be picked up by the Soviets. That would completely blow the operation. McGrath knew he was tough but not tough enough to resist the combination of physical and psychological torture. No man could. The days when prisoners gave name, rank, and serial number and were able to leave it at that were dead and gone. Nowadays name, rank, and serial number were just for starters.

He picked up the mike. "SAVAGE? You have problems. Enemy chopper in vicinity. Am not lighting flares. Repeat: Am not lighting flares."

Then he saw it, lumbering down out of the night sky, rotor whirring. It hadn't seen him yet. McGrath could see the lights in the cabin as the craft swung this way and that, searching. His thumb was on the button of the mike but he didn't press it. They were surely listening for him, hoping for a radio fix.

A short-barreled cannon was mounted at the rear of the jeep. McGrath managed to get it into firing position. He loaded it, checked the ammunition, and waited.

At exactly the same moment as the Soviet helicopter finally spotted the damaged jeep, the Chinese helicopter arrived on the scene. McGrath watched the dance of the two great machines. It was both lyrical and ferocious, as they twisted and spun in the air, diving and pirouetting, darting and soaring with a grace and agility unlikely for their bulk. The Chinese had the advantage of surprise: Their An-36 T-class machine came in for a full frontal attack, all guns blazing. But the Soviets had greater firepower. They pulled away and, in quick succession, released two Sidewinder-type missiles that barely missed their target. The first round was over. They both retired out of range.

When the second round began, the Soviets had the advantage of height. The Soviet pilot flew directly over the Chinese helicopter, firing downward. A spray of bullets hit the water around the jeep and McGrath, huddled by the cannon waiting for his moment, felt the breath of their passage. He watched the Soviet craft coming straight toward him, at upward of 100 knots. The Chinese craft pulled away to gain altitude. He saw flashes of light from their guns, and heard the sickening whine and thud of bullets. And then, when the range was less than 80 yards and it was clear the Soviets would pass not more than 20 feet above him, he pulled the trigger in one long and sustained burst of machine-gun fire. The Soviet helicopter exploded before his eyes. Debris flew all about him, and he threw himself to the ground.

A spark lit the circle of flares. Minutes later, McGrath grabbed hold of a sling and was hauled aboard the Chinese helicopter. The sling descended a second time to bring up the body of Ping Chen.

Colonel Ming was in the aircraft. "Shall we destroy the jeep?" he asked.

"No need to worry," McGrath answered. "By tomorrow morning, the jeep and the helicopter will be under fifty feet of water."

Half an hour later they landed at Chihsi.

"Oh, Ma Ga't!" Li moaned as she looked at the battered, shirt-less figure being carried off the helicopter.

McGrath looked at her with half-closed eyes. He smiled. He had failed to save Ping Chen. But the operation had succeeded. Li was waiting for him. He was thankful he had made it back alive.

20

General Bledsoe rose from his seat in the White House Situation Room with an air of satisfaction. Taking his place in front of the large-scale map, he first nodded toward the President and then began in a firm voice:

"You know all the preliminaries. We estimate that within about three hours of the explosion—that is to say, around 11 P.M. local time—the water was backed up sufficiently far behind the dam for the diversion of the Ussuri through the trench into the Bikin to begin. At about two in the morning, a state of hydraulic equilibrium was reached—that is to say, the rise in the water level behind the dam was being constrained by the satisfactory functioning of the diversion trench, and the necessary equalization between inflow and outflow had been attained. By first light, when the first reconnaissance was made, it was clear that the wall thrown up by the nuclear explosion had effectively achieved a total blockage of the Ussuri River. Seepage through the body of the dam was nil."

The President himself led the applause that followed.

After a moment, Bledsoe held up his hand to stop it. "Gentlemen, thank you. Believe me, I shall pass your congratulations on to the man who truly deserves them! John G. McGrath!"

Bledsoe let the renewed applause run on. He was pleased that

McGrath had done such an impeccable job. His own role had been a limited one, and if they applauded him, it was mainly because he was McGrath's old friend, the man who had known whom to go to and how to persuade him to take on the job. He was giving the briefing now only because McGrath was in the hospital.

"How is McGrath this morning, General?" the President asked as the applause died down. "I'm going to try to get out to see him later today."

"The people at Bethesda say he'll be right as rain in a couple of days. I'm sure he'd appreciate a visit."

"Back to the briefing now," he continued. By the time of the explosion, the Chinese military and civilian commands were ready to mount relief operations. They had been told to expect an earthquake at a particular time and, by golly, that was what happened! I can guarantee you that with the exception of maybe half a dozen people, the whole of China believes that the disaster that struck the village of Ch'i-li-pi and the surrounding area was the result of an earthquake."

He pointed to the map. "Of course, the Chinese used the cover of the relief operations to bring in massive reinforcements along the new frontier line. The deposit area is now occupied by two fully equipped divisions of the People's Liberation Army, Heilungkiang command.

"I'm afraid," he went on, "that there has been some loss of life. The town of Bikin, on the Soviet side, has been devastated. Until the big bang, the Bikin River was a pretty modest little stream. Houses came right down to the riverbank. Then, all of a sudden, this little stream finds itself the channel for the mighty Ussuri." He tossed some photos onto the table. "These came off the satellite this morning. You can see that all the low-lying land in the town of Bikin, habitations included, has been flooded."

They studied the photographs with concern.

"Has the United States offered any help yet?" asked the President. "We ought to offer help—blankets, tents, baby food, medicine. It will look odd if we don't."

"We made a general offer late last night," Kristof interjected, "indicating that we would be mobilizing both public and private assistance and that American aid would be available impartially to both sides to help them deal with the consequences of the earthquake."

The President nodded. "Did they accept?"

"The Chinese said that although their seismologists predicted with 100 per cent accuracy the time and place of the earthquake and they were prepared for it, they would accept some materials to help with the relocation of the Ch'i-li-pi villagers."

"What about the Soviets? Have we heard from them?"

Gordon Kristof thoughtfully shook his head. "No, it's rather odd. The Soviets have been completely silent. Not a squeak on the hot line. We haven't even seen the ambassador, and he's usually in and out of here like a yo-yo with some message or other."

The President turned to George Chisman. "How do your intelligence people read it, George? Does this mean the Soviets are going to take it lying down?"

Chisman's reply was both quick and confident. "What else can they do? They're not going to risk a war by forcibly taking the land back. They've been confronted with the *fait accompli* of all time. Now they've got to live with it."

A stark and jagged ringing suddenly came from the red-and-white striped telephone on a side table. The President himself picked up the receiver of the Moscow–Washington hot line. He said nothing, but the color drained from his cheeks as he listened. He put the receiver down and looked around the room. "That was Premier Chernetsov in Moscow," he said, gloom and frustration in his voice. "Chernetsov says he knows there was something fishy about the Manchuria earthquake and sooner or later he'll find out what it was. He also said that he had spoken personally to Chairman Yang within the last thirty minutes. He told Yang the Chinese have forty-eight hours to blow a hole in the dike and let the water run back into its old channel."

"And if they don't?" asked Kristof.

"Chernetsov says the Soviets will do it themselves. With laser bombs—the kind that can hit a fly from ten miles up. His exact words.

"Well, gentlemen. What the hell do we do now?"

That evening the President slipped secretly into Bethesda Naval Hospital. He found McGrath, looking remarkably fit, propped up in bed watching the news on television. They both turned to hear the latest reports.

"Mount Katla in Iceland," John Chancellor was saying, "was still erupting today forty-eight hours after the lava first began to flow. Icelandic authorities say damage has been slight. However, on the Sino-Soviet border in Manchuria, considerable flooding has resulted from the recent earthquake. Relief operations are under way. We are told that some localized skirmishing has taken place between Soviet and Chinese units engaged in relief work, but so far there has been no serious outbreak of hostilities. . . ."

McGrath turned it off and looked at the President.

"We've got problems with the Soviets, haven't we?" McGrath asked dejectedly. "I heard this afternoon from Thaddeus."

The President took a seat at the bedside. "Tell me, John, what would be the effect of bombing the dam? Would we really be back to square one if the Soviets did that?"

McGrath shook his head. "It's not quite as simple as that. If they bombed the dam today, maybe that's what would happen. When the Chinese blew up the dike on the Yellow River to stop the Japanese getting it, the river simply returned to its old course. But it depends on the different hydrological and geological factors. The Ussuri is a river with a good deal of cutting and scouring power. That means that every day the diversion trench is getting deeper and wider. It's a matter of time before it actually becomes the natural channel for the Ussuri, and once that happens, it doesn't matter whether the dam stays or goes."

"So time is crucial? The more time we can buy, the more likely it is that the situation will be irreversible?"

"Exactly. Time is of the essence."

The President stood up, paced once around the room, and came back to look down at McGrath. "How's the leg?"

"Getting better every day. The Chinese whisked me down to the Institute of Traditional Medicine in Shenyang, stuck in a couple of needles, and reset the leg within half an hour. I was conscious the whole time. One of the marvelous things about acupuncture is that you don't have the aftereffects of anesthetics."

"Maybe I'll try acupuncture myself one day," said the President. "Set a trend."

He pulled out a felt-tip pen and wrote on the plaster in clearly legible handwriting: "TO GENERAL JOHN MCGRATH. THANKS FOR A GREAT JOB AND BEST WISHES FOR A QUICK RECOVERY." Beneath the message, he signed his own name.

McGrath was visibly moved. "Thank you, sir. Do you really mean 'General'?"

"I do. It came through this morning. I thought I'd tell you myself."

They chatted for a few minutes, when McGrath remembered about Marshal Lu. "By the way, something odd happened earlier. I tried to call Marshal Lu to tell him that I'd gotten back safely and not to worry—he worries about me, for some reason. I asked the operator to get me his home number. It's been the same for years—he's one of the few people who has a private phone. After a minute, I could hear the Peking operator saying that the number was no longer available. I asked the Peking operator myself what had happened to Lu's number and she would say only that it had been disconnected."

"What do you make of it?"

McGrath took a pull on his pipe. "Frankly, I was somewhat alarmed. Of course, it could be some minor bureaucratic confusion. On the other hand, it could mean something more serious."

"Such as?"

"It could mean that some kind of power struggle is going on in China—radicals vs. moderates—and that Lu and Yang are on the losing end."

The President laughed. "Tell me a time when there isn't some kind of power struggle going on in China."

He looked at his watch. "Hell, I've got to run. One day when you're better, you should stop by. There's so much more I'd like to hear."

With the lithe strides of a man conscious of his own power, the President left the room.

21

BORDER CASE TO BE DECIDED BY INTERNATIONAL COURT OF JUSTICE. ARGUMENTS BEGIN MONDAY IN THE HAGUE. Ricker read the New York *Times* headline aloud to Richard Hosmer. It was a month after the Ussuri had changed its course. Hosmer, an ambitious and well-fed young academic who was Dean of International Affairs at Georgetown University, had just been appointed an official observer of the Court's deliberations. Over breakfast, he was filling Ricker in on the workings of international law.

"The fact is, Thaddeus," he said, his mouth full of marmalade, "that the Soviets stand a fair chance of winning. That's probably one of the reasons they've agreed to go to the Court. If the Chinese try running the *thalweg* argument, they may find themselves on pretty thin ice. The Soviets are likely to come back and claim that an earthquake is a case of 'avulsion,' a sudden unusual and unnatural shift in the river rather than a gradual process of accretion, and that the formerly established boundary isn't therefore in question."

Ricker nodded. He knew they ran a risk, perhaps a serious risk, of the International Court's finding in favor of the Soviets. But what was the alternative? The International Court was really the only option they had. The United States had negotiated energetically with both sides to get them to agree in advance to the Court's eventual judgment. That way the use of force would be avoided, and they would also gain time.

A week later Hosmer and Silcott, the other official observer, sat together in the courtroom watching the judges file into the splendid Chamber of the Peace Palace for the start of the proceedings.

"There's Golenski, the Soviet judge." Hosmer indicated a short bald man walking behind the President. "And there's Lewis Nagefo, from Nigeria. He's very sound. Next is Hoo, the Chinese judge. Strictly speaking, though, it's wrong to talk of them as Chinese judges and Soviet judges and so on. Once appointed to the Court, they are meant to act independently of any national affiliation."

Silcott nodded. "It will be interesting to see if they do."

The other members of the Court took their seats. Silcott looked down the line of faces. There was Kirmani, the Pakistani; Read, the New Zealander; Mercier, the Frenchman. Solemn, serious men, who had reached the pinnacle of their profession. Their air of gravitas was wholly in keeping with the stately furnishings of the room—heavy chandeliers hanging above the bench, stained-glass windows behind them, polished wood panels, thick carpeting.

The President, Dr. Enrico Campos, a Brazilian, banged his gavel to call the Court to order.

"Well," thought Silcott, "here goes."

Leonid Vorosilov, the tall, polished Soviet Ambassador to the Hague and one of Russia's finest lawyers, rose to present the Soviet case. The Soviets had instigated the proceedings, and were therefore the ones to speak first. Vorosilov faced the judges and, in perfect English (the rules of the Court requiring that it be addressed in either English or French), introduced his main arguments.

He was eloquent and impressive. He had complete mastery of his brief, and appeared to revel, perhaps excessively, in the presentation of detail. More than once the President felt constrained to cut him short. But when he sat down, there was a rustle of appreciation in the hall. The observers had to acknowledge that his case had been especially well presented. Wong Liu-ching, China's representative in the case, rose next. He was a total contrast to Vorosilov. A short, scruffy man with heavy black spectacles and dark untidy hair, he wore a somewhat outmoded blue-gray Mao suit and spoke in the old rhetoric of the Chinese Revolution.

"The renegade Soviet revisionist clique, which has inherited the mantle of the Tsar, vainly attempts to divide the world to establish world social-imperialist hegemony. In Europe, this clique has put Czechoslovakia under direct military occupation. In Asia, not satisfied with colonizing the Mongolian People's Republic, it has even tried to invade and occupy Chinese territory. In Cambodia, it encouraged an unlawful Vietnamese invasion. In the Middle East and South Asia, it is also making desperate efforts to widen its colonial influence. The rabid aggressive policy of the Soviet revisionists will be repulsed with a vengeance by the Chinese people and will certainly be denounced by liberated people everywhere."

Wong then turned to hard facts and figures. He traced the whole history of territorial disputes between Russia and China, demonstrating that the underlying pattern over the centuries was the ruthless annexation by Russia of Chinese territory.

There was a short recess after Wong sat down. Over coffee Hosmer turned to Silcott. "I have a feeling Wong is getting his points across. Campos isn't interrupting him the way he interrupted Vorosilov."

"What about precedent, though?" Silcott asked. "Surely international law would tend to support the Soviet point of view? All this historical argument—the unequal treaties and so forth—is interesting, but is it really relevant?"

Hosmer stirred extra sugar into his coffee. "Article 38, paragraph 1 of the Statute of the Court declares that the Court's function is to decide the disputes submitted to it in accordance with international law. The article goes on to provide that the law applied by the Court be derived first from international agreements, whether general or particular, establishing rules expressly recognized by the contesting states. In this case there have been various treaties over the years between Russia and

China, some of which have been denounced by one side or the other. The Court has to take these treaties into account, but it also has to take into account the fact of their denunciation."

With the opening speeches completed, the Court next took the opportunity to pursue points that seemed to require explanation. The judges asked some questions requiring answers then and there. Other questions would have to be answered later when further information or documents could be produced.

"It looks to me as if the Soviets are worried by the tone of the questions," Hosmer commented. "Vorosilov is clearly nervous."

Silcott could see it too. Vorosilov did seem somewhat ruffled. Wong, however, appeared calm and confident.

Campos banged the gavel. "The Court will adjourn for two days in order to give the parties time to assemble the requested information and to allow the registry to complete translation of the minutes. We will reconvene at 10 A.M. Thursday."

"My guess," Hosmer confided to Silcott, "is that on Thursday—which will be the final round of pleadings—the Soviets will try a new tack altogether."

By Thursday morning, Vorosilov had regained his poise. As Hosmer had predicted, he introduced new evidence "lately come to light," which he believed the Court would find interesting. He began by accusing the Chinese of making an "incursion" into Soviet territory, across the border from Ch'i-li-pi, in armored vehicles with Soviet markings. He argued that this was a preliminary reconnaissance.

"A preliminary reconnaissance for what?" Dr. Campos asked him.

"I shall come to that in due course," Vorosilov replied. "At the moment I am simply trying to establish that long before the so-called earthquake, the Chinese were showing an unusual interest in the area."

Vorosilov's second piece of evidence was a photograph, which he projected onto a screen above the judges' bench. "This picture of the Ussuri was taken by satellite six weeks before the 'earthquake.' The village you see is Ch'i-li-pi. Now I shall show you another picture of the same area, taken only ten days before the earthquake." Another photograph appeared on the screen. The judges did not appear to notice anything unusual. "There is an object on the bank of the river now," Vorosilov pointed out, "which was not there before. In the next photograph you will see it blown up."

The third photograph clearly showed a small hut, like a hunter's blind, camouflaged to blend in with the background. "Look carefully," said Vorosilov, "and you will see the outline of a pump at the water's edge. I suggest that the Chinese were in fact digging a tunnel under the river and that the pump was used to discharge the debris."

There was a gasp in the courtroom.

"What you see here," he said as another image appeared on the screen, "is the railhead at Hut'ou, also ten days before the 'earthquake.' Near the railroad, just off the track, is a dump of materials. Our analysts tell us that these are segments of concrete lining of the size and shape needed for construction of a large-scale tunnel."

The considerable rumble of interest in the Court gave Vorosilov confidence. "You have seen the preliminary evidence. I now publicly accuse the Chinese Government of deliberately engineering the diversion of the Ussuri River. The earthquake story was fabricated by them to hide the movement of troops. It is clearly nonsense to talk about natural causes." He pounded on the table. "And if there are no natural causes involved, Mr. President, members of the Court, but, on the contrary, wholly artificial ones such as"—and here he paused—"an underground nuclear explosion, which would account for the tunnel, then whatever merit there may have been in the *thalweg* argument is completely destroyed. I now ask the Court to find in favor of the Soviet Union."

Before Vorosilov had a chance to sit down, Wong was on his feet. "I object to the vile and unwarranted accusations by the representative of Soviet revisionism, and I protest that the Soviet Union has departed from the rules of the Court by introducing new material not part of the original proceedings. I request an immediate adjournment, and I warn that if this continues, I cannot guarantee the continued participation of the People's Republic of China."

Dr. Campos looked out from his seat on the dais, weighing his words carefully. His task, as he saw it, was to keep both sides talking. If they were talking, they wouldn't start shooting, and that was at least some contribution to world peace. He decided to talk procedure. It would give everyone time to think this out and calm down.

"Gentlemen," he addressed Vorosilov and Wong, "perhaps you will permit the Court a few hours to investigate whether all its rules regarding the submission of evidence have in fact been complied with. Until we know that, we cannot really complete our business. The Court will adjourn until 10 a.m. Friday."

Silcott made his way directly to the American Embassy, where he placed a call to Thaddeus Ricker at his Washington office. They would be able to speak frankly knowing that the Embassy's scramble phone would foil anyone who might be trying to tap the line. "Okay," Ricker said, "what's going on over there? Are we in trouble?"

"The Soviets are challenging the earthquake story," Silcott told him tensely.

"I know that. But why now? Why not at the beginning?"

"Hosmer says they were holding back because they thought they could win by presenting strictly orthodox arguments. When they saw Vorosilov wasn't making it, they had no other option. They must have been pretty desperate to reveal in open court the extent of their satellite monitoring of the border area. I doubt if Vorosilov even knew about the explosion hypothesis until this morning."

"What's the view of the Court?" Ricker asked. "Are they taking the Soviets seriously?"

"It all depends, I think, on whether Vorosilov has something else up his sleeve, some other evidence. That's what has me worried. It's the reason I called."

"What do you mean?"

Silcott frowned. "After the explosion, I looked over seismograms from all over the globe. You remember how delighted I was at the success of the evasion ploy. In every seismogram, including those from the sophisticated NORSAR array in Norway, the trains of seismic waves from the explosion were totally muddled up with the waves from the eruption of Mount Katla. No one could unscramble those tracings well enough to detect the true nature of the Chinese explosion. There are P waves and S waves from both sources all arriving together.

"But," he paused, "I haven't seen the seismograms from Iceland itself. It's just possible that because the station up there is so close to the source of the first set of shock waves, we may lose the masking effect. Instead of the two sets of waves being recorded almost simultaneously, and being all jumbled up as a result, there may be a clear separation, enough for the experts to figure out that the second shock was not caused by an earthquake. If that's so, and if the Soviets get hold of those seismograms—which, after all, are readily available scientific documents—then we have a real problem."

"Goddamn," Ricker said. "Short of destroying the Iceland seismograms, which would look pretty suspicious anyway, what options do we have?"

Silcott could not find an answer.

On Friday morning, Wong launched his counteroffensive. "What incursion?" he asked scornfully. "If armored vehicles with Soviet Army markings have been seen on the Soviet side of the river, it is because the Soviet Union maintains a state of warlike preparation there. Soviet tanks, Soviet guns, Soviet armor of every kind threaten us daily. If there have been any 'incursions' across the river, those incursions have been made by Soviet troops crossing into Chinese territory, not the other way around."

He cited the famous Chen Pao Island incident of March 1969, when Soviet soldiers occupied an island lying in the middle of the Ussuri, which at the time was frozen over. This land—according to Wong—was indisputably Chinese. He cited fourteen other similar incidents of Soviets occupying land clearly in Chinese possession. "Let us hear no more of these outrageous charges!" he cried.

"As for the photographs," he continued, contemptuously, "the Soviets have to rely on pictures taken by spy satellites. Do we admit the evidence of spy cameras in the International Court of Justice? And in any case, what is the charge? Vorosilov sees a pile of concrete and says these are tunnel linings! What rubbish. Cannot the Soviets recognize the material for a drainage system when they see it? Or do they have no sewers in the Soviet Union?"

Wong asked permission to call witnesses. Campos agreed, reminding him that the other side had the right of cross-examination. Wong called Fu Pu-po, who took the stand. Wong then produced a large batch of seismograms. Fu examined them and asserted that they were records of the recent seismic activity in Manchuria.

"What do they tell us?" Wong asked.

"They indicate that an earthquake occurred in the area of Ch'i-li-pi approximately six weeks ago. There is no evidence of a nuclear explosion, which would be distinguishable by the attenuation of surface waves, and by what we call the 'lonesome P-wave' phenomenon."

"Thank you, Doctor." Wong dismissed his witness.

Two days later the Soviets were ready for their cross-examination. Professor Vladimir Kuznetsov, director of the Geophysical Department at Moscow University, was brought in to assist with the interrogation. A scientist, his discomfort with this political arena was obvious, especially to Silcott, who recognized in the white-haired man a kindred spirit.

"Dr. Fu Pu-po," Kuznetsov began, "argues that there is nothing in the seismograms he has shown us to prove that the event in Manchuria was a nuclear explosion rather than an earthquake." He paused. "As a scientist, I respect Dr. Fu Pu-po's opinion and I agree with it. Because of the masking effect of seismic signals emanating from the volcanic eruption in Iceland, there is indeed no way of proving on the basis of the evidence so far presented, the occurrence of a nuclear explosion.

"However," Kuznetsov continued, "I do not believe that we have examined all the evidence, Dr. Fu." He turned to the witness. "It appears that you have not presented to the Court the seismogram from Iceland itself. Why not? Is it because you know it will show the lonesome P-wave and prove conclusively that a bomb was exploded in Ch'i-li-pi? If you are not afraid, will you now produce that evidence?"

Fu answered, embarrassed and uneasy. "I'm afraid we are not in possession of that seismogram."

"I thought not," Kuznetsov responded. "Fortunately, however, the Soviet Government has acquired copies of the Reykjavik seismograms. I shall now make them available to the Court."

Wong jumped up to protest. "How do we know these are true documents and not something fabricated by the Soviet renegades?"

Campos turned to Kuznetsov. "Are these certified copies of the Reykjavik seismograms, and are you prepared to surrender them later so that the Court can verify their authenticity?"

Kuznetsov nodded. "Of course."

"Very well then," said Campos. "Kindly proceed."

Wong sat down, crushed. There was no more he could do.

Kuznetsov projected the Reykjavik seismogram onto the screen. He pointed to the pattern of squiggly lines on the edge of the graph. "Dr. Fu, do you agree that these lines indicate a second set of shock waves? And that in this second set of shock waves there is clear evidence of the so-called lonesome P-wave phenomenon—that is, the presence of the P wave without accompanying S waves?"

"Yes, I agree," Fu answered.

"If you do agree," Kuznetsov lowered his voice, "that the evidence is proof of an artificial explosion, how then can you cling to your obviously fictitious earthquake story?"

As Kuznetsov sat down, the observers could no longer hold still. An excited buzz broke out in the room. Campos rapped his gavel. "Quiet!" When the noise died down, he turned to Fu. "What do you have to say?"

"With respect, sir," he addressed Campos, "I would like to see if Professor Kuznetsov has made an estimate of the location of the source of this second set of shock waves?"

Kuznetsov was exasperated. "I think it should be obvious that the second set of waves emanates from Manchuria. Nevertheless," he added impatiently, "if it makes our opponents happy, I will certainly calculate the precise location. It is a simple matter." Campos interrupted. "Perhaps, Professor Kuznetsov, you will be able to do the calculation right here in Court. I am sure we would all enjoy watching and it will give us a chance to learn something."

"Gladly," Kuznetsov answered. "The trigonometric calculation that I am about to demonstrate was first suggested as early as 1842. The key to it is that the time lapse between arrival of the P waves and arrival of the slower-moving S waves tells us how far the source is from the recording station. A 20-second lag means a distance of about 100 miles. Eight minutes of lag indicates 2,500 miles.

"To do the calculation, we need information from three stations. We put one end of a compass on the first station and draw a circle whose radius is equal to the distance from that station to the source of the waves. We repeat the process for the second and the third stations. The point at which the three circles intersect is the exact position of the source. In the present instance that intersection will be at exactly the site of the so-called Manchurian earthquake!"

Kuznetsov took up a large compass. "Let's start with the seismogram from the Rangoon Station. The time lapse between the P and the S waves is 7 minutes, 50 seconds, which means that the Rangoon Station is about 2,450 miles from the source of the waves." He put one end of the compass on Rangoon and drew a large circle with a radius equivalent to 2,450 miles. "You will note," he said confidently, "that this first circle passes exactly through the area of the Ussuri just south of Khabarovsk."

There was no sound in the room as the judges, the press, and other observers watched in fascination.

"Now I will draw the second circle. I am taking the information from one of our own monitoring stations, far north in the Soviet Arctic, on New Siberian Island." He looked across the room toward Fu Pu-po. "I hope our Chinese colleagues are prepared to accept seismographic data from a Soviet station."

Fu Pu-po nodded gravely. "Dr. Kuznetsov has a worldwide

reputation. We accept the authenticity of any evidence he may present to the Court."

"Thank you." Kuznetsov continued. "On the evidence from New Siberian Island, we have a time lapse of 8 minutes, 10 seconds, which means a circle of about 2,550 miles in radius." He drew the circle. "You can see," he exclaimed, "how this second circle intersects with the first exactly in the 'earthquake' area!

"I shall now draw the third and last circle. Let me remind you that the point where the three circles meet will be the source of the seismic waves. The Chinese have already agreed that the evidence from the Reykjavik Station signifies a nuclear explosion. If the third circle, drawn around Reykjavik, intersects with the first two circles at the 'earthquake' area, that will be ample proof that we are not dealing with an earthquake at all, but with the deliberate use of an underground explosion to engineer a diversion of the Ussuri River!"

He consulted his notes. "The Reykjavik station shows a time lapse of 10 minutes, 40 seconds, which makes the source"—his voice faltered—"3,200 miles. . . ." Something was wrong. He began to draw the circle around Reykjavik, driven to complete the calculation now that he had begun it. "I don't understand," he stammered. "There must be some mistake. The three circles don't intersect where they should!"

"Stand back, Professor," Campos interjected, "and let us see where they *do* intersect."

Kuznetsov sank into his chair, staring with them at the map. Suddenly Fu Pu-po was on his feet. "Mr. President," he declaimed, "it is obvious from the calculations Professor Kuznetsov has just made that the nuclear explosion we are examining took place not in the so-called earthquake area but deep within the Soviet Union itself. The three circles intersect in the heart of Soviet Siberia, in the Lake Balkhash area, which, gentlemen, is the main Soviet center for underground nuclear testing! I submit that these calculations all point to a crude attempt on the part of the Soviets to cheat on the new comprehensive Test-ban Treaty! I submit that the Soviets conducted an un-

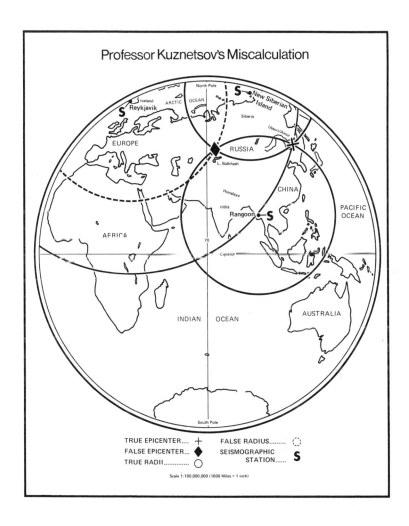

Professor Kuznetsov's Miscalculation

TRUE EPICENTER.... +   FALSE RADIUS.........
FALSE EPICENTER... ◆   SEISMOGRAPHIC
TRUE RADII..............○   STATION...... S

Scale 1:100,000,000 (1600 Miles = 1 inch)

derground nuclear test, of the kind banned by the new treaty, at the same time as the Chinese earthquake, hoping that in this way it would escape notice!"

Campos managed to silence the Court long enough to ask Kuznetsov if he had any comment. The professor could only shake his head. "I just don't understand," he mumbled, as reporters raced for phones and photographers snapped pictures of his carefully drawn circles.

That night Silcott was again on the scramble phone to Ricker in Washington. "Thaddeus, it's Wilbur. It looks as though we've won this round. I think you had something to do with this."

"Well," said Ricker, "it seems that someone who knew a lot of what you told me last week happened into the Reykjavik Station and touched up the seismograms. Just shifted the epicenter a few hundred miles west. The Soviets were obviously so convinced they were right that they never bothered to check the trigonometry. Made them look pretty bad, didn't it? That's good for us too. The judges will be sympathetic to China."

"But, Thaddeus, aren't the Soviets going to think they were tricked?"

"My guess," Ricker answered, "is that they're totally confused. They never talk to each other, anyway. The left hand doesn't know what the right hand is doing. I'll bet the professor, Kuznetsov, probably believes that the Soviet military, who hate the comprehensive Test-Ban Treaty about as much as the Pentagon hates it, were trying to pull a fast one."

Silcott sighed. "It was unethical and awfully risky, I'd say, but I guess that's what you guys are all about. I'm sure glad I'm not a politician."

Ricker laughed. "Speaking of politics," he said more seriously, "do you remember Roberto Delgado, our Brazilian friend? He turned up in China and we think he may have been in the Soviet Union as well."

"I remember. What about him?"

"George Chisman just called me to say that they think he's in The Hague. What the hell is he doing? The President of the Court is Brazilian. It's too much of a coincidence."

"Anything I can do?" Silcott asked.

"No, I'm just alerting you. If anything's to be done, we politicians will handle it." Ricker chuckled and hung up.

The fifteen judges of the International Court of Justice voted at 10:15 A.M. on the last Tuesday of August. The registrar read the final question aloud to them in clear, precise tones: "Is it the view of the members of this Court that the international frontier between the Soviet Union and China, in that area where it is not subject to dispute, should follow the *present* course of the Ussuri River? Members of the Court are required to vote either 'Yes' or 'No.' "

Alvarez, the Mexican, was first. "No," he said firmly.

"Judge Read?"

"No." The New Zealander was equally emphatic.

Dr. Campos jotted the votes down on his pad. Two votes and two "No's." It looked bad for China.

A third "No" as the Frenchman, Mercier, also voted for the Soviets.

Then there was a string of "Yeses" from the Nigerian, Nagefo; Hoo, the Chinese; and the American, Professor Sachs.

The Soviet judge, Golenski, made the score four to three for the Soviet Union. Then Rau from India and Carey from Ireland also voted "No." Poland's Zakonovski brought the score to seven to three.

Campos looked at his pad. There were four more judges and himself. They would all have to vote "Yes" if China was to win. Campos felt his palms getting slippery with sweat. He closed his eyes and saw the faces of his children.

Strauss from Canada voted "Yes"; so did Olembo from Senegal, and Haden-Guest from Britain.

"Justice Kirmani?" called the registrar, addressing the Pakistani.

"Yes," said Kirmani.

"Since the vote of the Court is seven "Yes" and seven "No," it falls to the President of the Court to cast the decisive vote. Mr. President, how say you?"

Dr. Campos removed his glasses. He had no choice; of course the Soviets were in the right—but now he had to think of other things—his wife, his children. "Think how tragic it would be," he heard Delgado's voice, "if tomorrow, after the vote, your family were to die in an accidental fire." He closed his eyes against the image of Delgado's smile. The Brazilian guerrillas would stop at nothing. They had decided to make their move and he was their first target.

"Dr. Campos?" the registrar called again. "Yes or no?"

Campos shuddered. "Yes," he whispered.

Silcott and Hosmer arrived early for the delivery of the judgment. The judges were already in their places, the cameras were set up, the reporters were taking notes. Campos banged his gavel, bringing silence to the room.

"For these reasons," he read shakily, "the Court finds *against* the application by the Soviet Union. . . ."

Silcott looked around and found Delgado, sitting alone, grinning smugly.

"There's no appeal from a judgment of the International Court," Hosmer told Silcott as they left the building after the verdict. "Each side is bound to abide by the judgment. If they don't, the United Nations Security Council will enforce it." He paused. "I'd love to know how the voting actually went."

Silcott smiled. Sometimes it was nice to be in with the politicians. "It so happens that we had a rundown on the voting from an inside source. It went pretty much as you expected. Apparently, there was one bad moment when the score was seven to seven with only the President left to vote."

Hosmer was astonished. "You mean Campos voted with the Chinese? That's incredible!"

"Why?"

"Campos is an international lawyer in the classic tradition—Lauterpacht, Fawcett, Jenks. He's been involved in arbitrating boundary disputes between several Latin American countries. He would never agree that changes in international frontiers resulting from 'avulsion' should be upheld. I can't believe he voted that way!"

"Well, he did," Silcott grimaced. He was glad after all to be going back to his ivory tower.

22

Chung ushered her into the Chairman's office in the Politburo Headquarters. She looked around. All evidence of the previous occupant, Chairman Yang, had been removed, and she knew that he himself had been banished to a remote post as a lowly Party official. Chung certainly moved fast.

"I wanted to thank you, Li," he said. "Without you I could not have succeeded."

She shrugged her shoulders. "Chung Feng, even without me you would have found a way to succeed. The Secret Service was behind you. All the radicals supported you. A hundred people, a thousand people could have done what I did."

"No." He regarded her across the desk. "You had access, unequaled access. You told me what was going on."

She laughed harshly. "You mean I betrayed my father. Instead of spending his old age in peace at home in the Village of the Summer Palace, he has been sent off to a rehabilitation center in Sinkiang."

"Betray. That is a strong word," Chung Feng rebuked her. "On instructions from the Party, the true radical Party, you brought me a recording of the conversation that your father had with the American, Ma Ga't. That was no betrayal. It was your duty!"

Li was hurt by the mention of McGrath's name. "I betrayed him too," she said. "I gave you tapes of the secret meeting in the Ming tombs. I kept you informed about the progress of work on the tunnel and the placing of the bomb. These were Ma Ga't's plans, Ma Ga't's work, and I betrayed it all. He was my lover!"

"I know, Li, I know. Don't forget, I was your lover too, once."

He moved around the desk and held her, letting her sob passionately. "You must console yourself, my dear, with the thought that you provided the tools for victory. Nothing was more important to the removal of Chairman Yang than the proof you provided that he had high-handedly undertaken negotiations with the Americans that were entirely to the detriment of China's strength and self-sufficiency. He had no right to give away, for almost nothing, 50 per cent of the most valuable mineral deposit ever discovered. What the tapes showed"—Chung's hand moved affectionately across her shoulders—"is treason of the highest order. Yang should not have discussed, let alone agreed to, a deal such as that one. The whole effort by Yang to make China dependent on American technology was outrageous. He brought in Coca-Cola, and he invited the capitalists to come rape China once again. He defiled the Revolution. He is lucky he has not been killed for it."

She looked up with a sorrowful face.

"And Ma Ga't?"

"Ma Ga't will understand. He too has a concept of duty."

Suddenly her face cleared. "You mean I shall be coming with you to Washington?"

"Of course you will come, Li. You are still our top interpreter. I will need you for my conversation with the American President."

When Chairman Yang had finally named a date for his visit to the United States, the White House was elated. The excitement dissipated when Washington got news of the change in power in China. The pundits and professional China watchers assumed that the new Chinese leader, Chung Feng, a radical with strong anti-American leanings, would hardly be likely to fulfill this commitment to visit the United States. The whole Chinese-American rapprochement of the late 1970s seemed endangered. Now that word had come from the Chinese Embassy, however, that the visit would be going ahead, the Administration was again looking forward to massive television exposure and lots of good press praising its peaceful, forward-looking trade policies. The official machinery was set in motion. Chinese flags were ordered for the streets of Washington and New York—Chung intended to put in an appearance at the United Nations General Assembly. Protocol officers at the White House and the State Department prepared invitation lists. Chefs drew up menus for the official banquets. Blair House was made ready to receive an honored guest. Staffers were busy drawing up documents, statements, and agendas for meetings. Members of both governments had to meet at the official level to work out, as the State Department press release put it, "the modalities of cooperation."

The Chinese arrived quietly in the evening. The next day the crowds were ten deep along Pennsylvania Avenue. Chairman Chung came out of Blair House to the sound of enthusiastic applause. The limousine drove him across the street to the White House. Along the way he saw hundreds of smiling faces of Americans, eager to make friends with the little Chinese man with the severe face.

The President, with his wife and family, was waiting for Chung on the steps of the White House. The national anthems were played while the leaders shook hands and stood at attention. Flashbulbs popped and television cameras whirred. A few minutes later, forgoing speeches or other formalities, the President graciously ushered Chung into the Oval Office. Only one person accompanied them—China's top interpreter, Li Lu-yan.

The President shook hands with her warmly. "Hello. I'm glad to meet you. I've heard a lot about you."

The two men sat down side by side in armchairs next to the fireplace. Li's chair was placed between them in such a way that her presence would not interfere with the personal contact that was meant to develop. They talked for an hour and covered all the topics the joint communiqué would say they covered.

"Well, I guess we've gone over all the official business," the President said. He was glad things had gone so well. "I can tell you I had a bit of trouble with Congress over the Economic and Cultural Treaty. They were very reluctant to ratify. They seemed to think that the United States had given too much away and not gotten enough in return. I had to have the Congressional leaders in for breakfast to tell them the basics about the Secret Protocol. After that it was fine."

Li was leaning forward in her seat, straining to hear. She interrupted. "Secret Protocol, sir?"

"Yes," replied the President impatiently. "Secret Protocol. The one our people negotiated in Peking. The one that deals with U.S. access to the Ch'i-li-pi mineral deposit in return for our help in locating it and ensuring that it became part of Chinese territory, and also for signing a treaty that is, as you know, highly favorable to the People's Republic of China."

Li translated all this into Chinese. When she had finished, Chung looked impassively at the President. "Please tell the President of the United States that I have no idea what he is talking about. I know of no Secret Protocol. I know of no mineral deposit. China needs no help from any country in finding or exploiting its natural resources. As for his statement that the Economic and Cultural Treaty is highly favorable to China, that is a matter of opinion. In my country, there are many people who believe we should not have entered into any treaty with a hegemonistic superpower such as the United States."

The President took a long, deep breath. "Wait a moment! We've got a ten-page plan for getting the plutonium out of the area. And the Uranium 235. Our people have it all worked out. You can't tell me you don't know anything about it!"

Chung shrugged. "I know nothing."

Desperately, the President appealed to Li. "You were there. You know about the deposit. You know about the Secret Protocol."

Li looked at him blankly. "I am just an interpreter," she said quietly. "I translate what people say."

The President took another deep breath and picked up the phone. "Thaddeus, come in here right away. Bring Kristof. And bring the 'Secret Protocol' too, if you can find it. I'm having a little communication problem."

A few moments later, Kristof came in, followed by Ricker, who was carrying a document.

Kristof was officially introduced to Chung and Li.

"Here's the treaty, sir," Ricker said, handing over the document. "And here's the text of the Secret Protocol. It exists in English and Chinese. Both versions are authentic."

The President examined the Protocol. It was there in black and white. He handed it to Chung. "Look at the signatures," he said triumphantly. "There's Ricker's—for and on behalf of the United States of America. And there's Chairman Yang's—for and on behalf of the People's Republic of China."

Chung examined the signatures uninterestedly and handed the document back to the President. "That is Chairman Yang's signature, not Chairman Chung's. Whatever the agreement may be that is contained in this so-called Secret Protocol—and I do not intend to read it—Chairman Yang had no authority to commit China. Only the Chinese people can do that, and he had no mandate from them!"

Chung stood up to leave. The President, feeling very near to violence, forced himself to his feet. "I see," he sounded somewhat aimless. "So that's the way it is. Good-bye, Mr. Chung. See him out, would you, Gordon? Thaddeus, I'd like to talk to you."

"The bastards!" the President yelled as soon as they were gone. "Let us do the work and then keep the whole thing for themselves. Damn them. And what about those Brazilians? You know the revolutionary underground in Brazil has suddenly become very active. Terrorist activity, strikes. What if it was the guerrillas and not the Brazilian Government who knew about the anomaly? They could have gone to China with the information in return for support. Chung would certainly have been the man to give it to them."

"Of course!" Ricker suddenly understood. "That's it. You know, one of the Brazilians was in China. I saw him in the hotel, but I couldn't remember why the name was familiar. They must have seen Chung. That would explain his quick takeover—he knew about the deposit even though we thought he was out of the way in Tibet. He probably used the time to plan his strategy. When he got back, he worked on stirring up a lot of radical sentiment and latent anti-Americanism."

The President interrupted. "As for the International Court, the guerrillas must have put enormous pressure on Campos. It was in their interest. Think of the start they'll have if they take power—with the promise of even a part of that deposit."

A few minutes passed in silence. "What about the trade treaty?" Ricker finally asked. The United States has signed it and Congress has ratified it. Can we go back on that now?"

The President shook his head. "I don't think so. There's a tremendous desire in the business community to trade with China. We need it for our balance of trade. Maybe we can go a bit slow in implementing some of the provisions."

"Well," Ricker said, "I guess I better get back to my desk. Looks like we lost this one. Maybe we'll win the next."

"Sure." The President looked glum. "See you later." He heard the door close as Ricker left. The President was furious, and sad, and he felt powerless. What good was all his prestige and influence? His strategic command? His arsenal of missiles? His fleets of bombers? What were they to do? Bomb the dam themselves so that the river, if it hadn't already cut a new channel, would revert to its original course? That would be handing the deposit over to the Soviets. Denounce the Chinese for breach of a secret agreement? Impossible. The truth about the nuclear explosion and the diversion of the Ussuri would come out. It would be clear that the United States had encouraged the subversion of justice at the International Court. No. The President groaned. He had been had.

Li was traveling in a black unmarked Ford belonging to the U.S. Government Federal Service Agency car pool. As they crossed the Potomac, she used the car phone to call McGrath and let him know she was on her way.

He heard the car pull up and hobbled out onto the veranda, followed by his dogs, as he had once—how long ago it seemed now!—come out to greet his old friend Bledsoe and his new friend Ricker. She got out and the car turned around to go back.

"How are you, Li?" Their embrace opened up all his passion and longing like a sudden ache.

She felt tears welling up. Did he know? If he knew, would he ever understand? Would he believe that there were issues, commitments, ideals more important than the love two people might have for each other? Would he know the anguish of dealing with such divided loyalties?

Suddenly awkward with each other, they went inside. He sat on the sofa; she sat primly on a chair.

"Is that your wife?" she asked, picking up the photograph on the table.

"Yes."

"She looks like a good woman."

"She was. I loved her."

"And you loved me too!"

"I still do."

"How can you? You must think that I betrayed you, that I betrayed your friendship with my father. You know, don't you? I'm sure you know."

He looked at her with overwhelming tenderness. "Li, I know and I understand. Each of us must do what he thinks right. You believe in the 'purity' of the Revolution, you side with the radicals. I know that now. I imagine you told Chung about the meeting in the Ming tomb. You told him details about the tunnel and the bomb. Perhaps that was why I found you down there in the cavity that evening. But you were only following your loyalties. What seems like treachery to one man is an act of trust to another. And I shall never forget what you did for me in Ch'i-li-pi. You saved my life! That was not a betrayal!"

McGrath stopped speaking, remembering how hurt he had been when the President called to tell him about the meeting with Chung and how Li had been there and had said nothing. He wanted to remember only the happy moments—how they had walked in scented woodlands and listened to the song of the summer birds; how they had taken the boat on the river, the talks they had had sitting together late at night in the village. He could not bear the thought that even in their most intimate moments she had had other things on her mind. The President had asked him to talk to her. "I can't think of anything else for the moment. Perhaps she can get Chung to change his mind," he had said. McGrath had agreed to try. Now, however, he could see that things were both more complicated than that, and simpler.

She came to sit beside him on the sofa, passing her hand lightly over his brow. "Can we watch our efforts be washed away?" she whispered, as if in explanation.

"Ah," he exclaimed. "You heard even that, did you? How?"

She smiled, a small, tragic smile, and mimicked herself. "I'll leave you the tea in the flask," she said, "while I go to my navigation class."

The thermos flask! Set beside them as they talked. How obvious, how easy, thought McGrath! But, then, it didn't seem to matter. All he knew was that he was glad, unbelievably glad, to have a chance to be alone with her again.

They went out and she drove the jeep around the farm.

They went up into the foothills of the Shenandoah Mountains, where the sap was already beginning to fade and the first hint of red and gold was appearing in the trees. "What would the villagers of Ch'i-li-pi say if they knew all this belonged to one man?" she said.

On the way back, he turned to her. "You'll stay, won't you?" I'll cook dinner. It must be my turn."

"What if I'm missed?"

"Missed?" McGrath cried. "Of course you'll be missed! When you leave here, I shall be missing life itself and all that makes it sweet."

"Oh Ma Ga't! Of course I will stay. And I will make dinner. I would like to cook for you one last time!"

They ate the meal on the veranda, watching the last light fade on the hills to the west.

"Why did Chung come to Washington at all," McGrath had to ask, "if all along he knew he was going to renege on the agreement?"

She shrugged her shoulders. "Chung is a strange man. He believes passionately that China must be independent and self-sufficient and avoid dealing with political enemies. Yet at the same time he is consumed with curiosity to see what the American style of life is like."

"You mean he wants to try hamburgers and french fries?" She laughed. "Perhaps."

"I have to ask you a question, Li."

She nodded, knowing what it was and that she would have to answer.

"Was Chung your lover? Tell me. I need to know."

She took his hand. "What does it matter, Ma Ga't? Yes, Chung was my lover."

"Was or is?"

"Was."

"I'm glad, Li. I'm so glad you are not Chung's lover now," he said, tears beginning to fall down his face.

She held him and whispered, "Ask me to make love to you before we part forever."

He did, speaking softly to her in Chinese, in the private language they had used when they were alone together by the Ussuri River.

The following day, Wilbur Silcott went out to the farm to visit McGrath and congratulate him in person on making general.

"I'm sorry you weren't in The Hague, John," he said over coffee. "That was quite a scene. The Soviets really had us worried. They had the whole story—Panda crossing, tunnel, nuclear explosion—but they just couldn't make it stick. The fact is they weren't able to produce a convincing motive. Without a plausible explanation for why the Chinese would have gone to all that trouble to divert the river, the whole thing sounded like a fairy tale."

McGrath smiled. "Hell, it's a good thing they didn't pick up the radioactivity in the waste from the tunnel. We discharged it into the river, you know, just like the other waste. I was worried about it at the time. If the Soviets had had an effective pollution-monitoring unit downstream—at Khabarovsk, for example—they would have detected it."

"What do you mean? What radioactivity?" Silcott felt a little panicked.

"Remember we had to put the diversion tunnel over on the Soviet side. We went far enough east through the rock to be sure that when we exploded the charges the trench would cut all the way through, so that the Ussuri could flow into the Bikin. Well, right at the end of the tunnel, when we had almost finished digging, we found we were running into pretty high levels of radioactivity. We took precautions. All the diggers wore protective clothing and worked short shifts. But getting rid of the radioactive spoil worried me. I knew we were putting something into the river that would be pretty difficult to explain away if the Soviets ever picked it up. It would certainly have given them a major clue as to the Chinese motivation. Thank God they didn't!" He looked up. Silcott had gone pale and was shaking. "Wilbur, what's the matter? Is there some problem?"

"Problem?" Silcott screeched. "My God! It's more than a problem. It's a disaster! What fools we were! We should never have taken the risk!

"Right at the beginning"—he grabbed onto facts in an effort to calm himself down—"Otis Oman suggested that if we didn't want the Soviets to have the deposit, and if we couldn't think of any other viable plan, why didn't we just go in there and blow it up? Well, of course, it was a damn-fool suggestion and the NSC rejected it out of hand. Nobody in their right mind goes and blows up a deposit containing enormous quantities of plutonium."

"Go on." McGrath didn't yet understand what Silcott was driving at.

"Okay," Silcott continued. "The night in the Ming tombs, remember, our initial plan was to explode one 100-kiloton device under the middle of the river. We knew the rough contours of the deposit from the satellite evidence, and when we went over in the Pandas we verified that the western edge of the deposit was a considerable distance from the place where the nuclear explosion would take place. Then, when it looked like we needed 150 kilotons, which would be impossible to mask, we decided to blow out the diversion trench."

"What are you afraid of, Wilbur? You think something went wrong, don't you?"

"I think something *may* have gone wrong. When we made the Panda trip, we never established the deposit's *southern* boundary. To be honest, we were frightened after the encounter with the Soviet patrol." He saw McGrath's raised eyebrow and swallowed hard. "All right, I admit it. I was frightened. We should have pressed on and we didn't. Up until this afternoon— in fact, up until you just spoke—I was confident that the line of the diversion trench was well clear of the southern edge of the deposit. The satellite images we were working on put the deposit way north of the latitude on which the village of Ch'i-li-pi was situated.

"But now you tell me," Silcott went on, "that at the end of your tunnel you were getting highly radioactive spoil. That means the deposit may in fact extend much farther south than we supposed. In other words, we may have exploded those 1-kiloton charges very near or even within the deposit area itself!"

"And if we did?"

"John, if the high-pressure shock waves generated by the explosion have compressed or imploded even a part of the deposit in upon itself, we could be generating a critical mass that might blow at any time! And the first explosion would release further shock waves and achieve further compression until the whole deposit blew up in one great big 'whoosh'!"

Silcott's voice sank to a whisper. "An explosion like that could, quite literally, blow the world apart and send the two halves spinning off into space!"

"I guess we'd better call Ricker," McGrath said.

Ricker put down the phone, sent immediately for his official car, and had himself driven to Goddard Space Flight Center. He did not look out the window; he stared ahead, deathly solemn. The guard recognized him and waved him through. He went straight to the Data Interpretation Center in Building 6.

Ella was amazed to see him. "Thaddeus, what on earth are you doing here?"

"Ella, show me the latest LANDSAT 3 images of the deposit area. And get out the first set of tapes for comparison."

"Is that an order from the top? Any images on that set of co-ordinates are kept under maximum security. Thaddeus Ricker's personal instructions." She smiled.

"Ella, better get the stuff." She was chilled by his lack of humor.

They took the tapes into the small viewing room. "Let's see the first set," said Ricker, "and then the most recent set. Better yet, can we see them side by side?"

"We can. I'll run one set on this screen and the other right here next to it."

"Do you have any calipers?" Ricker asked when both sets of images had been projected. "I'm not sure I like the look of this." She handed him the instrument. He took the dimensions of the incandescent blob as it appeared on the first LANDSAT tape and as it appeared on the latest one. "Damn it. The blob *has* grown, Ella. Not by much. Just a fraction. But you can measure it."

Ella checked the measurement. "You're right." She sounded alarmed. "The question is: Is it still growing? How fast is it growing? Thaddeus . . . could this mean there's a reaction going on out there?"

He did not reply.

She looked at her watch. "The latest images are about a week old. If we wait a couple of hours, we'll be able to get instantaneous transmission from LANDSAT 4, which we've just put into synchronous orbit."

"What do you mean, synchronous orbit?"

"It means LANDSAT 4 is moving in orbit at exactly the same speed as the rotation of the earth. In effect, it's stationary with reference to one particular area; in this case, the Pacific. When it starts transmitting in a few hours, we'll be getting moment-by-moment images of the deposit area."

He turned to the window. "A couple of hours will be all right. There's an emergency Cabinet meeting at nine. The President called it when Chung double-crossed us, but now we've got this new complication to look at too. I want to be awfully sure before I send up a rocket on this one—we ought to see those new images first." He turned back to her. "But it does look bad."

"Yes . . . yes, I guess it does." Her face was ashen.

He took her into his arms. "Look," he said, his voice husky, "there's no point waiting around here. Let's go over to your house. I want to be with you."

Arms around each other, they walked slowly toward his limousine. It was getting dark. "The stars are beginning to shine," she said. There was a faintly hysterical timbre in her voice.

"Yes."

"There's Polaris, just over from the Big Dipper. The North Star. Maybe Polaris has just gone out."

"I know what you're getting at."

"Every time a star goes out, it means a world has vanished. Of course, it could have happened millions of years ago, but we see it now because that's how long the light takes to reach us."

He let her go on.

"So you see," she said, looking up at him, "things do come to an end. Maybe suddenly. There are billions of live stars out there, but billions of dead ones too. And each one was once a world, maybe like ours. Who knows what caused their destruction?"

She stopped and then realized she was trembling. "I'm frightened, Thaddeus."

"I know, darling, so am I."

They got in the car, and he wrapped her in his arms. She was crying now. He groped in his pocket and took out a piece of paper. "I want to give this to you, in case . . ."

"In case what? . . ."

"In case . . . the worst happens. I copied it down last night. It's from 'Dover Beach.' "

She couldn't read it because of her tears, so Thaddeus read it to her with a crack in his voice and an ache in his chest.

> Ah, love, let us be true
> To one another! for the world, which seems
> To lie before us like a land of dreams,
> So various, so beautiful, so new,
> Hath really neither joy, nor love, nor light,
> Nor certitude, nor peace, nor help for pain;
> And we are here as on a darkling plain

Swept with confused alarms of struggle and flight
Where ignorant armies clash by night.

"Oh, Thaddeus." She hugged him tighter and kissed his mouth. The poem he had chosen was cold comfort: all too appropriate. But there was something about the idea of Thaddeus copying out a portion of his beloved 'Dover Beach,' for her, that filled her with a kind of joy.

When they reached her house he made two calls: one to McGrath and one to Gordon Kristof. And then for two hours they lay quietly together on her bed, grateful for each other.

Just before eight, they said a wrenching good-bye. Thaddeus went to the White House for the emergency meeting, and Ella returned to Goddard. In an hour the synchronous satellite high over the Pacific would begin transmitting its fateful message.

23

The Cabinet met in formal session at the White House.

"I've called this meeting," the President began, "to discuss the consequences of an operation that was recently undertaken, clandestinely, in Manchuria. Some of you know all about it, and some know almost nothing. I need your help now, though, and so I'm going to tell you the whole story."

An hour later, he began summing up. "What are the pluses?" he asked. "Well, the deposit no longer lies within the territory of the Soviet Union. There is much less danger of our major enemy discovering and exploiting it, for either peaceful or war-like purposes. The new international frontier between the Soviet Union and China has been upheld by the International Court of Justice, the world's highest legal and judicial authority, and there can be no going back on that ruling.

"There are, however, a few minuses. We have to admit that. First of all, for reasons beyond our control, the United States is not at this present time in a position to profit from the existence of the deposit. We had hoped to stockpile, for energy purposes, the enriched uranium, while effectively neutralizing the hazardous plutonium. The change of regime in China, however, has meant that agreements that the United States entered into in good faith—secret agreements, admittedly—are no longer considered operative by the other side. Of course, the pendulum may very well swing back again in China toward the moderates. For the moment, though, we have to chalk up a minus. The Chinese took us for a ride."

The President drank from a glass of water. "Now I come to the difficult part. Our scientists have expressed the fear that we may have failed to take into account the consequences of exploding nuclear devices so near to the deposit itself. My people tell me that while they are satisfied that the main explosion could not have caused any harm, one or more of the subsidiary explosions that excavated the diversion trench may have been too close for comfort."

"What do you mean, sir, when you say 'too close for comfort'?" asked William Porter, the Secretary of State.

The President took a deep breath. "The danger is," he said hoarsely, "that these smaller explosions may have impacted the deposit in such a way as to induce a state of incipient criticality. We have no way of estimating accurately the extent of the possible damage, but we do have some theories.

"At one end of the scale," he went on, "I am told we might have a nuclear bang of about 100 kilotons. In that case there would be no venting, no release of radioactive material to the environment, no problem at all really."

They looked a little less worried for a moment.

"Moving on up the scale, however, we can imagine considerable quantities of plutonium or uranium being involved in a chain reaction. In this case, there could be venting and a fallout problem that is unlikely to be entirely local. The Japanese fishermen who died from radioactive poisoning," he reminded them, "were several thousand miles from Bikini Atoll. We must also imagine the secondary consequences on a geopolitical scale. If an explosion of this kind occurred in Manchuria, the Soviet Union might suppose that China was launching a preemptive nuclear strike. Or China might suppose the same thing about the Soviets. Each might attack the other, leading to a major war."

Otis Oman, the Secretary of Defense, interrupted. "If that

happened, sir, if the Soviet Union and China became involved in a major war, would that be such a bad thing from the United States' point of view?"

The President looked at him icily. "I wouldn't care to comment on that point, Mr. Oman. At the present time, we're simply discussing in an objective way the possible eventualities. Any other comments?"

There were none. The President sipped his water.

"I come now," he continued reluctantly, "to what our scientists somewhat colorfully refer to as the Doomsday hypothesis. In other words, they postulate a scenario in which the deposit attains a state of supercriticality and the whole thing literally explodes as one single gigantic fission-fusion bomb!"

There was a shocked silence in the room.

"There are two possible results from such an explosion. One is that the radioactive fallout resulting from the eruption of a major plutonium-uranium deposit would be so extensive as to render the planet, or at least large parts of it, unfit for life, except perhaps for the cockroach."

This time the silence seemed to lengthen into an eternity.

Finally, Kristof asked in a small voice, "And what is the other possible result?"

"The other possible result is that the explosion might in fact shatter the structure of the earth itself. The globe as we know it and all the life that it contains would be destroyed. The world egg would be cracked and the particles voided into space. The planet would cease to exist. The poet, gentlemen, may have got it wrong—the world may end with a bang, not a whimper."

William Porter was distraught. "What are we doing about it, sir? Surely we ought to be doing something?"

"Well, William, we've got a satellite in synchronous orbit over the deposit area. The minute-by-minute images it sends back are being monitored out at Goddard right now. If the deposit is going to go critical there should be a period of marked intensification of the thermal images just before the 'big bang.' " The President sounded strangely offhand, matter-of-fact; almost as though he had given up worrying.

"That's not enough!" the Secretary of State cried. "When is all this going to happen? How long do we have? Are we going to die sitting here in this room?"

The President spread his hands and looked at them for help. "I'm afraid I have no answers for you. I just don't know."

When he finished speaking, only the ominous ticking of the grandfather clock by the window could be heard.

It was funny, Ella thought, as she sat down in front of the display screen, how the wheel had gone full circle. This is how it had all begun—with Shirley Lewis punching the buttons to receive the LANDSAT images.

She tapped the keyboard, requesting data, and, just as she had months before, on the morning of her fortieth birthday, waited for the image to appear. In moments she was once more looking at the familiar scene. Now the river had changed its course, and there was a dam and a body of water where once the village of Ch'i-li-pi had been. But basically it was still the same picture. The incandescent blob that denoted the deposit was still there, burning.

She blinked. My God, that blob was bright! She reduced the intensity of the image. That was better.

She left her seat to get a pair of calipers. When she returned to her desk, she saw immediately that the blob was as bright as ever. That was odd, she thought. Someone must have come by and turned the intensity control up again.

But then, as she touched the control, she realized that it had not been turned up again. It was still on LOW. She spent half a minute verifying that the machine was functioning correctly. Then she picked up the phone.

"Get me the White House," she said, trying to keep the panic out of her voice.

The telephone rang shrilly in the Cabinet Room.

Kristof, who was nearest to it, picked up, listened, and motioned to Ricker. "It's Dr. Richmond from Goddard," he whispered.

Ricker went to the phone, feeling all their frightened eyes

staring at his back. He listened to Ella and then said quietly, "I think you'd better talk to the President. He's right here."

The President took the phone. "Hello."

"Mr. President, this is Ella Richmond. I'm calling about the blob."

"What about it, Dr. Richmond?"

Ella wondered for a moment whether she had imagined it all. What an idiot she would look like then. But no, she had not imagined it. She was quite sure about that.

"Mr. President," she gasped, "I'm looking at the blob on the screen in front of me as I speak. AND IT'S GETTING BRIGHTER ALL THE TIME!"